TWILIGHT OF EMPIRE

By

Stoney Compton

Eric Flint's
Ring of Fire
PRESS

Sharing stories around the campfire since 1632

Cover designed by Stoney Compton

This book is a work of fiction. Names, characters, places, and incidents either are products of the author's imagination or are used fictitiously. Any resemblance to actual persons, living or dead, events, or locales is entirely coincidental.

by Stoney Compton
Visit my website at https://stoneycompton.com/

Printed in the United States of America

First Printing: Aug 2019
Eric Flint's Ring of Fire Press

ebook ISBN-13 978-1-948818-40-7
Trade Paperback ISBN-13 978-1-948818-41-4

CONTENTS

Prologue 1
1 5
2 7
3 9
4 11
5 13
6 15
7 21
8 23
9 27
10 31
11 37
12 41
13 47
14 51
15 55
16 59
17 63
18 67
19 69
20 75
21 79
22 87
23 91
24 95
25 99
26 103
27 107

28 111
29 115
30 119
31 123
32 125
33 129
34 133
35 137
36 139
37 141
38 143
39 147
40 149
41 151
42 153
43 155
44 157
45 163
46 167
47 169
48 171
49 173
50 177
51 181
52 185
53 187
54 189
55 193
56 195
57 199
58 201
59 203
60 205
61 209
62 213
63 215
64 219

65..223
66..225
67..227
68..229
69..235
70..239
71..243
72..247
73..251
74..255
75..259
76..261
77..263
78..267
79..269
80..271
81..273
82..277
83..281
84..287
85..291
86..295
87..297
88..299
89..301
90..307
91..309
92..311
93..313
94..317
95..321
96..323
97..327

PROLOGUE

Tee Harbor, Alaska Prefecture
Late August 1967

Light rain lazily drifted down over the Japanese patrol boat as it motored quietly into the placid waters of Tee Harbor, turning toward the north, and longer, arm of the small bay. Cabins and small houses populated the rocky beach, some sitting back in the tree line of the huge forest that seemingly sheltered this beautiful place from the surrounding mountains.

Next to the shore, beneath a heavy netting covered with live foliage, lay a U.S. Navy Higgins patrol torpedo boat. PT-245 had sat lovingly maintained in the same concealed berth dug out of the rocky shore for over twenty years. Many of her original crew now stood at their stations, along with apprentices who couldn't remember a time when Japan did not rule Alaska Territory, and avidly watched the Japanese boat slowly move toward them.

Word had come down that the reign of Nippon was finished. Both of the twin 20mm Oerlikons and the big Browning .50 caliber mounts were all locked and loaded. The United States was back in the fight.

Damn, I hope that message was right, thought Lieutenant Brian Wallace, skipper of the venerable craft. Chief Radioman Dennis Harris had turned off their communications as soon as the lookout up on the ridge spotted the approaching Japanese vessel. Some of the Jap boats carried radio detection gear.

Chief Gunner's Mate J.W. Foster manned the Browning. He could tear down every weapon on the boat *and* reassemble them while blindfolded. Captain Wallace had asked Chief Foster not to sink the patrol boat; they could use it once the crew was eliminated.

✳ ✳ ✳

Senior Lieutenant Noguchi had his crew quivering with anticipation. The squadron commander had put all of Southeast Alaska Prefecture on Full Alert yesterday morning. Noguchi didn't know why, but he loyally followed orders.

Commander Sunnichi, visibly troubled, had told all six of his patrol boat commanders, "Be ready for anything. The world has changed and we must be vigilant if we wish to continue ruling it. From this moment forward, where ever you patrol, keep all weapons loaded and ready for combat."

Senior Lieutenant Noguchi wondered, *Who would attack us? We are masters of the Pacific and all lands touching it.*

His patrol boat was one of the hundreds of fishing vessels seized by the Empire when they moved into Southeast Alaska Prefecture. Only in this part of the prefecture did the Imperial Japanese Navy dominate; the Imperial Army remained honcho of the rest of the vast territory.

Patrol Boat 96 had been a 48' fishing trawler. Now it boasted twin Nambu machine guns on either side of the foredeck, and a 40mm cannon on the afterdeck. The wheelhouse held three men, the radar and ASDIC units, as well as the radio.

His nine-man crew had one man who had served in the Great Pacific War. Chief Petty Officer Horiuchi had been a seaman second class on the *Yamato* when MacArthur surrendered to Japan in Australia. The chief operated both the radar and the ASDIC in addition to being the leading petty officer aboard.

Senior Lieutenant Noguchi was terrified of Chief Horiuchi. If Noguchi had any doubts about himself as an officer the chief seemed to sense it and issue a pithy koan. The crisp Fall air chilled his ears and nose, but Noguchi's eyes didn't stop moving as they constantly swept the dark bank. He hated being in a situation where he was universally hated by the populace, and lacked the authority to shoot any of them. The Alaskans always bowed, always carried out any orders with dispatch, and always stared at him with dark, smoldering hate in their eyes.

He didn't trust them and wore his service pistol even on holidays. A raven made a clacking sound that bounced over the water and magnified in his mind. The teachings of his animist-minded grandmother about ravens surfaced and he suddenly felt they were in great danger here.

He was torn. He would need a reason to leave Tee Harbor before completing the full circuit and fear wouldn't suffice.

He should have listened to his grandmother.

＊ ＊ ＊

The Jap trawler slowly traversed their field of view no more than fifty feet from the bow of PT -245. One of the Jap gunners seemed to stare directly through the falling rain, netting, and camouflage at Captain Wallace.

"Open fire!" he shouted.

Both Oerlikons fired directly into the pilot house amidship and then raked the deck in either direction.

"Cease fire!" Captain Wallace yelled. "I think you got them all, boys. Bosun, lift the canopy, we're taking her out."

Chief Motor Machinist Mate Spike Walsh carefully revved all three Packards, examined the gauges, laughed, and bellowed over the engine noise, "We're ready to go, Brian, I mean, Skipper!"

Chief Bosun's Mate Clyde Andrews grabbed a rope and pulled the front of the canopy off the berthing space. Seaman First Class Dean Long raised the radar dome and dogged it down.

"All secure, captain," he yelled as the engines gained strength.

Brian Wallace slowly idled the boat out of its berth for the first time in a year and the first time in daylight in twenty-two years.

"Stand by to board!" Captain Wallace ordered. Chief Foster motioned for his striker, Seaman First Class Jerry Kohler, to take over the Browning. Foster pulled his Thompson .45 caliber submachine gun off its rack and made sure he had the chamber loaded and the safety off. Bosun Andrews threw a line around a cleat on the trawler, which had continued its slow course toward the end of the harbor.

Andrews slipped over the side along with Chief Foster, Chief Walsh, and Seaman Long. All carried Thompsons. Chief Andrews pushed the body at the helm out of his way and took the trawler out of gear.

"We kinda shot the shit out of the control panel," Andrews observed. He glanced around at the bloody deck. "Not to mention the crew."

"I'll check below deck," Seaman Long said and disappeared down a hatch next to the pilot house.

"Wait, dammit!" Chief Foster yelled.

Before anything else could be said a shot rang out from below.

"Gawddammit!" Bosun Anderson shrieked.

Shouts in Japanese sounded from below deck and the foredeck hatch banged open while simultaneously a Japanese sailor with a machine-gun popped up where Long had disappeared.

Chief Foster fired a burst into the Japanese sailor who dropped from sight. A second Imperial sailor emerged from the forward hatch and aimed a rifle at Foster.

Two 20mm rounds from the PT-245 suddenly blew the man's head and upper torso into a gruel splayed across the deck.

Silence reigned. Chief Foster held his hand up and made a *wait* motion. He slipped over to the fallen Japanese gunner and plucked a hand grenade off his belt.

Without pulling the pin he threw it down the hatch and screamed, "Grenade!"

Everyone heard the grenade stop bouncing and roll to a stop. Silence.

"Ain't anyone alive down there, skipper," he yelled.

The explosion blew off the aft hatch cover.

"I didn't pull the pin!" Foster blurted.

"Now you've messed up the engines, John!" Chief Walsh yelled.

"Sorry, Spike, it wasn't on purpose, but this *is* war."

Seaman First Class Jerry Kohler vomited over the side.

1

Imperial Japanese Navy Headquarters
Patrol Section
Juneau, Alaska Prefecture

#

"Commander Hokama, Patrol Boat 96 does not answer," the senior radioman said with a deep bow. All motion stopped in the operations center.

"Lieutenant Chiba, What course was 96 to follow?"

"Commander, Patrol Boat 96 was to perform standard patrol of Sector 2."

"Chief Izumi, are any of the other patrols experiencing radio problems?"

"No, commander. All other boats and stations have reported in, following protocol. Perhaps Patrol Boat 96 has experienced equipment failure?"

"Have your men continually monitored all radio traffic today?"

"Yes, commander. Just as you ordered. All they heard was routine traffic from the fleet."

"Fleet!" Hokama said contemptuously. "We haven't had a fleet for over twenty years thanks to Tojo's bastards."

Silence fell throughout the room. Despite the Imperial Navy's contempt for the Imperial Army it was very dangerous for anyone to disparage the late General Tojo. Both the Tokkō and the Kempeitai, as well as the Navy's Tokkeitai could have planted informers among their ranks.

Hokama immediately sensed the caution in the room.

"Excellent. Tell the air wing to send a reconnaissance aircraft to follow the standard route of Sector 2."

"Yes, Commander Hokama!" Chief Izumi snapped to attention and gave his superior a three-quarter bow. He turned to the technician manning the radio and spoke to him in a low voice. Moments later he once again came to attention.

"Commander Hokama, the air wing has sent up an observation aircraft."

"Make sure someone stays on the radio with the pilot."

"Yes, Commander Hokama!"

2

Reconnaissance Floatplane 535
Juneau, Alaska Prefecture

Flight Sub-Lieutenant Goro Seta taxied his N1K1 floatplane into the middle of Gastineau Channel and accelerated down channel into the wind. Once above 4,000 feet he turned north.

"This is Recon 535," he said over the radio. "I am searching Sector 2 beginning with Shelter Island."

"Acknowledge, Recon 535. Keep us informed."

Light rain reduced visibility more than Goro liked. He flew low around the small islands in Lynn Canal so he could easily see the beaches. Shelter Island required a complete circumnavigation and the smaller islands received a mere glance. At the northern-most point of the sector he flew along the mainland beach.

Dusk arrives early in the Alexander Archipelago and visibility had dropped accordingly. Lieutenant Seta neared Tee Harbor and glanced over at the largest portion, the south end, and moved his heading to the right. Totally as an automatic gesture, he glanced in his rearview mirror.

"Is that a floating dock or two boats?" he blurted.

"We did not copy that transmission, Recon 535," the operations radioman said.

"I am going back to Tee Harbor for a fly-over."

"Acknowledged."

Stoney Compton

3

PT-245
Tee Harbor, Alaska Prefecture

Seaman Second Class Jerry Kohler, still embarrassed about puking, heard the plane first.

"Aircraft!" he screamed.

"Battle stations!" Captain Wallace bellowed. "Gunners, nail that son of a bitch!"

Chief Gunner's Mate Foster grabbed the 20mm, led the plane and then raised the muzzle two inches and fired four times. The first three erupted from the barrel, but the fourth round didn't fire.

He pulled the trigger again. When nothing happened he cursed and ran to the starboard Oerlikon and pushed Bosun Andrews out of the way. The late Seaman First Class Dean Long had last manned that position.

"Let me get it, Chief!" Foster said. He aimed the weapon and pulled the trigger. "It's a Rex, they're nasty!" he shouted.

The fighter screamed down at them, seemingly impervious to their fire. The plane's engine abruptly blew apart, sending the propeller spinning off in a high arc into the growing darkness.

The Rex kept firing as the burning plane continued to head straight for them.

"He's going to hit us!" Foster screamed. "Blow him out of the air!"

The 40 mm Bofors on the fantail pounded away and the plane disintegrated in an explosion. The crew of PT-245 stared in shocked relief as debris rained down across the south arm of Tee Harbor.

"Chief Harris, get the radio warmed up. We need to talk to central command."

"Aye, aye, skipper." Harris was already inside the small radio room, on the other side of the bulkhead from where Captain Wallace stood at the wheel.

"We're getting out of here, guys," Wallace yelled. He hit the boat horn three times. The sound echoed back from the shoreline.

People came out of their cabins all around the cove and he picked up a bullhorn. "The Japs will be here soon and they're gonna be pissed. You should all evacuate. Good luck!"

Every family in Southeast Alaska had an emergency plan and now they would be tested.

PT-245 accelerated out of Tee Harbor and into Lynn Canal on her first war patrol in 22 years.

4

Juneau, Alaska Prefecture

Joseph Coffey wasn't surprised to hear pounding on the door to his house. Six hours ago the word had filtered through the community and he had immediately destroyed every document in his house that could throw blame on him or anyone else.

He opened the door and beheld a stern Japanese in a suit backed by three armed marines. All wore Tokkeitai armbands.

"Yes?" Joe said as evenly as he was able.

"You will come with us, Mr. Coffey, as will everyone else in the house."

"I'm the only one who lives here."

"This is not auspicious, Mr. Coffey, you have already lied to me. You have been seen entering this house with the same woman many times."

"I'm not even married. Please, feel free to search my home." He stepped to one side.

The man nodded and two of the troopers shot through the door and ran from room to room. In three minutes they returned, bowed from the waist, and said something to their boss.

"It is nothing, we shall find her. Follow me please."

Joe used the railing to go down the steps, he didn't want them to see his fear and shaking legs.

Why the hell did we decide against cyanide pills?

Dusk lay on Juneau, the late August evening would be one of the last pleasant ones until spring returned. He took a deep breath of the fragrant air and resigned himself to his fate.

A Japanese civilian walked down the street and stopped to watch the soldiers hustle Joe to the waiting car. Joe recognized Kijan Kimura, an eminent artist and printmaker.

"Why are you arresting my friend?"

"This is none of your affair, citizen," the man in the suit snapped. "Go about your business."

Kimura bowed deeply. "I understand your attitude, you do a thing that is demeaning and unwholesome. But, I know you have some rationale behind your actions and I would like to know it."

"This is Tokkeitai business! You will leave now or risk being incarcerated with this traitor to the Emperor—" his voice abruptly stopped and he looked down for a moment as if to gather himself.

Joe watched the man's face shift from apoplectic to haunted in the space of a breath.

My God, it's really true! Joe thought, forcing himself not to show elation.

"Please, citizen," the plainclothes Tokkeitai officer said, his voice oozing supplication. "We are bringing this man in for questioning. Allow us to perform our duty."

"I vouch for Mr. Coffey. I have been his friend for over a decade."

"Your words are noted and appreciated, citizen. Now be about your business and we shall do the same."

As the car rolled down Seward Street toward the old federal building, Joe wondered what the Japs would do next. Without an emperor they were adrift in an unforgiving world.

5

Tlingit Provisional Navy HQ
Angoon, Alaska Prefecture

Bleary-eyed and exhausted, Captain Wallace edged the PT-245 up to the fuel dock in the Angoon small boat harbor. He waited until his crew had moored the boat fore and aft before telling Spike to shut down all three Packards. A single overhead light provided the only illumination in the star-filled darkness.

"Permission to come aboard," someone said on the dock.

"Permission granted." Wallace rubbed his eyes, all he wanted to do was go to sleep.

"Brian, it's Gabriel George," the newcomer said as he walked carefully across the deck to the small cabin. "You made good time."

"Hey, Gabe, good to see you, brother." They shook hands. "What is the mayor of Angoon doing up at 0400?"

"When you radioed your departure from Tee Harbor I figured we had about six hours before you showed up, so I set my alarm."

"There were a couple of Jap patrol boats we had to evade, so the trip took longer than it usually does."

"Did you guys really shoot down one of their planes?"

"Yeah. Also took out one of their trawler patrol boats. What do we hear from the Underground Liberation?"

"Fairbanks and Anchorage are mostly in UL hands. We have people attacking a shit load of German positions east of the Rocky Mountains, but no idea how well they are doing. We have the go-ahead to eliminate Japanese naval elements."

"Are there any other warships than mine?"

"It seems we have destroyer escort down near Ketchikan."

"Someone hid a DE? I'm impressed, we felt pretty good about hiding PT-245."

"You people have done a beautiful job. I have two guys on their way to refuel your boat. Then I want you to take it up to the berth in Stillwater Anchorage. There are people waiting there to help you rig camouflage before daylight."

"So what's your rank now, Gabe?"

"I'm a commander in the TPN at the moment. Now that the balloon has gone up I suspect we'll all be getting higher rank, but the pay will still suck. Captain Williams wants you to come down to headquarters as soon as you can and give us the official version of your combat yesterday."

"Can I get some sleep first? I'm at the end of my rope."

"Of course. How about 1300 today?"

"I'll be there."

Bosun Andrews assisted the two fuelers as they filled the tanks. All of the crew stumbled around and were nearly asleep on their feet by the time the tanks were topped off.

Gabe went ashore and Brian motored the PT-245 toward its berth. It had been a long day.

6

Valdez, Alaska Prefecture

"**M**ajor, what do you want me to do?"
Kempeitai Major Katsu Miamatsu regarded Sergeant Norio Hamada through grainy eyes. Exhaustion leaked from every pore of his being and all he wanted to do was sleep for at least a week. He also had no desire to become a prisoner of the surprisingly well-organized rebellion that had swept over northern Alaska Prefecture. Nor had they the desire to go into the war zone of Anchorage, so they went south toward Prince William Sound.

"We need to find some place safe to sleep, we're both at the end of our strength."

"The last time I was here there was a small garrison to protect the harbor." Hamada peered down at the fuel gauge on the lorry they had requisitioned. "It is below the empty mark, major."

"Park somewhere unobtrusive so we can get some sleep."

"Maybe we can get to the harbor," Hamada said as he drove slowly through the small fishing settlement. "Perhaps we can hide on a boat."

"Good thinking." Miamatsu yawned. While they had traveled through the mountains the weather had thrown one storm after another at them. After the flood in Fairbanks neither of them had wanted to see water in quantity, and here they were almost to the ocean.

"Major, there's an Imperial Army patrol!"
"Stop the lorry."

Hamada complied and switched off the engine.

15

A young lieutenant and two enlisted men approached them. The lieutenant held a pistol in his right hand and both soldiers carried rifles with fixed bayonets.

Hamada cranked his door window down.

"Good evening, lieutenant."

"Who are you people?" the lieutenant shrilled in a high-pitched voice. "Get out of the lorry so we can see you."

The soldiers weren't pointing their weapons at them, but they weren't at ease, either.

"Do as he says, Norio, we'll sort this out."

Miamatsu climbed down and braced himself for a moment. He had been sitting on the bench that passed for a seat for more hours than he could count and it had been a long bumpy gravel road. He stretched and walked past the soldiers to face the lieutenant.

They are all so young!

"I am Major Katsu Miamatsu of the Kempeitai. This is my assistant, Sergeant Norio Hamada. What is the situation here?"

"Kempeitai?" The lieutenant's tremulous voice instantly acquired a an edge of fear. "May I see your identification, major?"

All three soldiers seemed ready to bolt, or worse. Miamatsu reached into his breast pocket and pulled out the leather-cased badge, held it out for the lieutenant to inspect.

"Attention!" he barked, he and the soldiers snapped to perfect parade ground rigidity. "I am Lieutenant Todo Saito. Are you the vanguard of a reenforcement column, sir?" Hope suffused his voice.

"No, Lieutenant Saito, we are inspecting our outlying districts. What is the situation here?"

"I ask that you speak to my commander, sir. He gave me instructions to not tell anyone of our situation."

Miamatsu stifled his impulse to smile. "Excellent, lead on, lieutenant."

"Do you wish to secure your vehicle, major?"

"Not necessary. It is requisitioned, and it's out of petrol anyway."

A captain too old for his rank looked up when they entered the small one-room building. "Well, what do you have here, lieutenant?" he snapped officiously.

Miamatsu nudged the lieutenant aside and walked up to the desk. The captain had to crane his head back to look at him with widening eyes. Lieutenant Saito quickly left the building.

"I am Major Katsu Miamatsu of the Kempeitai. Who are you and what is the military situation here?"

Instantly on his feet, the captain swayed at attention.

"I am Captain Hirayama of the Imperial Coastal Defense Force, Major Kem– ah, Major Miamatsu."

Nodding back at Sgt. Hamada, he introduced him and stepped back from the red-faced captain. "Why don't we all sit while we talk, do you have anything to eat?"

"Eat? Yes, of course." He turned to the bug-eyed private still standing at his desk. "Hammura, get these men something to eat, now!"

The private braced. "Yes, captain, at once!" He all but ran from the room.

"Please," Hirayama said, indicating two chairs. "Sit, and I will tell you all I know of the situation."

Miamatsu nodded to Hamada and both men sat down on government-issue bamboo chairs.

"If the major doesn't mind me asking, from where did you and the sergeant journey?"

"Are you the senior officer in Valdez?"

"At the moment, yes, sir."

"Who is in charge of this district, captain?"

"Commander Ito of the Imperial Navy, major."

"Where is Commander Ito at this moment?"

"I wish I knew," Captain Hirayama said wistfully. "He went out on patrol with his second-in-command three days ago and has yet to return."

"Is this standard procedure?"

"No. This is the first time he has accompanied a patrol. He told me he would be gone for a few days but I am now worried."

"Why?"

"They didn't have enough fuel to patrol a great distance and then return."

The private hurried in with a tray holding two bowls of noodles mixed with seafood. He sat the tray on the captain's desk and deeply bowed. "This is the best I could do with what we had in the galley, major. Would you like some rice beer or saki?"

The aroma of the food overwhelmed Miamatsu. He and Hamada hadn't eaten in over thirty hours and saliva threatened to drown him.

He swallowed. "This is excellent, private, you are to be commended. Yes, rice beer would be most welcome."

While they ate and drank, Miamatsu pondered the local situation. He harbored no doubts about the former commander; the officer had absconded with his staff and everything he could carry. Captain Hirayama was so far out of his depth it was remarkable he hadn't already drowned.

"How many are in your garrison?"

"I have thirty-three men, an auspicious number."

"Indeed, it is. Please show me a chart of your patrol areas and the rest of the coast for comparison."

"Ah, right here." He pulled on a cord and a large curtain covering one wall opened to reveal a huge chart of the Alaska coastline from Prince William Sound all the way south to Ketchikan. "This is the area the Alaska Prefecture branch of the Imperial Navy covers. The red lines indicate our patrol area."

Miamatsu and Hamada closely studied the huge chart. Even to the untrained eye, there was a lot of water between Valdez and anywhere else of any size.

"The red stars are our naval bases, captain?" Hamada asked.

"Yes, exactly. You will note that the closest to us is Yakutat."

In a musing tone, Miamatsu asked, "Would it be possible for a patrol boat to get that far without refueling?"

"Only if it carried extra petrol, major."

"How much extra?"

"A fifty gallon drum at a minimum."

"I see," Miamatsu said in a casual tone. He yawned. "The sergeant and I have come a great distance since we last slept in anything resembling a bed. Do you have quarters we can use?"

"Of course, major. The sergeant can take one of the rooms in the NCO barracks and there are at least five unoccupied rooms in the officers' barracks."

"If you could have someone lead us to these places I would be most gratified."

"At once, Major Miamatsu!" The captain gave them a quarter bow and shouted at the private to deploy guides.

The private rushed from the office and returned in less than five minutes with two equally bug-eyed privates who deeply bowed before standing at quivering attention.

"What time would you like to be awakened, major?" Captain Hirayama asked.

"An hour before dawn, please."

The privates led them out.

Miamatsu edged closer to Hamada. "Tomorrow we must get out of this place if we wish to evade capture. Find out what you can about boats."

"Yes, major."

The privates moved away from each other in different directions and their guests followed.

The only way out for himself and Sergeant Hamada was further escape, but to where?

Stoney Compton

7

Tlingit Provisional Navy HQ
Angoon, Alaska Prefecture

"**C**ongratulations, commander, you did a hell of a job in Tee Harbor."

Brian glanced over his shoulder to see if anybody had followed him through the door.

"*Commander*, Captain Williams? I'm a lieutenant." He saluted and the captain pointed to a chair.

"As of midnight last night you are a lieutenant commander, congratulations."

"Lieutenant Commanders don't skipper PT boats," Brian said as he sat down. "I don't want to lose PT-245, that boat has been my life."

"Don't worry. If we were going by 1945 Navy regs you wouldn't have much of a crew left anyway, all your people are far too senior for their billets. Hell, so am I."

"Colby, you aren't old, you've got all of three years on me."

"Hard to believe we're over fifty, ain't it?"

"I feel like I'm still in my late twenties, early thirties on hard days."

Colby laughed. His barrel chest made for a lot of lung power. He was the only Tsimpshean Brian knew. Most Tsimpsheans lived on Annette Island, southwest of Ketchikan to where they had migrated from Canada in the 1880s.

All other Alaska Native peoples grudgingly admired the Tsimpsheans for their financial shrewdness and sharp bargaining. Colby was one of the smartest people Brian knew and he freely trusted the man with his life.

21

"Ain't none of us getting any younger, Brian. Here's the thing, we don't know what the hell to do next."

"When you say 'we' you mean the TPN, right?"

"Right. We've gotten some pretty wild radio messages in the past week. Supposedly Berlin and Tokyo were wiped out by atomic bombs at the *same* time. The Underground Liberation has taken Fairbanks and Anchorage. The Japanese Air Force has been virtually wiped out north of us, and we're at war with Japan and Germany again."

"Shit!" Brian said with feeling. "Who told you all that?"

"The Liberty Underground by way of the Annette Island and Queen Charlotte Island groups. They always vet the messages they receive and send on what they believe to be true."

"Then all that must be true! Holy crap. Did the UL take out Berlin and Tokyo?"

"They didn't exactly say. Somehow, I doubt it. The problem is, they haven't given us any instructions or information as to what we're all supposed to do now."

"Brother, we stirred up a hornet's nest back at Tee Harbor. We need to get our ducks in a row. The Japs are going to stomp on us hard, and we have to be ready for them."

"I know, Brian, believe me, I know. But what the hell am I supposed to do?"

8

Imperial Japanese Navy HQ
Juneau, Alaska Prefecture

Vice Admiral Eikichi Kato glared at the situation map on his office wall. He viewed recent events as a personal affront. In four months he would have retired with full honors, a pension from a grateful nation, and time to devote to his massive collection of artistic pornography.

Now the Emperor was dead along with Tokyo and over two million people. The future stumbled through a dark haze lacking definition. Deep in his heart he knew the odds of him leaving Alaska Prefecture outside of an urn were negligible.

I have my duty, he thought grimly, *and will retain my honor.*

"Where is the Alaska Squadron?" He stared up at his Chief of Staff with eyes so devoid of empathy they could be mistaken for pebbles.

"It was on patrol near Ketchikan, Vice Admiral Kato," Captain Tanaka said, his face exuding even more sweat in anticipation of his next words. "It was ordered south to San Francisco twenty-six minutes ago."

"By *whose* orders?"

"Admiral Nakagawa, sir."

"Did an explanation accompany the order?"

"No, Vice Admiral."

"You realize that we are all ronin now. The Emperor is dead and all direction from Tokyo has vanished. There will be a scramble for power throughout the Empire in addition to Nazi perfidy and war with the Reich."

"Vice Admiral Kato, I and the rest of our forces in Alaska Prefecture will always be loyal to you. Tell us what to do and we will make it so."

Admiral Kato nodded. "Leave, I must think."

* * *

Without another word, Captain Jo Tanaka fled the room and quietly shut the office door. He would rather be in battle than in a room with the vice admiral. His stomach roiled in pain and he hurried toward his office and private medicine chest.

"Captain Tanaka," the signals petty officer called as he snapped to attention. "We have a priority message from Yakutat."

"A moment," Tanaka said, holding up his hand and increasing speed toward his office. In moments he gulped down half a bottle of the chalky liquid that soothed his stomach yet made him want to retch from the taste.

Is it possible to retire from the service at this point? He wondered.

"Show me the message," he snapped as he reentered the office.

The petty officer handed him the flimsy and stood at attention.

"As you were." He scanned the message quickly, then carefully reread the words. The situation required attention from someone above his official station. His stomach twinged.

He didn't want to bother the vice admiral, but they were faced with a new wrinkle in what had become a desperate situation. Chewing his lip, he knocked on the admiral's door.

Nothing. Not even the usual grumble.

Captain Tanaka knocked again, more vigorous than before.

Still nothing.

He opened the door and beheld the vice admiral sitting in his chair, head slumped over his prodigious stomach from which a katana protruded, glistening with blood and viscera.

"Everyone get in here at once!" Tanaka screamed. He ordered himself to not vomit.

In moments the office was crowded with the signals petty officer, the two seaman first class typists, the ensign officer-of-the-deck, and the chief petty officer who actually ran the office.

The chief took one look and ordered one of the seamen to call for the doctor and two medical orderlies. "Tell them to bring a litter!" he added.

Ensign Matsuda, his face ashen and swallowing often, addressed Captain Tanaka. "You are now in charge of Southeast Alaska Prefecture, sir. What are your orders?"

The doctor and two medical orderlies hurried in. Doctor Nakamura pushed everyone aside as he closed on the admiral. For a moment all went quiet.

"He's dead," Dr. Nakamura said. He stood up and stared into Tanaka's eyes. "You are now in charge of this district, Captain Tanaka. May the spirit of the emperor smile upon you."

This was not supposed to happen!

Captain Tanaka would never again be the subordinate of anyone for thousands of miles. He had to make all the decisions and be responsible for them. The concept terrified him.

He nodded to the doctor and gazed around at the other men in the office.

"Is the *Hamiba* still in port?"

The orderlies staggered out of the office carrying the litter weighed down with the covered corpse of Admiral Kato. A trail of blood followed them.

"Clean up this mess!" Chief Izumi snapped at the typists.

Ensign Matsuda, looking pale, turned away from the gory sight and stared into Captain Tanaka's face.

"Yes, captain, the Destroyer Escort *Hamiba* is tied up at the dock. Every other capital ship is with the Alaska Squadron. We have twelve, uh, eleven patrol boats and a company of Imperial Marines."

"You are now a full lieutenant as well as first lieutenant."

Matsuda bowed deeply. "Thank you, captain, I will not fail you." He hurried out of the office.

"Chief Izumi, I need to confer with the captains of our remaining fleet within two hours."

"Hai, Captain Tanaka. It shall be done."

"I am not be disturbed for an hour."

9

Juneau, Alaska Prefecture

Kijan Kimura made a final delicate cut into the flat surface of the block and eased back from the work bench and sighed. Andy King examined the block with as much critical assessment as he could muster.

"Does not the final cut offset the balance of the scene, sensei?"

"If one looks at it that way, yes. Consider, however, the new dynamic of the piece. It now contains an undeniable urgency rather than an unnatural balance. Make a test print and we will discuss it further."

Andy bowed low. "Yes, sensei."

While Andy ran the brayer over the patch of ink on its sheet of glass, Kimura spoke.

"The Tokkeitai arrested Mr. Coffey a few hours ago. I tried to reason with them but they ignored my entreaties."

Andy stared down at the rich, black ink on the brayer and willed himself not to panic.

"Did they have a reason?"

"I am sure they did. However, they chose not to share it with me when I asked."

Andy forced himself to roll the ink onto the block, continuing to roll until the ink had the right sound and consistency. After carefully laying the brayer down he picked up the sheet of rice paper and laid it across the gleaming block.

"You actually asked them what they were doing?"

"Yes. I also told them that Mr. Coffey was a friend as well as neighbor and I would happily vouch for him."

Andy picked up the bamboo baren and slid it over the rice paper, pushing it down onto the block and absorbing the skin of ink where the block held firm. After replacing the baren on its shelf, he carefully pulled the paper off the block and laid it face up.

"I agree with you, sensei. The last cut did make a difference."

The five by seven inch print portrayed a fishing scene, the fisherman has just pulled the salmon from the water. Without the final cut it would have portrayed a humdrum event. The added line on the print gave the salmon life, urgency, and the intimation of struggle.

"Perhaps you should not return to your home tonight, Andrew."

"Thank you for your consideration, sensei, but where else would I go? Juneau is a small town and the Tokkeitai knows where every one of us live."

"True. I am told the world has just changed in a most dramatic way. I believe the Tokkeitai are grasping at straws while they struggle to maintain what no longer exists."

Andy held his teacher's gaze. "Why do you think I am in danger?"

"Because you are part of the resistance, no?"

"How long have you known?"

"Since the day they recruited you, Andrew. Four years now, I believe."

"Why didn't you turn me in to the authorities?"

"I stopped kowtowing to authority many years prior to that. There exists a higher order that we must honor, and turning in those who righteously combat a growing evil has no positive place in the greater scheme of things."

"We are fighting the Japanese Empire! If they discover that you helped in that case they would kill you instantly."

"I won't tell them if you won't."

"You would fight your own people?"

"I have lived in Alaska since the end of the Great Pacific War. I came here to cleanse my soul of the things I did as a soldier for the Imperial Japanese Army. I can not support the militaristic regime that enveloped my country and now rules half of the world. The Emperor is dead as is Tokyo—"

"What! Dead?"

"I thought you knew. Two days ago Tokyo and Berlin were targets of atomic bombs. Both capitals are gone from the face of the Earth."

"W-who did that?"

"They did it to each other." A smile ghosted over his lips and disappeared. "My heart smiles at the application so much karma in such a short time."

"How do you know this? Maybe it's just a ruse to get the resistance out in the open."

"I was an intelligence officer during the war. The Imperial Army allowed me to retire if I would report any sedition I became aware of to the authorities. I agreed."

Andy felt his blood run cold.

"Do not be frightened. I have never reported anything to the Tokkeitai or Kempeitai. When asked, I point out that I am now an artist and teacher and have uncovered no sedition in my students.

"I own a radio that can monitor military broadcasts. My evenings are spent listening as I sketch ideas for new woodcuts and engravings. Fairbanks and Anchorage are both in the hands of the Underground Liberation.

"Yesterday at Tee Harbor a naval scout plane and a patrol boat both fell victim to hostile action. The naval district is on full alert and they are desperately trying to maintain control. What else may I tell you?"

"Where are they holding Joe Coffey?"

"In the basement of the Administration Building."

"Why have you shared all of this with me?"

"After all of these years I am on your side, Andrew. How may I be of further help?"

Stoney Compton

10

Prince William Sound, Alaska Prefecture

Major Katsu Miamatsu had joined the Imperial Army all those years ago because he hated boats and deep water. With his knees wedged firmly against the small table in the galley of the FV *Auspicious Provider* he kept his gaze on the constantly undulating horizon through the window. Sergeant Hamada had told him he would not suffer as much if he could constantly observe the surface of the sea.

"How do you know that?" he had asked his subordinate.

"My father was a fisherman. This boat makes me feel nostalgic for my childhood."

"Between the constant movement and the reek of fish I feel something entirely different."

Hamada kept his face professionally still but Miamatsu could see humor glint in his eyes.

"You say I will become accustomed to this after a day?"

"Yes, major, you possess a strong constitution and even stronger resolve. It will get better."

That had been early in the morning before the sun made its welcome appearance. It did help to see the ocean and the sky. Sergeant Hamada had located the boat prior to going to sleep the evening before.

The Japanese skipper had readily agreed to take the men to Yakutat for a mere 500 yen. The fishing stocks suffered from over harvesting and ready money was scarce yet always welcome. His crew of two said they would enjoy the change of scenery.

Miamatsu wondered if the three of them had heard the news from the north but decided he wasn't going to bring up the issue as long as they didn't. The Tlingit crewman remained stoic and the American crewman carried constant worry lines across his forehead.

The seas seemed especially rough but the skipper said the waves should only get to two and a half meters at the most. The constant up, down, and rolling to left and right bothered him less and less, however he could not imagine trying to work out here.

"How's your stomach?" the American asked as he came into the galley.

"Much better than earlier, thank you."

"I'm going to fix something to eat, can you handle that?"

"What do you plan to serve?"

"Ham sandwiches. Would you like one?"

Miamatsu took stock and decided that since he hadn't lost his dinner from the previous night he would probably survive a ham sandwich.

"I would be most appreciative, Mr...."

"Jones, Oscar Jones. You're Kempeitai, aren't you?"

"Yes. How did you know that?"

"Valdez is a pretty small place. News gets around fast. Are you after someone?"

"I have never before met an American who asked so many questions. Usually people are very quiet around me."

"Yeah," Oscar said, cutting bread with a large knife. "I imagine they are."

"Yet you evidence no hesitation in conversing with me, why is that?"

Oscar flashed a quick grin. "Because I'm not hiding anything nor have I committed any crimes. I have nothing to be afraid of."

"An honest man, impressive."

"I'm as honest as I can be. It makes it easier to keep track of things. Here's your sandwich. I'm going to pass these around to the other guys." He picked up the plate of sandwiches and disappeared up the ladder to the bridge.

The sandwich tasted wonderful and he hadn't known he was hungry until he started eating. Hamada descended the ladder, eating his sandwich. They nodded to one another.

Hamada dropped onto the bench across the small table from him.

"Captain Inoue says we have at least another ten hours before we reach Yakutat."

"Have you looked around for evidence of fishing?" Miamatsu asked in a low voice.

"Yes, major, I have." Hamada kept his voice low. "I suspect these fellows do more smuggling than fishing."

"That's why they took us on so readily?"

"I hope so. They could be taking us anywhere."

"I think it is time to stretch my sea legs." Miamatsu stood and braced himself on the bulkhead.

"The trick is to let the deck come up to your foot instead of lunging down after it."

"Thank you, sergeant."

He climbed the ladder to the flying bridge. Captain Inoue stood braced behind the helm steering back into the wind that constantly tried to force them off course. When the boat would nose down into a trough the resulting spray would fly back over them like salty rain.

Gripping the line that ran the length of the upper deck he made his way forward to stand next to the captain.

"How are you doing?" Captain Inoue asked.

"I believe I am getting the feel of the boat, thank you."

When the boat crested a wave peak he could see a smudge on the horizon far off to their left.

"That's land over there?"

"Correct. There are a lot of reefs along this stretch so we're safer out here."

"Tell me about Yakutat."

The captain shot him a questioning glance and faced forward again.

"Small place, mostly Indians, Tlingits that is. Great hunting and fishing around there. The Imperial Navy has a contingent stationed there, damned if I know why."

"Is the town accessible by road?"

"Oh, hell no. It's surrounded by glaciers. You couldn't walk out if you wanted to, and nobody in their right mind would."

"Do you have a radio on this vessel?"

"Of course I do. It would be suicide to be out in the Gulf of Alaska without one. Why do you ask?"

"What have you heard about events north of Valdez?"

"I heard the Liberation Underground is fighting the Japanese garrisons and winning. Where were you, Anchorage or Fairbanks?"

"Fairbanks. It was a mess. First the flood and then the revolt."

"So you and the sergeant are refugees?"

"Not quite, but close. I want to get to San Francisco if I can."

Inoue regarded him, his eyes bright in a weather-creased face. "Pardon the impertinence, but why?"

"Once I loved a woman who lives there…"

"You are more mature than most men who would say a thing like that, Major Miamatsu, if you will forgive me for saying so."

"Everything else has turned to dust in my hands. I saw the shelling of Fairbanks. The Americans have been hiding artillery all these years! Only the gods know what else they have secreted away waiting for this moment."

"You and your sergeant are adrift, major. May I offer you a haven?"

"Why would you do that?"

"You have a reputation of being a stern, but fair, man."

"How would you know that, even if it were true?"

"The Kempeitai are not the only ones in Alaska Prefecture who keep dossiers on people. Your fair treatment of prisoners is known, and appreciated. You asked permission to come aboard *Auspicious Provider* rather than commandeering the craft, which you could have done under the circumstances. It all adds up you see."

"You are Japanese," Miamatsu said, frowning. "Why would you…"

"I am an Alaskan. What that means is I do not believe in a system where the military makes all of the decisions that govern my life. I do not adhere to the Code of Bushido nor any of the ideologies it embraces, I never did."

"So you are part of the Liberation Underground?"

"In a manner of speaking, yes. Now I ask you to listen very carefully to my words and give them deep consideration."

"I owe you that much," Miamatsu said with a nod.

"Here are the things we know. You have been an integral part of the Imperial Japanese Army for many years. Your superiors have ignored your intellect to the point of their own demise. You put your life on the line to save prisoners who would have drowned in Fairbanks otherwise."

"That was just a few days ago! How could you know that?"

"Do you believe you are the only disaffected member of the Kempeitai?"

Miamatsu couldn't say the name that immediately came to his tongue. "What do you wish me to consider, Captain Inoue?"

"Join us. There are many Japanese, not all of whom were born here, who have joined the effort to replace the Empire with a more enlightened form of government. But first we must get the militants off our backs and out of power. We need people like you who understand the inner workings of the occupiers."

"You were one of those born here, weren't you?"

"Yes, and so was my father. We were Americans and Alaskans long before the Great Pacific War, and that will never change."

Miamatsu suddenly saw the koi in the Army Park pond in Fairbanks again. He wondered if the colorful carp had survived the flood. Their world had changed from a stable, carefully managed environment into chaos.

I never imagined I would compare myself to a fish, he thought.

"So I could stay after this is all finished?"

"That's what I have been saying."

"What if I refuse to be part of your organization?"

"We put you ashore a few miles north of Yakutat and you fend for yourself. However, I believe you will join us since you are not a fool."

"I *have* been a fool, a long time ago in San Francisco."

"Haven't we all?"

Stoney Compton

11

Juneau, Alaska Prefecture

The front door of the Juneau Public Library swung open with unusual vigor and Betsy Phillips snapped her head up from behind the front desk.

"Sue, you startled me."

"I have just heard the most amazing thing," Sue Ann Freeman said, quickly looking around in the small building. She lowered her voice. "Are we alone?" The small woman radiated energy and excitement.

"Yes. What's up?"

"Someone has been hiding a PT boat out at Tee Harbor all these years! Can you believe that?"

"Where did you hear this?" Betsy kept her voice as calm as possible.

"One of my contacts just told me. He said–" Sue abruptly stopped talking and stared at Betsy. "You're not even surprised, are you?"

"Of course I am!"

"About the boat being there or me finding out about it?"

"How is this suddenly common knowledge, Sue?"

"Because yesterday it shot up a Jap patrol boat and then shot down a Jap plane, all right there in Tee Harbor. Everybody who lived there has skedaddled into the bush. The Japs are shitting themselves."

"You always have such a colorful way of saying things."

"You knew about that PT boat, didn't you?"

"I will neither confirm nor deny that statement." She successfully stifled a smile.

"The PT boat left. Nobody knows where it went or who was on it. Oh, before I forget..."

"Battle stations!" Betsy snapped in a low voice.

Two Japanese men opened the front door and entered at a brisk pace. Betsy recognized them both as Tokkeitai agents.

Betsy and Sue bowed.

"Good morning. How may I help you gentlemen?" Betsy asked, straightening up. She felt gratified that both men were of short enough stature they were obligated to look up at her.

"We have need of information," the first man said, staring at her through thick glasses.

"I would be honored to provide you with what I can. What, in particular, do you request?"

"The census records for the Tee Harbor area."

"I apologize, sir, but we do not have those records. They would be at the court house up on Telephone Hill where all official territorial government records are stored."

The man seemed to deflate.

The second man said something in Japanese and both men turned and left the library.

"Fuck!" Sue Ann muttered as the door swung shut behind them.

"You curse like a sailor. In this instance I completely agree with you."

"Why do they want the census records, aren't they twenty-five years out of date?"

"So they can get the names of the people who live there, easier to round them up that way."

"Omigawd!"

"They won't find them."

"Where–, uh, never mind."

"Sue Ann, did you have a reason for coming in today other than passing on information?"

"Yes! I have this for your collection." She handed Betsy a bound book.

She immediately examined the book.

"The UL edition of *The Sun Also Rises*! You can end up in a penal colony if they catch you with this."

"You're welcome, Betsy. A warning delivered with pleasure is always appreciated. See ya."

When Sue opened the outer door Betsy lowered the book so it could not be seen by a casual passerby. From here on out she would be the one they caught with a proscribed book. The Nipponese might be losing their grasp on the situation, but they still made and executed the laws in Alaska Territory.

I wonder where she got this? Oh, Christ, what if she was followed!

As if reading her mind the front door opened. Her heart ceased racing when she recognized the familiar face.

"Addie! Oh, God, I'm glad it's you!"

Assistant librarian Adrienne Johnson pushed the door shut. "Are you ill, Betsy?"

"Please, lock the door and turn over the sign. No, I'm not ill, just a little more paranoid than usual. How are you?"

"I'm great. Have you heard the news?"

"About the PT boat?"

"PT boat? What PT boat?"

"It can wait, what have *you* heard?"

"Tokyo and Berlin have both been vaporized by atom bombs. The Emperor and Göering are both dead."

Betsy stared at the healthy, rounded young woman. "What's the source of this information, Addie?"

"The Imperial Navy. Our code people swear that message is being sent to all military installations. There's more."

Her legs felt weak and Betsy dropped into a chair. "Tell me."

Addie relayed the information about Fairbanks and Anchorage, ending with, "And the Imperial Navy Alaska Squadron has been ordered south to San Francisco."

"Why not Seattle or Vancouver?" Betsy muttered. "Unless they are circling their wagons. That means Admiral Kato is now the supreme commander for all of Southeast Alaska."

"Maybe," Addie said.

"Who else would it be?"

"I'm not sure about who is next in line, but I think something happened to Admiral Kato. I had three different reports that a military ambulance, no emergency lights operating, removed a covered body from the old capitol building. The size of the body was close to that of Kato, who hasn't been seen since."

Betsy's mind raced as she bounced conjectures and facts against each other. "Do you think they're fighting for dominance up there?"

"Nobody heard gunshots."

"What is going on?"

"Betsy, if they are losing their grip will they take it out on us? Have you heard anything from the Council?"

"I don't know, and no, I haven't heard anything. We all need to be on our toes and ready to jump in any direction."

"Do you think it's time to dig up our guns?"

"I've already done that."

"So the locker is no longer empty?"

"No. The UL has put everyone on alert. We're supposed to be ready for anything."

Addie pulled out a chair and dropped into it, her eyes suddenly large. "What's this about the PT boat?"

Betsy related the facts as she had heard them. "I'm sure Brian and the guys are going to be fine, they got away, didn't they?"

"He won't take me seriously, you know."

"There is a bit of and age difference," Betsy said gently.

"Fourteen years isn't much! He's such a nice man."

"*He's* the one you need to convince, not me."

12

Imperial Headquarters, San Francisco, Pacific States

Crown Prince Akihito sat silent, remote, and regal on a dais close to the front wall of a large, ornate chamber. Fifteen feet away, a massive table of California redwood stretched forty feet from one side of the room to the other. Generals, admirals, and consular ministers populated the chairs behind it and conferred in quiet tones with their staffs as they met with their new prime minister in the presence of the heir apparent to the Chrysanthemum Throne.

Prime Minister Keizō Komura, elevated to his position just that morning, quietly conferred with his soon-to-be emperor.

"The ceremonies have been finalized, majesty. All of us fear for your safety in this city. If the Nazis can destroy Tokyo they certainly can vaporize San Francisco."

"Please find a chair, admir–, ah, Prime Minister Komura. There is no need to stand."

"As you wish, majesty." He turned to an aide standing at attention ten feet away. "Chair."

Ten seconds later the minister sat in front of his emperor. "We have been combing the empire for senior officials and ministers. Unfortunately, those most knowledgeable of the governing structure were lost along with your father. Maintaining a mirror government here in the Pacific States lessened the mountain we must climb, but it remains seriously steep."

"You were able to find enough senior ministers to make my ascension both legal and honorable?"

"Of course, sire. Most of us find it auspicious that you were here on your official visit. Otherwise we would have faced nothing but chaos and factional fighting among our own."

Crown Prince Akihito nodded. The same thoughts had occurred to him, also.

"I am stunned and saddened by this turn of events. To be truthful, I never thought I would actually ascend to the throne due to my lack of military training."

"Majesty, you are not unprepared for the task. Your grasp of the inner workings of the empire cannot be matched by any other. We have ample military men who will give you any martial directions on any subject you deem necessary."

"I am fortunate that you were here, Mr. Prime Minister. Filling General Tojo's shoes will not be an easy matter. What must we do first?"

"Start the meeting. I will be your voice. If I err, please tilt your head to the left and we will confer."

* * *

The Prime Minister stood and bowed to Crown Prince Akihito. As he turned to face the chamber the aide made the chair vanish. He sat in a chair with a small desk in front of the massive table.

"Councilor Akakabe, have final plans been made for the Crown Prince's investiture?"

"Yes, Prime Minister," Councilor Akakabe, seated in the center of the table, said in a funereal voice. "Three days from now, on the last day of *hachigatsu*. We felt it would be more auspicious for Prince Akihito to succeed his father in the same month of his cruel death."

"I concur. What news of the insurrections?"

"It seems we have lost Alaska Prefecture, Prime Minister,"

"It cannot be found councilor, or has it eluded our grasp?" the minister snapped.

"The major portion is in revolt. The insurgents have taken all of our bases in Fairbanks and Anchorage. Only a few small ports, the Alexander Archipelago, and the Aleutians are still under our control."

"What an inauspicious time to lose the emperor and his cabinet. Are the people there remaining loyal?"

"Unfortunately, no. We have lost military units near Juneau and Dutch Harbor although there is yet no open conflict."

"What is being done about these insurrections?"

"All available forces have been ordered to hold at all costs."

"Do we not have a naval squadron in Alaska Prefecture?"

"We did, Prime Minister. Admiral Nakagawa ordered it to San Francisco yesterday." The councilor nodded toward a profusely sweating admiral sitting toward the end of the long table.

"Admiral, why did you make such an order?"

Although seated, the admiral bowed to the prime minister. "Prime Minister, I deemed it important to protect the Prince and San Francisco first and the outlying areas secondly."

"The insurgency is being fought in those outlying areas. How could the fleet help the empire while in obviously safe waters? Your orders reek of cowardice and defeatism."

"Prime Minister, we know not where the next conflagration will erupt. The prince regent's safety and the safety of our headquarters must not be neglected."

"Remind me," the prime minister said, "Are there any Imperial Army garrisons in those places?"

"Dutch Harbor is administered by the Imperial Army, Prime Minister. Juneau and the southeast portion of the prefecture is administered by the Imperial Navy under the command of Admiral Kato." Sweat beaded the admiral's face and his hands quivered.

The councilor bent over and said something in the prime minister's ear.

"I believe I understand the problem. Have we heard from General Yamashita?"

Admiral Nakagawa bowed again and looked down the table at General Hokita.

General Hokita bowed and spoke bluntly in his tobacco-scarred voice, "The last message we received from the Chrysanthemum Project indicated German paratroopers were attacking and most of the personnel on the base were dead. No mention of General Yamashita was made then, or since. It is our assumption that he died a hero with his command."

"Has the Imperial Army Air Force performed air reconnaissance to enlighten us?" Prime Minister Komura asked.

"Not as yet, prime minister. All of our air power in Alaska Prefecture has been nullified or destroyed. With the retreat of the Imperial Navy the Empire now lacks air support of any kind over the northern portion of the prefecture."

The Prime Minister returned his gaze to the three naval officers at the table.

"Admiral Nakagawa, for your information, Admiral Kato has committed seppuku. We have a Navy captain running Alaska Prefecture. You are relieved of your duties as of this moment. Leave us."

The admiral shot to his feet and bowed from the waist. He turned and left the room without a word.

"Vice Admiral Nishiawa, you are now Grand Admiral of the Fleet. Turn the Alaska Squadron around. I want them at Juneau as soon as possible. Ascertain which aircraft carrier group is closest to Alaskan waters and dispatch it to Cook Inlet immediately. I want a full reconnaissance of Fairbanks and Anchorage immediately."

"Hai, prime minister!" The small, spare officer bowed and turned to a captain for a quick whispered conversation. The captain bowed and hurried from the room.

More couriers arrived and various officers quickly scanned messages while still paying close attention to the Prince.

"What is the latest intelligence on the Reich?"

General Hokita cleared his throat. "Prime Minister, the eastern side of the Rocky Mountains is burning with thousands of insurrections. The Nazis have been attacked everywhere. Whether or not the Underground Liberation will carry the day is anyone's guess. It is my observation that Americans do not believe they have been conquered, merely presented with a twenty-two year set-back."

"General, they cannot possibly win the day against the two major military powers in the world." The Prime Minister's tone was more pleading than placating.

"Prime Minister, *we* believe that, I am not sure *they* do."

"Have there been any insurrections between Alaska and here?"

"Some of our more isolated stations in Canada, Washington, and Oregon have gone silent. All are being investigated as we speak."

"San Francisco has been quiet?"

"Yes, Prime Minister, which I am sure is due to the massive amount of Imperial Army and Navy personnel in the Bay Area."

"Pay close attention to the cricket network, general. That is where the first warning chirps will be heard."

Stoney Compton

13

Juneau, Alaska Prefecture

A large dash of cold water in the face woke Joe Coffey from his pain-induced fog. He hung from the ceiling by his manacled wrists. His hands and arms had gone numb so long ago that the blood from his wrists had dried on his arms - not that he felt it.

The large Japanese sergeant gave him a wide grin. "So happy to have you back with us, Joe. Would you like to answer my questions now?"

Joe worked his mouth, wishing some of the water had assuaged his incredible thirst. He tried to grin in return but couldn't manage the expression.

"I've answered every question you asked me," he croaked, wincing at the pain in his chest. He knew what a broken rib felt like, therefore he knew he now possessed more than one. His face exuded agony and he wished they would just shoot him and get it over with.

"But you have not answered them fully, Joe. This makes me angry, and when I am angry I must hurt things."

"Have you discussed this problem with your doctor? He might be able to–"

The sergeant's fist smashed into Joe's face and he felt new rips in his skin.

"Why the fuck don't you just kill me?" he gasped.

"I cannot do that. My superior has forbade me from mortally injuring you. Also, I would then have nothing to do with my time."

He hit Joe again. The pain took on a new dimension, obliterating all other sensations before it. His mind surrendered actual thought and his consciousness dove beneath his core to bask in the serenity of total absence of will.

At some level he still registered the angry blows of the Tokkeitai sergeant but they only elicited a faint disdain for someone too stupid to listen. The blows finally ceased and he hung in his limbo of being to the point of awareness that he might willingly allow himself die without further assistance.

Something cool touched his face and the seeming caress and soothing aftermath brought him to confused reality. He fought his ravaged face until one eyelid opened. The Japanese medic caring for his wounds barely registered his return, but Joe understood the man knew it.

"Ww-ut-r," he ground out, trying desperately to keep his shrieking eyelid up.

The medic dropped his swab and picked up a bottle, held it to Joe's lips.

Joe let his eye close and accepted the bottle as best he could, his battered lips and broken teeth were all new territory; he finally, gratefully drank. The water brought him back to a semblance of cognizance. He knew he was severely dehydrated.

"Please, may I have more water?"

The medic again put the bottle to Joe's lips and he sucked in all that he could. They might deny him more. His body lit up with desperate messages, all of them involved damage and pain.

He found it easier to open his eye, the other seemed to be swollen shut. The medic continued to dress Joe's facial wounds. Some of the pain receded and he wondered if they had some new, more horrific way of inducing pain and merely wanted him awake for the application.

Gotta stop being so analytical, he thought. *I need to be stupid.*

The medic began working on the cuts and bruises on Joe's shoulders and upper arms.

A voice snapped a command in Japanese, which Joe understood.

"Enough! Dismissed!"

The medic corporal immediately snapped to attention and bowed at someone behind Joe's back. Abruptly, he wasn't there any more.

The Tokkeitai officer who arrested him sat down across the small table and stared into Joe's eyes.

"You are quite resilient, Mr. Coffey. Your mental strength is a wonder to behold."

"What do you base that on?" Joe carefully asked through his damaged throat and mouth.

"The fact you have not yet told us all we have asked of you, that's what."

"What the hell do you think *I* know? I'm a foreman in the AJ Mine. I can tell you about hardrock gold mining and bossing Chinese *guest* workers." His lips were aflame with pain and he wanted to stop talking and maybe cry.

"We believe you are a member of the resistance. Do you deny this?"

"What resistance? This is a model community for the Japanese Empire."

"You and your friends are to be congratulated on that deception. Until yesterday I would have agreed."

"I don't understand," Joe said with a gasp. His pain-racked body made it difficult to concentrate on the man's words.

"This community has hidden a vessel of war from the Japanese Empire. The punishment for that is death, as you all have been told for two decades."

"Vessel?" Joe tried to focus on the man's face but it kept fading out.

"A combat vessel capable of destroying an aircraft and a patrol boat!" The voice rose and Joe felt the anger and lack of understanding it conveyed.

Joe weakly shook his head. "I don't know what you mean." The words came out as a croak again. "May I please have more water? My throat—"

The officer slapped him hard enough to knock him off his chair. Somewhere deep in his mind he felt surprised they hadn't tied him down.

Too bad I can't just jump up and run. The thought was as close to humor as he would get in this room and he made a quick grimace to disguise a smile.

"Pick him up and put him back on the chair," the officer said in Japanese.

Unknown hands on each side of him lifted Joe onto the chair and allowed his chest and face to fall forward onto the table.

"Tell me what I wish to know or I will have your friends executed," the man said with a flat tone. "Do not doubt my words."

"Water."

The bottle again found his ravaged mouth and he sucked greedily, nearly choking with the effort. He took a deep breath and said, "I do not doubt you. I cannot tell you what I don't know."

"Put him in a cell," the officer said tiredly in Japanese. "We have others to question."

Two sentries pulled him up and dragged him down the hall. The cracked linoleum on the floor seemed to send him a signal, but he couldn't decipher it before consciousness again faded.

14

Yakutat, Alaska Prefecture

"I don't understand, Major Miamatsu," the naval commander said. "You are Imperial Army yet you are here. Why?"

The small office held three desks and three chairs for visitors. An IJN lieutenant sat at one desk, a chief petty officer at the second and the commander sat at the third. Major Miamatsu sat on one of the chairs and Sergeant Hamada stood near the door, leaning nonchalantly against the wall.

"Call it a strategic retreat, commander. I am sure you are aware of events in Fairbanks and Anchorage."

"You deserted your post and are in flight?"

"I was on an ordered reconnaissance and my command was destroyed by insurgent artillery. Fairbanks is under water and Anchorage is under attack. I felt it imperative to go where my hard won intelligence could be used."

"I am not convinced–"

"Commander," Miamatsu interrupted, "is there a Kempeitai or Tokkeitai officer in this place?"

"Not to my knowledge, major. Even if there was it would not explain your presence in my district."

"There is some discrepancy in what you say, Commander Ito. Your command was at Valdez, was it not? Yet you are here."

The lieutenant quickly looked down at his desk, searching for something to occupy his attention.

Ito's cheeks turned ruddy and he frowned. "Who are *you* to question *me*, major?"

"I am part of the law enforcement for Alaska Prefecture, commander. The last I heard the Imperial Army was still the dominant service up here. Do you have a copy of your orders to desert Valdez?"

"I did not desert!"

"Transfer?"

"I am the senior naval officer for the three northern sub-districts in Alaska Prefecture. I have the right to shift my flag wherever I so choose."

"Without telling your staff what you are doing? There is a very confused Captain Hirayama sitting in Valdez at this moment, wondering what became of you. Have you communicated with the Imperial Navy Command at Juneau?"

"Yes, I am waiting for clarification of my orders."

"How long have you been waiting?"

Commander Ito swallowed. "Twenty-two hours so far."

Miamatsu toned his voice down to reasonable. "It is my considered opinion that the command structure in Southeast Alaska Prefecture is in a great deal of turmoil. Rather than have a pissing match like two peasants, why don't we try to work together to solidify our position?"

The lieutenant glanced over at Commander Ito, hope lightened his features and Miamatsu wondered where the former officer in charge of this station might be at the moment.

Not my problem, he decided.

"I suggest you radio Juneau and request direction," Ito said smoothly. "They already know I am here."

"That is an excellent idea. If you would direct us to the radio room?"

"Next building to the west. Look for the large antenna."

Miamatsu gave the commander a quick quarter bow and turned before the officer had a chance to respond. Sergeant Hamada opened the door and held it for his superior. As they walked down the short stairway together, Hamada quietly asked,

"Any idea where the original occupant of that chair is at this moment?"

"None. How many people did Captain Hirayama say the commander took with him on patrol?"

"All he mentioned was the commander's second-in-command."

"So, a lieutenant commander or a senior lieutenant."

A brisk wind blew in off Yakutat Bay. Clouds scudded across the sky as the light faded.

"Something is amiss in this place, and I don't think it is just the new war," Hamada said, his gaze ceaselessly sweeping from side to side.

Midway down the long dock running out into Yakutat Bay the *Auspicious Provider* sat at the fuel dock with hoses pouring oil into both tanks. They both knew the American, Oscar Jones, watched them through binoculars as he guarded the boat. Captain Inoue and his Tlingit first mate, Cliff Didrickson had vanished into the small town.

A single petty officer jumped to attention when they entered the radio room.

Miamatsu showed the man his credentials although he suspected the petty office already knew who they were.

"How may I assist you, major?"

"I want to see your copies of all radio traffic for the past twenty hours."

"I need authorization to do that, major."

"I am a Kempeitai major, and you will follow my orders of face the consequences."

Sergeant Hamada stood up straight, let his coat swing open, and flexed his shoulders. The petty officer was a small man and didn't appear well fed, let alone overly fit. He turned and picked up a large book and sat it in front of Miamatsu.

"As you ordered, sir."

"Hamada, lock the door. Signals, you sit down."

53

Stoney Compton

15

IJNS *Genda*
Prince William Sound, Alaska

Captain Tatsuya Mihashi watched the four aircraft of Lotus Flight launch into the blue skies over Prince William Sound and wondered if this operation would be as easy as it seemed on the surface of the situation.

"What is their flight time to Fairbanks?"

Officer-of-the-Deck Lieutenant Commander Kanegasaki glanced at his clipboard and allowed his eyes to follow the jets while he said, "Approximately an hour and a half, captain."

"Excellent. Now launch the Anchorage group."

The IJN *Genda* sloughed through the medium seas off the coast of Alaska Prefecture as the first Fuji F-1NJ of Cherry Blossom Flight taxied over to the starboard catapult, and the second bird moved into place on the port catapult. The aviation boatswain mates connected the aircraft to the catapults and quickly moved away from the planes, signaling all was ready. Behind each aircraft a section of steel deck rose up wedge-like to redirect the exhaust force of their engines.

The flight deck petty officer gave the first pilot the circular wave to bring his engine to full thrust. With an exaggerated swing the petty officer snapped his fist level with the deck and pointed forward. The pilot released his brakes as another crewman punched the launch button and the Fuji was hurled down the flight deck and into the air.

Moments later the second fighter followed his wingman. The third Fuji was an F-1R looking no different than its mates, but loaded with cameras fore and aft as well as a wide-angle, high-resolution camera in the belly of the plane. The other three would give their lives, if needed, to protect this aircraft.

The third F-1NJ lined up on the port catapult as the recon bird launched. Anchorage awaited.

"Any surface sightings from our escorts?" Captain Mihashi asked.

"A few fishing boats, captain, nothing more."

"Keep in mind that we use armed fishing boats for patrol vessels up here, commander."

"Cherry Blossom Flight is reporting in, captain," the radioman said.

"Put it on the speaker so we all can hear."

"...smoke drifting from the coordinates of the Yamamoto Aerodrome. No movement to be seen. We will do a fly-over and return for a second look."

A different pilot's voice said, "Over there toward the mountains, are those tanks?"

"The army has a heavy armor division here, let us make sure they are Japanese vehicles," Cherry Blossom leader said.

"This is Cherry Blossom two, I will go down and examine them more closely."

"Agreed. Everyone else hold formation."

"Cherry Blossom three to Cherry Blossom leader, I see ground fire!"

"Where–" A crump sounded over the speaker.

"Cherry Blossom three just exploded! Evasive action, break, break!"

"They're *our* tanks and they are firing on *us!*" Cherry Blossom two shouted.

On the bridge of the *Genda,* Captain Mihashi said, "Tanks can't hit jets! They must be using them as decoys!"

The speaker went quiet.

"Radio!" Mihashi bellowed, "what is happening?"

"They are not responding, captain. It seems there is no one there."

The captain's bridge phone rang and he snatched it to his ear. "Yes? I don't know, Commander Agawa. No, don't launch any more aircraft until we know what happened to Cherry Blossom flight." He sat the phone on its cradle and looked around the bridge. "I want a meeting with all senior staff in the wardroom in five minutes."

"I will pass the word, captain."

"Radio, notify Lotus flight of what transpired. Instruct them to stand well away from the city area."

"Hai, captain."

16

Juneau, Alaska Prefecture

Tobacco smoke mixed with hints of marijuana, beer, and whiskey added to the dissolute atmosphere of the Lucky Lotus, one of Juneau's more notorious bars on South Front Street. Japanese sailors in uniform and merchant mariners from diverse origins comprised the majority of the clientele mixing with young women of many nationalities. In the back of the main room a door swung open and an inebriated young woman shrieked with laughter as the man accompanying her shouted a remark in her ear.

A large man with a well-trimmed beard and mustache wearing a white linen suit filled the doorframe, glanced around, and nodded to the bartender before closing the door. Angus, the bartender, a massive Samoan with huge arms nearly covered in tattoos, leaned over to a small round-eye wearing a dark, three-piece suit.

"Dave will see you now."

The man picked up his drink and wound through the noisy crowd to the door.

Dapper Dave Hammond looked up from his desk when the man entered his office, quickly assessed his visitor, stood and held out his right hand.

"You're either new in town or a cop I don't know yet. Welcome to my den of iniquity. Have a seat and help yourself to the good stuff." He nodded toward a bottle of twenty-year-old scotch in the middle of his desk.

The man sat down. "I need help." He pulled off his hat and revealed a well-cut head of hair that matched his small mustache. His eyes all but jittered in agitation.

"Who are you?" Dave asked in a soft voice. "And who sent you to my place?"

"Alfred Davis, I'm Alfred Davis," he said nervously. "I've got to get out of town right away."

"Who told you to see *me*?"

"Oh, yeah, sorry. Uh, Marla, over at the—"

"I know where Marla works. Why did she send you to me?"

"She said you could get things done if the price was right."

"Did her recommendation go into more detail than that, or did she just say 'things'?"

"She just said that." Davis glanced around. "Look, this might have been a bad idea. Maybe I should leave?"

"We haven't discussed business yet, Alfred. Calm down. You saw Angus out there, *nobody* gets past him without me knowing about it."

"Does he ring a bell of something?"

"No, he usually throws them through that door, without opening it first. Where is it you wish to visit?"

"Big city, Anchorage, Vancouver, Seattle, any of 'em."

"I don't think you want to go to Anchorage right now."

Puzzlement made him squint. "Why not?"

"They're fighting a fucking war there at the moment. Why are you in Juneau anyway?"

"I was a courier and they didn't like my message. They said they would kill me if I didn't come up with money."

Dave blinked and his good humor dwindled. "Oh fuck, the Yakuza are after you, aren't they?"

"H-how did you know?"

"If it was the Kempeitai who thought you screwed them, you would already be dead or very close to it. The, ah, other organizations in the area wouldn't use you in the first place. The Yakuza try to make a profit on everything they touch."

"Oh. Can you help me?"

"No. Life here in Juneau is a delicate balance of greed, self-preservation, and abject fear. Right now I'm heavily in the grip of the last part." Dave took a sip of scotch and made a mental note to have a long, painful chat with Marla; who would be bearing the pain.

"I don't have that much money! I have no way of getting it. I thought I could get out of town with what I do have." Alfred seemed close to tears.

"How much does the Yakuza want?"

"Ten thousand yen! I've only got six."

"I'm going to tell you what Marla should have, Alfred."

"What?"

"You're fucked. You might find a fishing boat that needs a crew member, but not dressed like that. If you ask the wrong boat they'll turn you in to the Kempeitai on the spot."

"What would it cost me to get your help in picking the right boat?"

"There's a closet over there where I keep spare clothing for unfortunates. Go find something a bit more fisherman looking and I'll think about this."

Alfred made a small smirk quickly quashed and hurried over to the door and opened it revealing a small hallway and a very large man. The large man broke Alfred's neck before he could make a sound.

"Tiger," Dave said to the man. "Search him carefully, I think he's a cop. We'll split what money you find, fifty-fifty. Anything else on him comes to me. Okay?"

"You bet, Dave. It's a shame he didn't watch where he was going, huh?"

"Yes, in so many ways."

Stoney Compton

17

Angoon, Alaska Prefecture

"The whole Jap navy is up here!" Rear Admiral Colby Williams said. "I don't know if we can blame it *all* on you, Brian..."

The men and one woman seated around the conference table all erupted in laughter, including LCdr Brian Wallace.

"...but I am sure you started the whole thing."

"I think the events in Anchorage and Fairbanks had more to do with it than our little PT boat," Brian said through a wide smile.

"The fact remains," Colby said soberly, "there is a carrier group sitting up in Prince William Sound that just begs for our attention."

"That's about all we got, Colby, uh, admiral," Captain Gabe George said. "We have eight fishing boats fitting themselves out with armament, but none of them will be equal to the firepower or speed of Brian's PT boat."

"What about the destroyer escort I heard mentioned?" Major Ramona Didrickson asked. She had been an officer in the Marine Corps and home on leave in Hydaburg when everything ended. Her mental strength was more acute than her physical strength. She was famous for winning an arm wrestling contest in a fisherman's bar in Petersburg a decade earlier, beating all five challengers.

"Face it, people," Gabe said. "Even if we had a DE we would still be outgunned by one carrier group."

"They have our old *Kearsarge*, what they call the *Genda*, a heavy cruiser, three destroyers, and a destroyer escort." Colby ticked off his fingers as he went through the list. "That's a lot of firepower and it would be suicide to attack them openly. Everybody agree with that assessment?"

Nods and shrugs went around the table.

"Too bad we don't have a couple of submarines since they have maybe six and are all somewhere else," Brian said, looking into his coffee cup.

'The table went silent.

Brian looked up and found everyone else staring at him as if he had sprouted horns.

"What? Did I say something wrong?"

"You just pulled that thought out of your ass, right, Brian?" Admiral Williams asked in a calm tone.

"Yeah. Wishful thinking and all that." He saw they all still regarded him oddly and a thought burned into his mind. "Do we *have* a sub?" he said in a whisper.

"Maybe."

"How can that be?"

Admiral Williams glanced around at the others. "Anyone who agrees that Lieutenant Commander Wallace be granted Supreme Top Secret clearance raise their hand." He raised his hand. The other four people at the table followed suit.

"Here's the deal, Brian. You *cannot* be captured alive by the enemy. Do you understand?"

"Yes, admiral, I understand."

"Do you accept this clearance and all that it entails?"

"Yes, sir. I do."

"Excellent. I yield the floor to Major Didrickson."

She stared into Brian's eyes for a long moment. "You're the only person in the room I haven't known for at least twenty years. If I seem hesitant it's nothing personal, okay?"

"Okay, major."

"When the world turned upside down in the Spring of '45 a lot of skippers took the initiative and headed for small out of the way ports in hopes matters would turn around. As we are all aware, it took twenty-two years for that to even start, but here we are.

"Anyway, Lieutenant Commander Lawrence Edge, skipper of the USS *Bonefish* held an all-hands meeting and they voted on what to do. In the end they decided to take the boat to southeast Alaska Territory and find a place to hide. They decided to go to Klawak."

"I've never been to Klawak. Is it still there?" Brian asked, feeling dazed.

"Klawak or the *Bonefish*?" Major Didrickson asked with a smile.

"The sub. I know that Klawak is still there."

"Yes, it is. The people in the area helped the crew build a sub pen with enough cover to hide everything from the air. They even built a grid for the sub to be high and dry when needed to clean and paint the hull."

"Wow, and I thought we had done a lot in Tee Harbor."

"You did. And you guys pretty much did it without any heavy equipment. The guys at Klawak were fortunate there was an operating fish cannery with a lot of equipment to move heavy loads. The *Bonefish* had just come out of the yards in San Francisco and carried a full complement of twenty-four torpedoes plus ammo for her four-inch deck gun and the twenty and forty millimeter cannons."

"Shit, she's loaded for bear!"

Colby cleared his throat. "We have to figure out the best and most expeditious way to use what we have, and that includes the DE as well as your PT boat, Brian."

"Do we have any way of knowing how long this carrier group will stay in Prince William Sound?" Gabe asked. "Keep in mind they have air cover and aerial patrols, so we can't really sneak up on them."

The fifth person at the table finally spoke. He wore a pressed shirt with the silver tabs of a commander.

"It would have to be a night action, which would negate their air cover. If we use a lot of small boats they might not show up on their radar. I don't know how much discipline they have but they've been top dog in the Pacific for over fifty years and might be getting lax."

"I don't believe I know you, commander," Brian said.

The man grinned and reached across the table to shake hands. "Tom Richards, Jr., I served in OPS at Pearl Harbor until the whole thing came unglued. I'm an Unaligmiut Eskimo from Unalakleet."

"Pleased to meet you, sir. You're a long way from home."

"Aren't we all?"

"Brian, how many torpedoes do you have on your boat?" Admiral Williams asked.

"Four, sir, and they are all well maintained."

"I wonder how many the DE has," Major Didrickson mused.

"Does that ship actually exist?" Brian asked.

"According to Medusa, it does."

"Uh, Col-, admiral," Gabe said. "Who the hell is Medusa?"

"The head of our intelligence network in Southeast. I don't know his real name."

"Wasn't Medusa a female?" Major Didrickson asked.

"Damned if I know, Ramona. I don't even know where this person is located, but they are the keepers of all secrets for us. Whatever we come up with here has to go to Medusa for vetting and additional input, so let's get after it."

Rain tentatively splattered across the windows and then beat down in earnest.

"Summer's over kids. Okay, Tom, I like the idea of a night action. So how do we pull it off?"

18

Imperial Headquarters, San Francisco, Pacific States

"Prime Minister Komura, there have been coordinated attacks on Imperial military bases throughout California and Washington. Heavy fighting is reported at San Diego and Long Beach in California, and at Bremerton in Washington." The aide bowed from the waist.

"Have the insurgents done any real damage?" the prime minister, still in a silk robe and warm from his bed, said with a sneer.

"Four warships tied up in Long Beach have been sunk at their berths–"

"How?" The sneer dissipated.

"At this time we believe mines were attached to the hulls. All went off at the same time, midnight. It is thought they wanted all personnel on board when they detonated the weapons."

"What is the current situation?"

"The fire aboard the carrier *Yamamoto* is still out of control. Mortars are being fired from the hills overlooking the naval base. Troops sent to engage them have been ambushed and their vehicles destroyed by mines and anti-tank missiles."

"Send in an air strike!"

"It is *dark*, prime minister. The pilots wouldn't know where to attack. We have many senior officials living in those hills."

"Have the army and marines been mobilized?"

"Yes, unfortunately their bases are also under attack. Many buildings, mostly barracks, have been destroyed or are on fire, and casualties are mounting."

"I ordered an increased security alert two days ago! Was nothing done?"

"I have no answer for that, prime minister. Nothing has been said about it."

"Heads are going to roll! Has there been any movement on the part of the Reich?"

"Not that we know, prime minister. We are not reducing our vigilance."

"Not that we could do a damn thing about it if they did attack! Alert the council, I want an immediate meeting. Double the guard around the Emperor. This is a very inauspicious event for his first week on the throne!"

"Yes, Prime Minister Komura!"

As soon as the prime minister exited, the aide ran for the door.

19

Imperial Japanese Navy HQ
Juneau, Alaska Prefecture

"**A**dmiral, I regret that I am forced to leave you and your command to face the insurgents without fleet support, but I must obey my orders from the Prime Minister."

Admiral Jo Tanaka bowed from the waist. He had been elevated in rank only the day before and now bore the burden of maintaining the Empire in Alaska Prefecture.

"We will follow the orders given, Vice Admiral Shima, and dedicate our lives to the Emperor. The situation in California is very much worse than what we face in this relatively placid backwater."

"We do not lose patrol boats and aircraft in *placid backwaters*, admiral," Shima said in a flat tone. "However, we have great faith in your abilities and are confident you will succeed here in Alaska Prefecture."

Admiral Jo Tanaka watched his superior leave with his retinue, wondering if he felt relief at the man's departure or terror at the aspect he had nobody to back him up other than Captain Mihashi who commanded the *Genda* carrier group in Prince William Sound. He decided terror won and he embraced the emotion as a goad to carry out his mission.

"I said *relatively* placid backwater," he muttered to himself.

"Did you say something, admiral?" Lieutenant Hasama asked.

"Nothing worth repeating. Do we have the field reports I requested yesterday?"

"Yes, admiral. They are on your desk. Would you like me to go over them with you?"

"No, lieutenant. I want you to quietly increase the security around the aerodrome and the military docks. I believe the situation in California is a harbinger of things to come."

"Hai, Admiral Tanaka!"

"Also inform the chief investigator of the Tokkeitai that I wish to see him at his earliest convenience."

"It shall be done, admiral."

Jo retreated to his office. The bloodstains from his predecessor still lurked on the deck in the form of a dark stain the enlisted ratings had been unable to eradicate. He had never considered himself a particularly strong person, but the concept of killing himself in response to the actions of another seemed more of a weakness than a strength.

As a child in Iwate Prefecture he had been drawn more to books and art than martial matters. His father, a frustrated businessman had deemed otherwise and packed Jo off to the Imperial Naval Academy at Etajima. Graduating in 1941 he had served in the Great Pacific War and at the end of hostilities carried the rank of lieutenant commander.

"Now here I am, in charge of the largest prefecture in the Empire." He glanced around to make sure nobody heard his utterance. Of late he had become garrulous and he wondered if it was a sign of infirmity.

A knock on his office door brought him to the immediate present.

"Enter."

A Japanese man wearing a business suit entered the office and bowed from the waist.

"I am Lieutenant Commander Toji Nagano, chief inspector of the Tokkeitai in the Juneau District. How may I serve the admiral?"

"Please, shut the door and sit." Jo waved at the two chairs against the wall.

Nagano placed a chair in front of the desk and sat.

"I congratulate you on your promotion, admiral." He glanced at the floor.

"I would bring Admiral Kato back in an instant if I could. This position was not what I aspired to, but we all serve the Emperor."

"Exactly so," Nagano said with a nod. "How may I be of benefit to your mission?"

"How prevalent is the underground in southeast Alaska Prefecture?"

"They are everywhere, admiral."

"In what numbers?"

"I have come to the conclusion that every caucasian and Indian in Alaska is part of the underground."

"But you cannot prove it?"

"Not yet. The human body can withstand just so much abuse before the person tells you everything they know. It's a matter of self-preservation."

"How many people are you currently, ah, interrogating?"

"Five."

"Your results thus far?"

"Negligible, sir. They tell one what they believe one wishes to hear but hard evidence is nonexistent."

"I suggest you release them all."

"Admiral?" Nagano blurted in surprise. "What would be the profit in that?"

"Unobtrusively follow all of them. Have your people make a list of all persons they contact and—"

"Forgive me for interrupting, admiral. Juneau is a small town. Everybody talks to everyone else. I postulate that within five days time we would have the entire population on our list."

Nettled by the interruption, Admiral Tanaka frowned. The worst part was, what the commander said made sense. He lost the frown and nodded.

"You are correct, commander. I had not fully thought out the concept."

Nagano shrugged. "This is a something we have never before dealt with, admiral. The coordination of this rebellion would be impressive were it not so serious. If we can sever the head of the beast we might be able to contain the remainder."

"What are the chances of inserting a spy into their midst?"

"Again, negligible, sir. I would not trust a round-eye who would agree to be an agent for us. The other Americans would certainly know of his perfidy and either use him against us or eliminate him altogether."

"Unfortunately, I cannot argue with that assessment either, commander. I go to sleep at night trying to envision a method to keep the locals in check."

"Other than the destruction of the patrol boat and our aircraft, nothing untoward seems to be happening here."

"*Yet.* Are you aware of the situation in California at this very moment?"

"Yes, sir, I am. The positive side of being in a location with a small population is they have very few personnel to work with. That is to our benefit."

"Tell that to the sub-lieutenant pilot, and senior lieutenant patrol boat commander who both died a few days ago. We have yet to understand how that happened."

"We discovered an anchorage built into the inlet's bank. It evidenced many years of existence and very recently abandoned."

"That is news to me, commander. How large a boat would it have accommodated?"

The lieutenant commander pulled a small notebook from his pocket and flipped through pages.

"The space is ninety feet deep, twenty-four feet wide, and has a seven-foot depth below sea level. I am not conversant with the dimensions of boats to answer further."

Jo thought hard, mentally going through the list of possible small craft left over from the war.

"It couldn't be a minesweeper," Jo mused, "they're longer than that. Oh, hell! They have a torpedo patrol boat!"

"I don't know that one, admiral."

"PT-Boat, they called it a PT-Boat. Small, heavily armed craft that can carry up to four torpedoes and have heavy caliber guns. No wonder they were able to destroy an aircraft and a patrol boat!"

"Where could they have it hidden now? Certainly not locally."

"I don't know, commander, but it is imperative that we find out."

"Perhaps you could instruct the aerial patrols to watch for it in particular?"

"That is an excellent idea. I will see that it happens."

"Do you still want me to release our prisoners?"

"Yes. I feel our subjects have had ample stick and now require carrots."

Stoney Compton

20

Yakutat, Alaska Prefecture

"**I**s everything aboard the boat, Norio?"

"Yes, Major Miamatsu. Captain Inoue says we need to leave in the next half hour to best utilize the darkness. The underground will attack a half hour after we depart."

Katsu Miamatsu stopped for a moment and thought about the irrevocable step he was poised to take. There would be no turning back from this night, not for the rest of his life, however long or short it might be.

"Then we should leave."

Rain fell in waves of varying intensity and he felt it was the perfect way to end one part of his life and begin the next. They hurried past the patrol boat tied to the long dock. No hail or murmur came from the small boat, where a light gleamed from the galley.

The man on watch obviously felt all was well and decided to stay out of the weather. Miamatsu pitied him, knowing what sort of official retribution would descend on the hapless soul if he lived through this long night. From this vantage point all of Yakutat lay quiet and still despite the fire and destruction already kindled in the men and women moving quietly and resolutely through the darkness.

The *Auspicious Provider* sat quietly at her berth, the engine running but no light showing to give away her impending actions. Miamatsu and Hamada climbed aboard. Oscar Jones slipped the lines off the dock bollards and shot up the ladder behind them.

On the bridge Cliff Didrickson, the Tlingit first mate, gave Captain Inoue a thumbs up and the engine shifted into gear, and the *Provider* moved smoothly away from the rain-slick dock. Yakutat Bay yawned before them and beyond lay the Gulf of Alaska.

As they hurried into the cabin Miamatsu reflected that he would have never done this if he didn't absolutely trust the crew of this boat. They knew what they were doing in nautical terms and he felt he knew what he was doing in military terms.

Committing treason.

Somehow the thought didn't bother him. He looked back where he knew the village of Yakutat lay on the dark mainland.

As he watched, a flash of light evolved into a larger fireballs as the buildings of the Imperial Japanese Navy erupted in violent explosions. Smaller flashes of light briefly marked where vehicles and structures housing the IJN war machine were destroyed in carefully timed and executed assaults.

By morning all members of the Japanese Navy would be dead. The Underground Liberation had retaken this piece of Alaska Territory.

Cliff hurried into the galley where Miamatsu and Hamada sat. "Major, the skipper wants you on the bridge."

Inoue stared into the night, a wide grin on his face. When Miamatsu stepped up beside him he turned and laughed.

"We did it! Ben Williams just radioed that the naval station has fallen. They are going to step two."

"Did we lose anyone?"

"No. The Imperial Navy lost all of their people." He nodded. "Cliff got the radio working if you want to listen to their chatter."

Newly bolted to the console an official IJN radio chattered through a headset that Miamatsu carefully placed over his ears.

"...Yakutat, do you read? Imperial Naval Station Yakutat, do you read?"

Miamatsu turned to Cliff, whispered, "Can they hear us if we talk in here?"

"Not unless you hold the microphone button down." he was close to smiling, which seemed to be something he never did.

"Good to know," Miamatsu said with a nod. "Can I hear it without wearing this head clamp?"

"Skipper?" Cliff said.

Inoue gave him a thumbs up.

Ray fiddled with the radio and the speaker mounted on the bulkhead made a slight squawking sound before "Imperial Naval Station Juneau, do you read?" boomed out.

"We read you, *Genda*, what is your position?"

"On station in Prince William Sound. We have lost contact with the Yakutat base as well as Patrol Boat 29. Please advise."

"*Genda*, we have no other patrol boats in the area. Aerial reconnaissance at first light will be made. Juneau out."

"Is there any other traffic we can hear?" Miamatsu asked.

"Turn the large dial slowly," Cliff said, even closer to a smile.

Barely touching the dial elicited: "Fire aboard Yamamoto has been contained. Shelling by insurgents has ceased. Situation under control in Long Beach."

"It sounds like they are having a busy night," Miamatsu said.

21

IJN HQ
Sitka, Alaska Prefecture

"**C**ommander Issi, we have a request from the Alaska Squadron to reconnoiter our base at Yakutat."

"Yeoman Hattori, I need a little more information than that."

"My apologies, commander. Last night neither the *Genda* or Naval Station Juneau could raise Yakutat by radio. The *Genda* is in Prince William Sound and Juneau lacks long-range aircraft, so they have asked us to investigate."

"Now I understand the situation. Invite Lieutenant Hiro and Captain Tamashiro to join me in the wardroom in an hour."

"Hai, Commander Issi, it shall be done."

Captain Tamashiro, Imperial Japanese Marines was first to arrive, five minutes early. Commander Issi anticipated this and was already in his chair at the head of the table.

The captain went to attention and bowed from the waist.

"Reporting as ordered, commander."

"Please be seated, captain. I'm sure we will not have to wait very long—"

Lieutenant Hiro stepped into the room and bowed to the commander. Before he could say anything, the commander said, "Please take a seat, lieutenant."

The lieutenant sat across the table from the captain.

"Here is the situation…" Issi explained the lack of communications and the dual requests. "So Admiral Shima is watching from afar. Lt. Hiro, I want you to take the H8K3 Flying Boat with full combat crew and fly up to Yakutat with Captain Tamashiro and thirty imperial marines of his choice.

"I may be overreacting to the perceived problem, but there have been unusual events transpiring in Alaska Prefecture since the loss of the Emperor and Tokyo. I want you to take off in two hours."

The lieutenant shot to his feet and the captain snapped to at nearly the same instant.

"It is my honor to carry out this mission as you say, commander," Lt. Hiro snapped, bowing.

"We will bring honor to the new Emperor." Captain Tamashiro said, also bowing.

"Excellent. Dismissed," Issi said to a suddenly empty room. "I pity anyone they find there who cannot answer all their questions."

✳ ✳ ✳

The massive Kawanishi H8K Type 2 Flying Boat easily lifted off the waters of the Western Channel of Sitka Sound. The four massive engines droned into the sky, effortlessly carrying thirty-one Imperial Marines and a crew of seven. The large aircraft could have carried another thirty passengers.

"How far is Yakutat, Lieutenant Hiro?" Co-pilot Ensign Ogata asked.

"About forty-five minutes. Attention, crew! Have all weapons charged and ready when we land. We have no idea what happened in this place."

Five microphone double-clicks signaled the crew had heard and understood.

The clear sky made for perfect flying weather and visibility exceeded twenty miles.

"This is beautiful country," Ensign Ogata said.

"Yes," Lt. Hiro said. "It is also a brutal, unforgiving country. If you are not prepared for it you can die in some rather amazing ways."

"Flight deck, port gunner here. I see a small boat at ten o'clock."

"Use your binoculars, Nishida! Tell me if it is a threat or not."

"Yes, lieutenant." Another thirty seconds passed. "It is a fishing boat, lieutenant, flying a Japanese flag."

"I am gratified you are so alert, however, next time fully survey the sighting before announcing it."

"Yes, lieutenant."

"Captain Tamashiro, can you hear me?"

"Yes Lieutenant Hiro, loud and clear."

"I plan to land out in the bay and taxi in to the military dock. As soon as we set down your men should be ready to fight."

"My men were ready to fight when they boarded this aircraft, lieutenant."

Lt. Hiro rolled his eyes. "Good to know, captain."

Silence lapsed over the plane as they flew over the sun-sparkled water of the Gulf of Alaska. One man called out a whale sighting but otherwise all were quiet.

"Where the land goes in, is that Yakutat Bay, lieutenant?" Ensign Ogata asked.

"Indeed. You are most perceptive, ensign. Five minutes to landing!" he announced over the intercom.

They circled over the village of Yakutat and saw evidence of burning among the military structures. Only the three massive fuel tanks remained. Lt. Hiro flew out over the water and turned into a landing pattern that would take them into the bay. The aircraft touched down 500 meters off shore and they taxied into the bay.

All guns were locked and loaded, their handlers peering out, searching for reasons to fire. Nothing moved on the shore. The Kawanishi slowly made its way toward the long dock, which appeared undamaged as did the curiously quiet Patrol Boat 29 tied to the dock.

"Captain Tamashiro, have two of your men ready to jump onto the dock and secure lines to the aircraft on my command."

"As you wish, lieutenant." He signaled to two of his noncoms and they opened the upper hatch in preparation.

Lt. Hiro was torn as to where he should actually stop—halfway down the dock or closer to the patrol boat and the shore. Both prospects seemed to hold equal amounts of benefits and drawbacks. He turned the plane so it faced the open bay in case it needed to escape on a moment's notice, and taxied toward the dock.

He shut down the starboard engines and reduced the port engines to their lowest setting.

"Get them out there!"

* * *

Two sergeants leaped out of the plane and grabbed a line thrown from the starboard gun slot, grabbed one that was already secured to the right float, and wrapped them around cleats on the dock. They immediately unlimbered their machine guns and faced the quiet shore. The stench of burnt buildings permeated the salt air.

Captain Tamashiro and his remaining marines poured out of the hatch and onto the dock where they all took a defensive stance and faced the shore and patrol boat.

"First squad, move in and search the boat."

Fifteen marines instantly rushed the patrol boat and scrambled aboard. Less than five minutes passed before the first squad sergeant jumped to the deck and reported.

"Captain, there is no sign of life on that boat. We found some blood in the galley, but no bodies."

"Good work, get your men back on the dock."

The sergeant whistled and waved his arm at the marines on the boat. They immediately reformed on the dock.

Captain Tamashiro pointed toward the damaged fleet structures.

"Second squad, take cover behind the building on the right!"

Half of the marines thundered down the dock and onto the sand, where they went to ground surrounding the structure.

"First squad, follow me!" Tamashiro yelled and they all rushed toward the second building. They finished the perimeter started by the second squad, and lay in the sand, panting from the effort of their sprint wearing full packs.

The only sound to be heard was the flap of the large Japanese flag on top of the middle fuel tank. Somewhere in the distance a raven rattled a query.

"Fire teams one and two, search those structures!"

Teams of three men rose from the either end of the perimeter and warily advanced to the buildings and disappeared inside. Moments later they emerged and waved all clear.

Undamaged buildings, obviously not military structures, sat another hundred meters inland. Off to the left around the curve of the bay sat the remains of two larger buildings that had burned to the ground. From the map he had been given the captain knew them to be the barracks and mess hall for the small base.

Nothing else in the village seemed to have suffered damage. They had yet to find a body. According to the briefing there had been a total of twenty-three naval ratings here and four officers.

Were they all taken prisoner? He wondered. *Why would they do that?*

The radio hooked on his battle harness beeped and he pulled it off and depressed the send button. "Yes?"

"What have you found?" Lt. Hiro asked, his voice reduced from commanding to tinny and irritating.

"Nothing. No bodies on the patrol boat or on shore. Just burned buildings. I'll tell you if I find anything."

He released the button and replaced the radio on his harness. His situational awareness skills, already on full alert, hammered at him. Something about this was all wrong and he felt vulnerable, something Imperial Marines were not supposed to feel.

He wished he had brought his sergeant-major, he had seen combat in the Great Pacific War. The rest of his men, including himself, had never fired a shot in anger or felt threatened. He glanced back at the Kawanishi neatly blocked by the patrol boat and realized that if anything happened out here the aircraft gunners would not be any assistance.

"Sergeant Sakai, take two fire teams and probe those buildings."

The sergeant gave him a clenched fist in the air and snapped orders to six of his men. They crept into the building. The silence remained unbroken save for two ravens squawking at each other in the distance.

Captain Tamashiro was not fond of ravens, never had been. He thought them scavengers of the dead. The silence became oppressive.

He pulled his radio off and held the key down. "Sergeant Sakai, what is your situation?"

No answer. He felt sweat running under his helmet binding.

83

"Sakai, answer, damn you!"

Nothing. *Maybe there is something in the building that blocks radio transmissions,* he hoped.

"Sergeant Haruna, take two fire teams and go around the other side of the building that Sergeant Sakai entered."

The sergeant shot his fist into the air and made hand signals to his men. They crept out of sight. Four minutes ticked by.

Reluctantly Captain Tamashiro slowly pulled his radio from the harness and held down the button. "Sergeant Haruna, I want a report, now."

More silence. One of the corporals frowned questioningly at him but said nothing. Tamashiro made a command decision. He signaled to his senior corporal to take half the remaining marines around one side of the structure and he would lead the other half around the opposite side.

He checked his weapon to make sure the safety was off and waved them forward as he leaped to his feet and charged forward.

❋ ❋ ❋

Ensign Ogata fidgeted in his seat with his head all but hanging out the open window next to him and Lt. Hiro stifled the urge to censure him.

Where the hell were the marines?

They had heard nothing past the queries from Captain Tamashiro to his sergeants. No shots had rang out or human voices heard. It was as if the marines had gone into a cave and were swallowed up.

Another raven clacked from the trees and Hiro wondered if they were the only birds in this area. More than anything, he wanted to crank up the other two engines and get out of this place. Unfortunately, he had yet to complete his mission.

"Lieutenant," Petty Officer Second Class Shimada said, "there are four marines coming down the dock carrying a fifth man. All of them are limping badly."

"Get out there and help them!"

"Hai, lieutenant!"

The five gunners quickly exited the aircraft and hurried toward the marines. Ensign Ogata moved over to the hatch to watch. Hiro turned in time to see the ensign take an arrow through the chest that came four inches out through his back.

Lieutenant Hiro unsnapped the flap on his pistol holster and freed his seat belt assembly so he could rush toward the hatch. Before he could cover the distance two arrows hit him in the chest and neck. The pistol fell from his suddenly nerveless hands and he reached toward the wounds before shock overwhelmed him.

He died twitching on the deck of the aircraft. Two men wearing the bloodied tunics of dead marines bounded through the hatch with newly liberated machine-guns and quickly scanned the interior.

"We got all of them, Jimmy," one said.

"And now we got us a plane, too!" he replied. "Sound the all clear, Andy."

The other man turned and made a raven call into the silent village.

Stoney Compton

22

A-J Mine
Juneau, Alaska Prefecture

"Where is Mr. Coffey?" the shift sergeant asked.

"I don't know, Sergeant Ando, he did not notify me that he would be absent," James Flanagan said, still bowing to the Japanese soldier.

"I am forced to report this to the colonel's office," Sgt. Ando said. "Return to work!"

James straightened up and stared after the retreating sergeant and his private as they made their way to the lift.

Where the fuck is Joe?

Three coolies pushed a loaded ore cart past him. He ignored them, everyone had problems. Joe missing a whole shift without permission was unheard of, he had to be dead or in the hospital to pull that off.

James wondered how he could find out without giving anyone his name. It was one thing to wonder if they hung your best friend. It was another thing entirely to voluntarily stick your head through the noose next to him.

"Boss," a coolie said next to him. "Trouble on adit four."

"Shit!" Phone calls forgotten, James hurried toward the problem. As he pushed past indifferent workers he felt keenly aware of the vast social distance between him and most of the other men in the mine.

When he hired on for this job he didn't realize he would be working with slaves. Thank God they didn't make him use a whip. The trouble turned out to be a coolie lying on the powdered dust floor clutching a shattered leg resulting from an upset ore cart.

"Did anyone notify the aides?"

"Only white man or Japanese can do that," a coolie said through a frown. "You not know that, boss?"

"I forgot. Here's my chop. Hurry and get help." He tore off a piece of page from a small book. Without the printed chop the coolie would be unable to get anyone to even listen to him.

"Okay, you two carry him toward the aid station. The rest of you get that cart back on the track and loaded." He did his best to never shout or curse them, no matter how slow their actions or response.

His Scot's notions of individual freedom suffered heavily in this job. Thoughts of quitting were quickly supplanted with the knowledge that if he quit his job he might easily be thrown to the other side of the social divide. Those jobs didn't pay beyond food and shelter, both of which were minimal.

The clatter of picks against rock, steel wheels on steel tracks, and the tired murmur of enslaved men breaking themselves for gold ore beat on him like a cudgel. The hardest part of his job was not to cry.

"Mr. Flanagan!"

Sgt. Ando's pet private stood there glaring at him.

Now what the fuck have I done wrong?

"How may I help you, Private Shimono?"

"Report to the colonel's office at once!"

James bowed and as soon as the private stalked away, followed him. If Lieutenant Colonel Hirota wanted him to track dust on his fancy silk carpet he would damn well do it.

The colonel was the squarest man James had ever seen. He was nearly as wide as he was tall yet didn't look fat, his mass seemed to be all muscle. The colonel had been a miner in his youth and understood the process and the people.

He also had run a prisoner of war camp. James had never seen the colonel smile, even doubted the muscles in the man's face could create one. He stepped into the office and bowed from the waist.

"How may I serve the colonel?"

88

"You serve the Emperor, not me. Mr. Coffey no longer works in the A-J Mine. You are now the shift foreman and responsible for the quotas required by the Empire of Japan."

James bowed again.

"Thank you, Lieutenant Colonel Hirota. I will do the best I can for the Empire."

"That is understood, Mr. Flanagan. Dismissed."

His mind buzzing with questions, James hurried back to the workings.

Stoney Compton

23

Klawak, Alaska Prefecture

"I am so sick of cleaning up bird shit!" Second Class Torpedoman's Mate Russell Velie said. He and five other men wearing patched and stained dungarees slowly walked the deck of the USS *Bonefish*, (SS-223) seeking debris, rust, and bird droppings from the cave of carefully arranged foliage that roofed their sub pen.

"Did I tell you about that king salmon I caught the other day?" Velie asked Prentiss.

"Only five times, this makes six. You think there's anything to the scuttlebutt about going on a war patrol?" Third Class Torpedoman Bobby Lee Prentiss asked in a near whisper.

"Who'd you hear it from?"

"Sparks Paskin."

"He's a radioman, but who told him?"

"Said it came in from TPN HQ."

Velie scrubbed at the deck for a moment and straightened up, rubbed his back.

"I'm getting too old for this shit. Did you ask the skipper?"

"I'm new crew, not old crew. I always feel a bit shy around him."

"Crew is crew, Bobby. You made the cut and went through the training, so you're crew. You just don't have a patrol under your belt yet."

"All the same…"

"When did Sparks receive this message?"

"Two days ago, before they passed the word this would be an 'all hands' meeting today."

"Had to give the married guys time to get here. Chief Fuller lives down in Hydaburg with his wife's family. That's why the skipper only calls these all hands musters a couple times a year."

"Velie, Prentiss, everybody," Chief Johnson yelled. "All hands muster in five minutes!"

"Aye, aye, chief," Velie yelled back. "Well, let's go find out if the scuttlebutt is on the money."

Mike Kalinoff, Motor Machinist Mate Second Class edged unto them. "Think this is about a war patrol?"

"The word sure gets around," Velie said with a grin. "I fuckin' hope so. As much as I love it here, I would love to hit the Japs again."

The crew mustered on the aft deck of the *Bonefish*, just like always. The skipper, Commander Lawrence Edge, stood on the island and looked down at his crew. His dark hair had silvered over the last two decades but he had maintained the slim, muscular physique he started the war with as skipper of the *Bonefish* back in 1943.

The crew revered him. Like the other married men in the crew, by crew consensus he could have tried to get home to his wife and kids. They had voted on that issue.

Eighteen of twenty-one men had decided to attempt to return to their wives. Two of the chief petty officers were married to Australian women and knew there was no chance. Commander Edge had elected to stay with his boat and crew until they could strike back at the Japanese.

From the radiant look on his face, that seemed imminent.

"Officers and men of the USS *Bonefish* I have some exciting news." He told them about Fairbanks and Anchorage, Tokyo and Berlin. About the conflagrations erupting all over the former United States against Nazis and the Japanese Empire alike.

"Two days ago, as most of you already know..." a wave of quiet laughs eddied through the crew, "...we received a message from the Tlingit Provisional Navy. It seems there is a carrier group currently in Prince William Sound. They have six capital ships crewed by the Japanese Navy.

"The *Genda* is what we built as the *Kearsarge*, an *Essex* class carrier with an on-board squadron of jets. The *Amagi* is our old *St. Paul*, a Baltimore class heavy cruiser. The *Sagiri* is the former destroyer USS *Compton*, the *Hayashimo* is the old DD-702, USS *Hank*. They also have the

USS *Shannon*, another DD they named the *Nawaki*, and last but not least the *Sakura*, which was our destroyer escort USS *Cannon*."

He paused so they could all get a grasp of the force they felt would soon be hunting them.

"So it turns out that somewhere east of us, over near Ketchikan, another crew of crazies..." they all laughed out loud, "...like us, have hidden a DE. I don't yet know which one and it doesn't matter. It is as sea worthy as the *Bonefish*.

"To top it off, a crew has kept a PT Boat hidden up near Juneau all these years and it has already fired the first shots in our war of retaliation by taking out a Jap patrol boat and a fighter plane."

The crew applauded and whistled. Edge let them enjoy the moment. The chatter died down but they all kept the wide grins and hope emanated from all.

"We're going to hit them. At this point that's all I know. The TPN is still working out the details and planning for maximum effect.

"It's a shame we don't have any aircraft on our side. I will now take questions."

A dozen hands shot up.

"Beck?"

The burly Gunner's Mate First Class came to attention. "Skipper, do we have a timetable on this thing?"

"Not yet, I will let everyone know just as soon as I find out. Gus, you're next."

"Captain, are we talking about a daylight or night time attack?"

"All they told me is that to even things up a bit we would probably attack at night so they can't use their aircraft against us. I don't know if that pertains to us or not since they can't see us anyway."

A number of hands dropped and only two remained in the air.

"Prentiss."

"Captain, do we *all* get to go?"

"All the men, Bobby, you people are the crew and I can't do it without you. The women and the married and retired men will stay here."

They all applauded.

Stoney Compton

24

Angoon, Alaska Prefecture

The *Auspicious Provider* pulled up to the fuel dock. Oscar and Cliff jumped down and tied the boat fore and aft. On the bridge, Captain Inoue turned to Miamatsu and Hamada.

"You two stay up here until I tell you different. This is going to be delicate at first."

"Good luck, captain," Miamatsu said.

Hamada nodded.

Inoue left the bridge and Miamatsu found a scupper hole where he could clearly hear the conversation on the dock.

"You guys are from Valdez?" a new voice asked.

"Yes," Inoue said as he stepped off the boat onto the dock. "It's been a long trip."

"You run out of fish up there?"

"Actually, I think we caught our limit. Is Gabe George around?"

The dock attendant gave him a wary glance. "Who's asking?"

"My name is Inoue, Gabe and I are correspondents."

"Y'don't say. You want to fill her up?"

"Yeah, number one diesel."

The man put the hose in the fuel tank and started the pump.

"I'll be right back." He went into the fuel shack and shut the door.

Miamatsu called down in a low tone, "Should we arm ourselves?"

"No," Inoue said in a conversational tone. "We're in this now, one way or another. Don't worry, Gabe and I go back a long ways."

"People coming, major," Hamada said.

The outgoing tide had dropped the fuel dock low enough that the men coming down the long, cleated ramp could easily see Miamatsu and Hamada behind the bridge cowling. They sat and stared back as nonchalantly as possible. Miamatsu didn't like the feeling of total vulnerability that washed over him.

In for a penny, in for a pound, he thought.

The three men closed on Inoue and Cliff. Oscar was nowhere to be seen.

"Hey, Gabe," Inoue said. "How ya doing?"

"Spunky Inoue! It really is you!" Gabe said with a wide grin.

The two men hugged then stepped back, smiling at one another.

"So why'd you leave Valdez?"

"Things are about ready to come apart up there and it was a good time to leave. Besides, I brought you treasure."

"Anything to do with the two people topside?"

"You never miss anything, Gabe, that's one of the reasons I like you so much."

"So tell me about the treasure."

"IJN naval codebooks and two newly enlisted security officers from Fairbanks."

"Security?"

"Kempeitai, to be exact."

Gabe's eyes rounded in surprise for a moment. "Okay, maybe it's time I meet them."

"Just for the record, brother, I promised them a safe harbor."

"Good to know. Get them down here."

Inoue raised his voice a fraction, "You heard him, gentlemen, come on down."

✳ ✳ ✳

"Why did you bring the code book, Major Miamatsu?" Major Didrickson asked offhandedly.

"I thought you people could put it to good use. Was it a waste of time on my part?"

"No, it is incredibly useful, especially since the Empire doesn't know we have it. Did you plan to use it as a bargaining chip?"

"No. Sergeant Hamada and I had already decided to take the offer Captain Inoue suggested. Since we were going to destroy the naval station anyway, I thought it would be good to bring anything that might help us in the future."

Commander Richards cleared his throat. "According to the dossier Captain Inoue brought, you went against the orders of your superiors in Fairbanks to save prisoners. Why did you do that?"

"Wouldn't *you* do that too, commander? I have always felt that people in my custody were my responsibility, my *giri* if you will. I cannot ignore that."

"Are you an example of the new face of the Empire?" Richards asked.

"Unfortunately, no. I have always believed myself deviant in my thinking and lately also in my actions."

"This session was designed to assess your worthiness to be part of our organization." Commander Richards looked around at the others. "At this point I must recuse myself from the deliberations."

"Why is that, Tom?" Admiral Colby asked.

"This man had over twenty prisoners pulled out of flooding cells in Fairbanks and sent them south to Anchorage with no backing from his superiors. The Underground Liberation captured that train and liberated the prisoners. One of them was my cousin. The way I see it, I owe this guy."

"I am very pleased to know they are all safe," Miamatsu said. "Within hours of their departure the building was shelled by insurgents, killing everyone."

"That's in my report, too," Captain Inoue said from his seat against the wall.

"Major Miamatsu, would you and Sergeant Hamada go outside with Captain Inoue for a bit? The rest of us have things to discuss."

"Of course." The three men got to their feet and Miamatsu nodded deeply to the people at the table before leaving the room.

25

IJNS *Genda*
Prince William Sound, Alaska

#

"If we had not warned Lotus flight we would have lost them as well as Cherry Blossom Flight!" Vice Admiral Shima said, his voice heavy with emotion and saki.

"None of us had any idea the insurgents were as organized as they are," Captain Mihashi said, staring into his empty glass. "This is going to be a blot on my record." He felt like crying.

"You were only following my orders, Tatsuya," the admiral said. "We have to make this right with the new Emperor."

"There is no way to reconnoiter their positions without endangering more aircraft and pilots, admiral. We can send in air strikes, but on what positions? The images from the Lotus Flight photo plane showed us nothing."

"I believe we need to steam into Cook Inlet so that we can shell the city," the admiral said.

Captain Mihashi pointed to the large chart on the table. "There is not a lot of room to maneuver in there, admiral."

"There's nearly forty kilometers before the inlet begins to close. How much room do we need?"

"I prefer to have as much sea room around me as possible."

"They don't have a navy, Tatsuya. They don't have an air force, they barely have an army."

"You are the commander of this squadron, Admiral Shima. I will go where you direct me. This insurgency has surprised us on many levels and I take nothing for granted in terms of superiority."

"This does not sound like the Tatsuya Mihashi I have known since the Great Pacific War," the admiral said with a frown. "Do you wish to be relieved of your duties?"

"Not at all, Admiral Shima. I serve the Emperor through you. Perhaps age has made me more wary than I was as a young lieutenant, I apologize for creating a lack of confidence."

"You have my fullest confidence, captain," Shima said warmly. "I do appreciate your candor in suggesting caution and to a point I agree with you."

Mihashi kept his silence.

I have said too much already, he thought.

"So let us go look at Cook Inlet. Perhaps we can nip this rebellion in the bud. Wouldn't that be an auspicious gift for our new Emperor?"

"Hai, admiral. Indeed it would."

"I bid you good night, old comrade." The admiral left the captain's cabin.

Captain Mihashi pulled on his uniform jacket and buttoned it per regulations, put on his hat and headed for the bridge.

All illumination outside his cabin was from red lights to better enable night vision as the squadron slowly moved through Prince William Sound in the dark. The passageway between his cabin and the bridge was short. As he entered the bridge, the sentry shouted, "The Captain is on the bridge!"

Everyone from the officer-of-the-deck to the lowest ratings standing sea watch snapped to attention.

"As you were," he said, moving over to the OOD. "Anything of interest out there tonight, Lieutenant Maita?"

"No, Captain Mihashi," he said with a trace of nervousness. "Nothing to report."

"As I expected. Things are going to get more interesting. Plot a course for Cook Inlet for me."

"Hai, captain!" The lieutenant moved over to the chart table and examined the options. He put a clear plastic overlay down and quickly plotted a course. He went back over it and nodded.

"This would be my suggestion, captain."

Captain Mihashi looked over the plot and nodded his agreement.

"Very good, lieutenant. Radio the squadron and inform them of our new course. The *Sakura* is to take the lead with *Hayashimo* and *Amagi* preceding us. *Nawaki* and *Sagiri* will follow *Genda*."

"I will inform the radio room immediately, captain!"

Tatsuya Mihashi stared out into the dark night, not seeing the phosphoresce-tipped waves but envisioning the successful subjugation of the insurgency.

26

Angoon, Alaska Prefecture

#

"Major Miamatsu, wake up, please."

He opened his eyes immediately. For the briefest part of an instant he wondered where he was before it all came flooding back.

Angoon, we are in Angoon.

He looked into the eyes of a young man who had the longest hair he had ever seen on a male.

"I am awake. Who are you?"

A wide grin displayed perfect teeth and a good disposition.

"I am Andrew Soboloff, I am a lieutenant junior grade in the Tlingit Provisional Navy. My boss has requested your presence in an hour and a half. I was instructed to wake you and offer you breakfast."

"How thoughtful," Miamatsu said, sitting up. A quick glance revealed Sgt. Hamada's cot vacant. There had just been the two of them in the small cabin.

"Sergeant Hamada is already eating breakfast, he woke up on his own."

"I feel like a laggard," he said throwing back his blanket and locating his shoes. "Usually I wake up just after dawn."

"You and the sergeant have been through a great deal as I understand it. Sounds like you deserved to sleep in."

"You are going to go far in this navy, lieutenant." Miamatsu laughed and the lieutenant joined him.

103

"This way, sir."

The galley proved to be the largest single-story structure in sight. The odor of cooked meat wafted out and Miamatsu realized he hadn't eaten a real meal for a very long time. Oscar's sandwiches had given his belly needed ballast, but didn't compete with what he now smelled.

"I think you can take it from here," Andrew said with a hint of a salute before he turned away.

Inside the building Hamada sat with three other men at the table in the middle of the room. Five other empty tables waited for occupants. A large man filled a large window flanked by trays on one side and plates and utensils on the other.

"Good morning. What would you like for breakfast?"

"What are the choices?"

Ten minutes later Miamatsu carried his filled tray over to where the sergeant and his comrades sat drinking coffee or tea and chatting.

"Norio, you didn't wake me," he said, setting his tray down and sitting on the bench.

"No, sir, I did not. You needed the rest and there was nothing demanding your attention at the moment. Let me introduce some of our new friends…"

As he ate, Miamatsu was introduced to Frank Bagio, a young Filipino radioman originally from Juneau, Sam Patterson, an older bosun who was friendly but reticent to talk, and Charlie Simon, a yeoman who said he felt more Eskimo than white but was both.

"You are a major in the Imperial Army Kempeitai?" Frank asked unabashedly.

"Was," Miamatsu said. "Not any more."

"Why'd you quit?" Sam asked in a flat tone.

Miamatsu realized the man distrusted his conversion to the resistance. He had given a great deal of thought to the subject over the past week and decided this was as good a time as any to share.

"Throughout all of my military life I studied people. At first it was to decide if they were lying and about what. After a time I realized that all people were motivated by the same things and exhibited the same emotions.

"It became a study in contrasts for me. About that time I began observing my fellow agents, my superiors, and their superiors. We Japanese have a hierarchy of responsibilities to others in our culture.

"I began to privately question those responsibilities just as I began to ponder our unquestioned right to rule over so many other peoples. Age may have been a factor in my ultimate decision that we were no better than those we ruled, merely more fortunate in how the Great Pacific War played out. Although the Empire has taken great pains to recast the war in terms of our superiority as warriors, I know that until the Germans used atomic bombs we were losing, and so were the Germans."

"You're right about that," Sam said and his manner felt even more chilled.

"Sergeant Hamada and I unknowingly were on the periphery of the Empire's atomic weapon project. We investigated two murders that became a microcosm illustrating the lack of cooperation within the various parts of the Empire as well as the total ruthlessness pervading the Alaskan portion of the Empire's attitude.

"I decided I had endured enough soul shrinkage for one lifetime and it was time to atone for Japanese transgressions. I pulled Norio along with me because I felt responsible for his safety. I never asked him if he agreed with me or not."

Hamada laughed.

"Katsu, I have been at your side for nearly twenty years. As a young private I studied you and your methods so I might become a better investigator. After all this time I think I know what you are going to do before you do.

"You earned my respect and allegiance many years ago. I was very relieved when we left Fairbanks for Valdez."

Miamatsu turned to Sam.

"Did I answer your question?"

"Yes, major, you did. Welcome aboard."

"Thank you."

A young woman wearing an armband hurried through the door.

"Major Miamatsu, the admiral wishes to see you, sir. If you will follow me?"

He glanced down at his breakfast and was surprised to see he had eaten most of it.

"Of course, lead on."

Admiral Williams was in the same chair where Miamatsu last saw him. Captain George and Commander Richards stood to either side of him as they all studied a sheet of paper.

"Major, you have proven your worth," the admiral boomed. "This code has already been an incredible asset. Have a seat."

"I am pleased to hear this," he said as he sat. "What have you discovered?"

"The Imperial Alaska Squadron is moving into Cook Inlet to shell Anchorage."

"How is that a good thing?"

"We know they are going to do it and now so does Anchorage. They will be ready for them when they arrive. We hope to be ready for them when they depart."

"We are a terribly long way from Anchorage, are we not?"

"We have at least four days to get to the area of the Barren Islands, where the squadron will exit Cook Inlet. The odds are tremendous, but we will have surprise on our side and they will be hurting if all goes right."

"Hurting, how?"

"They don't think any danger exists between the Barren Islands and Anchorage, but they are wrong."

27

Juneau, Alaska Prefecture

"The shit is hitting the fan!" Betsy said as she hurried into the Juneau Public Library.

Addie looked up from her typewriter. "You're lucky, there is nobody else here. Do explain what you mean."

"The Alaska Squadron is on the move and we know where they're going!"

"Does that mean we activate the *Bates*?"

"Absolutely. Do you agree?"

"Of course."

"Where does she need to be and when?"

Betsy gave her the information. "You remember the code words, right?"

"Of course!"

"Then make the call."

Addie picked up the telephone and waited a moment before the Japanese operator came on the line.

"This is the operator, whom do you wish to call?"

"The Saxman Library north of Ketchikan."

"Do you have official authorization to make a long-distance call?"

"Yes, operator. This is the Juneau Public Library answering an urgent request from the Saxman Library. My authorization number is 14J."

"Stand by, I am connecting you to the number." The operator went away and Addie knew he was setting up a recording machine.

Suddenly she heard her cousin, Maxine say, "Hello, uh, this is the Saxman Library."

"Hi, Maxine, it's Addie up in Juneau," she said in Tlingit. " What is the *urgent* inquiry you had for us?"

"Oh, hi, Addie!" Maxine replied in Tlingit. "So good to hear you. I'm glad you're here to help *escort* me through this."

"What's the problem?"

"If all indications are correct, I just need to know how long my patient with the flu needs to rest."

"Oh, three or four days. No more than that."

"You are certain, three or four days?"

"Yes, I'm certain."

"Thanks, Addie, I'll see you one of these days."

"Take care, Maxine, and good luck."

* * *

Maxine Stout hurried out of the one-room library in Saxman. With only a few dozen books it barely merited the title, but people did borrow books now and then and it was a hub of information. She walked down to the Hooch Shack, the only bar between Ketchikan and Loring, which wasn't saying much.

Chief Crockett, wearing his beat-up CPO hat from the war, sat behind his bar reading a book. Since the clock had just struck noon, the place was empty. He kept reading when she came in.

"How ya doing Maxine? Kinda early for booze ain't it?" He looked up at her with a grin.

"Chief, you know I don't drink!" She looked around quickly. "Are we alone here?" she whispered.

"Yeah," his voice low, "What's up?"

"Got a call in Tlingit from Juneau. Things are happening. They want you somewhere in three or four days tops."

"Damn! Stand by there." He bent under the bar, pulled out a sound-powered phone and pushed a button. "This is Crockett. Find the boss. We need to get up steam immediately."

He frowned as he held the receiver to his head.

"Of course this is legit, you fucking idiot! Who trained you? I–, oh, hi, Barry. What did the kid tell you?"

"Yeah, get up steam right fucking now, we got no time to waste. Make sure sparks has his ears open. Get the boss, I'm on my way. Yeah, you, too." He replaced the phone.

"You got it from here, chief?" Maxine asked.

"You bet, Maxine. Thanks for the message. I gotta go." He turned to leave.

"Chief Crockett?"

"Yeah, what is it?" He turned back to face her.

"Be careful and God speed."

"Thanks, Maxine, we'll do our best."

She watched him hurry out the back door. After he was out of sight she looked around the dim room.

"Great, now I'm the librarian *and* the bartender!"

28

Squid Cove, Southeast Alaska Prefecture

"We have steam up, captain!" Lieutenant Phillips said, "and full tanks."

"Excellent, Mr. Phillips. Mr. Rogers, are all the crew aboard?"

"Still missing about twenty-five, skipper. We do have enough hands to sail the ship and fight the enemy."

"Cast off all lines aft."

The order traveled aft and the line handlers on the dock slipped the hawsers free of the bollards, then hurried to climb aboard.

"Cast off all lines forward!"

In moments the high speed transport USS *Bates* (APD-47) floated free of the shore.

"Quartermaster, steer 025, all ahead one third."

"Zero-two-five, ahead one third, aye, aye, captain."

All the crew broke into a cheer.

Lieutenant Commander Eric Henry Maher grinned and snapped a quick salute to the crew. Then he went over to the bosun of the watch. "Announce me, Boats."

Chief Bosun Tony Llerena said, "Aye, aye, captain." He opened the microphone and blew his bosun's pipe into it.

"Now hear this, now hear this. Attention, all hands! Stand by for the captain."

Bosun Llerena stepped back and Maher moved up.

"Crew of the *Bates*, we have waited over two decades for this day. You have worked for the success of this ship far beyond your enlistment contracts, you have all gone above and beyond the scope of your duties and the expectations of your country. All I can say to that is thank you.

"Your unwavering belief in the vision we all share has held us together as a crew and a fighting unit. We could not have done it without the aid of all the communities around us. Had we been discovered by the Japs they would have cleansed this part of Alaska of all human life in retaliation.

"We owe them and the people of the United States one more good fight, and it's waiting for us at the Barren Islands."

The crew broke into another cheer.

"You take us there, skipper, and we'll fight the bastards!" a sailor shouted.

"Here's the deal, men. From where we are now and until we reach the point where we engage the enemy, we need to fly a false flag. The *enemy* flag.

"We have damn near 900 miles to travel through waters the Japanese Empire has considered theirs for over twenty years. The positive part of the situation is that they do not heavily patrol these waters. The negative part is they do fly routine missions out of Sitka and Juneau.

"We have to look like a Jap when and if they see us. We have to wave like we love the bastards. We have to wait until later to shoot them down.

"We are going up against an *Essex* class carrier, a Baltimore class cruiser, three DDs, and the old DE, USS *Cannon*. We are outgunned and punching above our weight limit. To help us we have a bunch of armed patrol boats, an honest-to-God PT Boat, and a submarine."

"That makes it about even, right, skipper?" Another sailor yelled.

He grinned. "Yeah, *about* even. That is all, men. Carry on."

Lt. Jerry Toomey, the navigation officer, saluted Maher.

"Captain, once we're safely through Dixon Entrance I suggest we sail straight across the Gulf of Alaska to the Barren Islands."

"That is exactly what I thought, too. Let's do it. Where's Lieutenant Brown?"

"He's in CIC, captain."

"Thank you, Mr. Toomey, you have the deck."

"Aye, aye, sir."

The combat information center was a small space filled with dials, red light, and too many bodies.

"Captain on deck!" someone said.

"As you were. From now on when I come in here you all keep doing your jobs." Maher stood next to Lt. Jefferson Brown.

"How's the weather look, Jeff?"

"Right now we're blessed with a high pressure cell that covers half the Gulf of Alaska. Unfortunately, about half way across we hit an occluded front and then a wicked low pressure system that will throw some prodigious seas at us."

"How prodigious?"

"Probably thirty to forty foot waves. Nasty is the only word that comes to mind."

"Then we should make hay while the sun shines! Thank you, Jeff."

"I am here to serve, skipper." His wide grin gleamed in the glow of the battle lanterns.

Maher stepped back onto the bridge.

"Mr. Toomey, once we are through Dixon Entrance, go to full speed on a course for the Barren Islands."

"Aye, aye, captain. Full speed it is!"

29

Klawak, Southeast Alaska Prefecture
#

The setting sun offered enough light for the USS *Bonefish* to navigate from its long time berth through Iphigenia Bay and out into the open ocean of the Gulf of Alaska. Sonar showed multiple fathoms below them but they stayed on the surface to run as fast as they could and save battery power.

Lawrence Edge loved being on the open bridge with the wind against his face. For far too many years he had waited for this patrol. He had no premonitions or fears about the future, he just knew this was the way it was supposed to be.

The communications officer ghosted up next to him.

"Captain, we received a message from TPN, we're not alone out here!"

Edge gave his radioman a long look.

"We're not? Who the hell else is out here besides Japs?"

"The USS *Bates*, a DE converted to a fast troop carrier. They are on the same course as we are. TPN wanted us to know."

"Good thinking. So that's the mystery DE we've heard mentioned, huh? I would love to rendezvous with her and have a long chat with her skipper."

"Maybe we can arrange that, captain."

"Let me know what you find out."

The *Bonefish* motored through the dark waters of the Gulf of Alaska and he wondered how long the good weather would hold. The sub didn't have a meteorological specialist aboard, they had to play it by ear. He had been in Southeast Alaska long enough to know the good weather would not hold.

We'll use it while we have it! he thought.

He had his youngest strikers on sea watch. Good binoculars and young eyes were the best security available. Both radar and sonar were active and operating flawlessly.

The older crewmen all had at least two apprentices who had been born after the war ended. Some of the new men were apprenticed to their fathers. Once they had found the perfect spot to build a sub pen back in 1945 they had worked 12 and 16 hour days to complete it before the Japanese surveyed their new spoils of war.

Once the *Bonefish* was hidden in her new berth, the majority of the crew had scattered to surrounding towns and villages in an effort to blend in. Relationships formed, marriages performed, and the maintenance of the boat became a nearly religious ritual that filtered through the communities.

It took the accidental deaths of two crew members to goad Captain Edge into setting up an apprenticeship program. Not only did the young men and women learn a skill, they also kept alive the values and very idea of the United States. The most difficult part of choosing new people for sea-going berths (they all knew they would return to the sea at some point) was sex.

He couldn't figure out how to keep young men and women apart in the close quarters of a Gato-class submarine. Much to their distress, he couldn't allow women to be part of the sea-going crew. The younger crew members were also disappointed, but the older guys felt relief–in some cases the women left behind were their daughters.

As the *Bonefish* surged through the dark waters, the moon peeked over the eastern horizon. He estimated it to be nearly full.

I wonder if that's a good omen, to make an attack on a full moon?

The soft tone of the muffled ship's bell sounded and the first watch relieved the second dog's watch.

Lt(jg) Abel took over as the OOD and quietly joined Edge at the blast shield.

"Good evening, Mr. Abel."

"Good evening, captain. We couldn't ask for a nicer night."

"No, we couldn't. We need to maintain as much speed as possible because we both know this lovely weather isn't going to last. We are racing both time and the elements."

"We will make the rendezvous, sir. Every man on this boat is busting his ass to insure that."

"I couldn't ask for a better crew, and I am a grateful man for that. You have the conn, Mr. Abel. Wake me if *anything* changes."

"Aye, aye, sir. I have the conn."

Edge went below, lay down on his bunk in the telephone booth he called a cabin and fell instantly asleep.

Stoney Compton

30

Homer, Alaska Prefecture

#

"**M**ike, Mike wake up! We have a priority message from the TPN!"

Mike Armstrong blinked away the dream and rubbed his face.

"Barney, how'd you get in here? I had the door locked." He sat up and peered around in what little light the moon provided through the window.

"Did you hear what I said? We have a priority message–"

"I heard you. What does the TPN want with us? We're not even in their neighborhood."

"Just read the gawddamned thing, would ya?" Barney Benson shoved the flimsy into Mike's lap.

"Light the lantern on the table, I can't see in the dark."

In moments Barney had the lamp lit and held it so Mike could see the message.

"The Japs are sending a carrier group to Anchorage? Are they nuts?"

"Probably just arrogant, but it works out the same," Barney said with a laugh.

"Put some wood in the stove, would you? It's cooling off in here. Does the UL in Anchorage know about this?"

Barney spread out the remaining embers and quickly loaded the firebox. He shut the stove door.

"There you go. Yeah, they know."

"So, are they planning to attack Anchorage?"

"Looks like it."

"Why?"

"Near as we can figure they are pissed about losing four jets over Fairbanks two days ago."

"They did? I hadn't heard that. But why attack *Anchorage*?"

"Because it has also fallen into the hands of the UL and the Japs can't shoot far enough with their ships to hit Fairbanks."

"This doesn't mention transports. Do they have any with them?"

"We don't think so. This just looks like a high-stakes pissing match to us."

"Are the Homer Hellfighters ready to jump into this?"

"Mike, you *know* we are!"

"So we're really going to do it, huh? Well, the dumb bastards asked for it. Give me a half hour and I'll be over to the hall."

"Okay, see ya there." Barney left the small cabin.

"I gotta figure out how he can always get in here," Mike muttered to himself. He went through his morning routine without actually thinking about it. He had mass murder on his mind.

The Homer City Hall was glowing with light when he arrived. Most of the Hellfighters Action Committee was already sitting in a circle, drinking tea and coffee, arguing over how to best proceed. He poured a cup of coffee, put a dollop of honey in it and joined them.

"Glad you finally made it, sleepyhead," Arnie Weimer said with a grin.

"I was up late. What's the consensus?"

Orin Beeder, the mayor of Homer crossed his hands over his ample belly and said, "We think we should mine the inlet after the Japs have gone north. On their way back they won't be expecting trouble, and if we're lucky, they'll be licking their wounds."

"We only have six mines," Mike said. "They could miss all of them."

"Not if *we* detonate them when the Japs get close," Bill Thompson said.

"Have you perfected the trigger switch?" Mike asked, "The last I heard it wouldn't work in water."

"Wax was the solution," Bill said proudly. "I've successfully set off three different quarter-sticks of dynamite in the water."

"Good to hear. Congratulations. So that helps the cause a bit."

"We have more help than that," Orin said. "Once the Japs get back down to Barren Island they're going to run into a Gato-class sub, a DE, and a PT-Boat."

"The DE isn't just a tall tale?"

"Nope, it's real. So are the sub, and the PT Boat."

"I'll be damned, I thought it was all bullshit."

"My question is," Orin said, "do we want to send out armed fishing boats?"

"Only if you want to lose them," Mike said. "They wouldn't have a chance against a Japanese man of war."

"That depends," Arnie said, "on how they are perceived."

"Go on," Mike said. "We're listening."

"If they were gill netters and pretty much covering the inlet, the Japs would have to slow down."

"Or run them down," Mike said, "depending on how shot up they were."

"The point is, they probably wouldn't shoot at them from a distance, or if they did, it would be a warning shot to get out of the way. Either way, the fishing boats would be out there next to them. They can't depress their guns enough to hit them with heavy fire."

"They also have 20 and 40 millimeters on board, they can damn near shoot down the side of the hull with those, Arnie."

"At least they could hit the Jap ships first."

Orin cleared his throat.

"Arnie, I think we should lay the mines and get the hell out of the water. The only way a fishing boat could hurt one of those ships would be by filling it with explosives and ramming them. You want to skipper something like that?"

"Nope. I'll take my theory and go home."

Mike laughed. "Hang around, Arnie, we need people who think outside the box."

"Are you making a comment on my art work?"

"No. I am making a comment on your way of thinking."

Marion Matthews sat down next to Mike and sipped her tea.

"So, gentlemen, have you figured out how to win the war yet?"

"No, Marion, we were waiting for you," Orin said through a grin.

"Perhaps we could use a log raft that *somehow* got away. The Japanese would slow to go through that rather than chance damaging their hulls. And our mines would be attached to six of those logs."

"That's brilliant!" Mike said. "Leave it to a librarian to find the right answer."

"That *is* a good idea," Orin said.

"How do we keep the logs where we need them?" Arnie asked.

"We post a lookout up near Ninilchik. When they see the Japs retiring south we push the logs out into the inlet," Mike said. "That's the best we can do."

"I like it," Orin said. "I vote we do exactly that."

"Where's the rest of the city council?" Mike asked. "We need this to be a legal vote."

"What about survivors, Orin?" Arnie asked.

"What do you mean?"

"If we actually sink one of those ships, do we rescue survivors?"

"Only if they make it to shore," Orin said. "And that's damn unlikely in 39° water."

31

Anchorage, Alaska Prefecture
Underground Liberation Headquarters

"The Japs are sending a carrier group to shell us, general. We have no more than two days to prepare."

"Damn! Any transports with ground troops?"

"None reported, General Cole. But there might be."

"That's not much help, Pete. How many artillery pieces did we capture at Fort Tojo?"

"Twenty-five or thirty. We captured the armory intact so we have all the ammo we need for the pieces we have."

"Excellent, Colonel Blewett. Let's look at the map."

The map table held the focus of a number of personnel. Gunnery Sergeant Keith Bush chatted with Lieutenant James Wright as the general and his adjutant walked over. LtCol Sarah Barenz studied the map intently and carried on a whispered conversation with Major Lillian Pletnikoff.

"Got it all figured out, colonel?" General Cole asked.

"We have some suggestions, general," LtCol Barenz said, "...any time you want to hear them."

For the next hour a heated discussion about tactics, fields of fire, possible casualties, and potential air strikes filled the room.

"We can't concentrate our forces, it would make it easier for their aircraft to take them out," Blewett said.

"How many of those surface-to-air missiles did we liberate?" General Cole asked.

"Somewhere in the neighborhood of fifteen." Col. Blewett scratched his head. "But we have no idea yet how they work, the instructions are all in Japanese."

"Surely we have people who can read Japanese, don't we?" Cole asked.

"We have people working on it, but there are a lot of technical terms that need to be interpreted in a couple of ways," LtCol Barenz said.

"We don't need to know how to repair them, we just need to know how to aim and shoot the bastards. They have no idea where our troops are, or even if we have troops." General Cole ticked off the points on his fingers. "There are a lot of Japanese owned businesses in downtown so I doubt they'll indiscriminately blow the place up."

"I wouldn't put anything past them," Gunny Bush muttered.

General Cole cocked an eye at him and continued, "But sure as we're sitting here, they will fly over the whole Cook Inlet Basin looking for targets of opportunity. Eventually they will have to land back on the carrier to refuel. *That's* when we hit them with everything we have."

"*If* we can see the carrier," Barenz muttered.

"We'd better get our armor and artillery dispersed immediately," Lt. Wright said. "It's going to take time for them to dig in if we want them to survive this."

"I wish we could get some artillery across Turnagain Arm," Blewett said. "We could get them in a crossfire if they went up into the arm at all."

"Aren't there some barges down at the dock?" Barenz said. "The Imperial Army brought in a about six tons of supplies and were in the process of unloading them when the shit hit the fan."

"Find out, now," Cole ordered.

"Lilly, would you check with the comm shack? I know we have people down there who know the port."

"On it!" Major Pletnikoff hurried out of the room.

"If we can get artillery, maybe even tanks barged across the inlet, we could really ruin their day." Cole looked around at the others. "So where do we put what, people?"

32

IJNS *Genda*,
Gulf of Alaska

#

"Admiral, the *Amagi* reports it will take a minimum of six hours to repair her propulsion problem." The ensign stood waiting with sweat beading at his temples. Admiral Shima's legendary temper might erupt and the hapless ensign would bear full brunt.

"Then they can catch up when they're sea worthy," he said with a grunt of annoyance.

Captain Mihashi asked, "What is the nature of their problem?"

"One of the four drive shafts suffered metal fatigue and shattered, sending debris into the other three shafts."

"Poor maintenance!" Admiral Shima said with a snort. "Captain Kodo assured me his ship was ready for action."

Captain Mihashi cleared his throat and nodded for the ensign to leave. With a quick bow the young man hurried out of the admiral's cabin.

"Admiral, I doubt it is poor maintenance. She is an old ship and desperately needs a refit. Is it wise to leave the *Amagi* without any backup?"

"They have radio communications. If anything unexpected should transpire they could summon us immediately."

"If we are more than a few miles away we would not be able to assist in a reasonable amount of time."

"Do you believe they are going to be attacked by natives in canoes? There is nobody else in these waters besides *us*."

"What about the losses we had in Juneau a few days ago, sir?"

"We are a *long* way from Juneau, Tatsuya," he said tiredly.

"I meant no disrespect, admiral."

"I know. You are a conscientious naval officer and as such you look for any potential flaws in a situation. I appreciate that but I must insist the *Amagi* catch up to us when she fixes her problem."

"We could order a tug out of one of the small naval bases and have it stand by until the *Amagi* is repaired, or tow it into port if needed. This situation sounds serious to me."

Admiral Shima sighed theatrically and smiled at his friend and subordinate.

"Very well, Tatsuya, call out a tug."

"Thank you, admiral, and the *Amagi* thanks you."

Captain Mihashi exited the admiral's cabin and went straight to the radio room. The two men on duty stayed in their seats when he entered but straightened in their chairs.

"Have we heard anything from Yakutat?"

"No, captain. The scout plane did not report again after landing."

"How long ago was that?"

"This morning, captain."

Mihashi picked up a sound-powered phone and called his air boss.

"Commander Agawa, this is the captain. I want two recon jets launched immediately to fly over Yakutat. They are to report as soon as they sight the area. ... Excellent, well done."

He hung up the phone and turned to the lead radioman.

"Contact Valdez. I want an ocean-going tugboat out here to assist the *Amagi* as soon as possible. Give them her coordinates."

The radioman made the contact and passed the order.

"Valdez said it would be a minimum of six hours but probably closer to eight hours before a tug can be on station, captain."

A lot can happen in that amount of time, he thought. "Very well, tell them to move as fast as they can, it's important."

As he reentered the bridge, two F-1NJ Fujis launched off the bow of the *Genda* and screamed in a long turn to the east.

"Quartermaster, resume course to Cook Inlet. Notify the rest of the group."

As orders flashed over the airwaves, Captain Mihashi peered out at the *Amagi* in the early afternoon light. It would be dark in another three hours and he worried that the hapless cruiser would come to grief with no other ships around. He wondered at Admiral Shima's nonchalant attitude.

A fully manned cruiser would be a terrible thing to lose due to neglect. I would not make such a decision under the same circumstances. He shrugged mentally and glassed the horizon ahead of them.

He had a ship to command.

"Captain, the recon aircraft are reporting," the bridge talker said.

"I'll be in the radio room." In a few steps he entered the space. "Put it on the speaker so we can all hear it."

"...sitting at the dock. I repeat, there is what appears to be an unmanned Kawanishi float plane sitting at the dock as well as a patrol boat. There are no signs of life, even when we buzzed the village. Over."

He picked up the microphone.

"This is Captain Mihashi. Are there any signs of violence?"

"All naval buildings have been destroyed by fire. The fuel tanks are still there. Other than that there are no signs of violence or humans."

"Well done. Return to the *Genda.*"

"Yes, captain."

He left the radio room, went into his sea cabin, and lay down on the bunk. He was responsible for an Imperial Navy aircraft carrier. He also was obligated to follow the orders of an old man who had seized on an idea and would not look past it.

Nor would he look anywhere else. The Japanese Pacific States and the Alaska Prefecture were in the midst of serious turmoil. Ignoring the enemy at your back was tantamount to suicide.

Did his old friend Admiral Shima seek a glorious death and had decided to take the Alaska Squadron down with him? Captain Tatsuya Mihashi felt very alone and very vulnerable. He did not care for the experience.

Stoney Compton

33

Juneau, Alaska Prefecture

"There is a man staggering up our front walk, James."

James Flanagan jumped to his feet and hurried out the front door. He was just in time to catch Joe Coffey when the man collapsed in his arms.

"Jesus, Mary, and Joseph! What happened to you, Joe?"

Joe's battered mouth moved but James couldn't hear anything other than a low croaking sound. He helped his friend up the three steps to his front porch and got him inside.

"Shut the door, Amelia, and then get some hot water and soap."

She ran into the kitchen while James helped his friend sit down.

"How did you get away?" James whispered.

Joe's eyes wandered a bit before focusing on his friend.

"They let me go," he wheezed. "They beat the shit out of me and I wouldn't talk..." he stopped and breathed heavily for a moment.

Amelia returned with a basin of hot water, soap, and a soft cloth. She immediately sat next to Joe and began bathing his ravaged face.

"I thought they were gonna kill me," he gasped and swallowed. "I, I was ready to die, cause I wasn't gonna tell them anything. I'm sorry, I didn't know where else to go."

"You know you are welcome here. You've been gone for two days!" James said. "Christ, what they did to you..."

"They, they, ouch, that hurts!" He rolled his eyes at Amelia who continued as though he had said nothing. "They worked on me for a day and a night. Then they just stopped. What has happened?"

"The Emperor is dead and they already got a new one. Tokyo has been destroyed and so has Berlin. Shit is hitting the fan all over America and the Japs are running scared."

"But why did they let me go? Did they follow me?"

Amelia snorted. "It doesn't matter if they did. We are all old friends, that's why you came here for help."

James grinned. "She's got bigger balls than I do, doesn't she?"

Joe tried to laugh but it ended in a painful cough and he spat blood into the basin.

"You need a doctor. Rest easy and let Amelia clean you up. I'll be back soon."

James hurried down the street to Doctor Anderson's house and knocked on the door. The doctor's elderly sister sung the door open and said, "Mr. Flanagan, whatever is the matter? You look white as a sheet."

"Good evening, Miss Anderson. Is the doctor in?"

"Yes, he is. Please wait here and I will fetch him directly."

James dropped into a chair and realized his legs and hands were shaking as if stricken with palsy. Dr. Anderson hurried into the room and looked down at him.

"Whatever is the problem, James?"

"The Kempeitai abused Joe Coffey something awful. He's spitting blood and his face looks like chopped liver. He's over at my place, can you come?"

"Of course. We can talk as we walk. Harriet, please fetch my bag."

Walking through the crisp, dark night, James related everything he knew about Joe's ordeal.

"But they released him? That is unheard of, you know."

"I don't think Joe told them anything, he's a tough son-of-a-bitch."

"He is that," Anderson agreed. "Oh, good, we're finally there."

When the doctor helped Joe take his jacket and shirt off, James thought Amelia was going to be ill. His torso was heavily bruised from below his belt all the way to his ears. As the doctor applied unguents and bandages he closely questioned Joe as to who the people were who had beat him.

"I'm going to give you a sedative and I want you to sleep for at least twelve hours, understand?"

"I don't want to get any of you in trouble with the Japs," Joe said with tears in his eyes. "You've all done more for me than I thought possible."

"We're friends, Joe," James said. "You would do the same for me."

"God, I hope so."

"Come on, let me help you to the guest room."

"I've already made up the bed," Amelia said as the two men walked slowly out of the living room.

When they were out of earshot, Dr. Anderson gave Amelia a searching look.

"Do you both really think he didn't talk?"

"Yes, I don't believe he did. If it had been me or James we probably would still be blathering out everything that came into our heads. But not Joe. They picked on the wrong fellow."

"What this tells me," Dr. Anderson said firmly, "is that the Japanese are losing their grip. They are more frightened than we are. That in itself can be a threat beyond any we have yet witnessed. Keep your heads down."

"I believe it might finally be time to mobilize," Amelia said, her voice hard.

Stoney Compton

34

PT-245
Gulf of Alaska

#

"How long can we go without refueling, captain?" asked the freshly minted Lieutenant John Hart, PT-245's new executive officer.

PT-245 raced across the water at maximum speed, all three engines screaming. Off to starboard the coastline two miles away seemed to amble past.

"No idea, lieutenant. However, we are making 39 knots and our range, fully loaded with gas, is 550 miles," LCdr Brian Wallace said. "As you can hear, our engines are in perfect operating order and Chief Walsh can fix anything that could break."

"So that's why we have to hug the coastline instead of going straight across the gulf."

"Correct. We'll pull into Yakutat where we'll be met by the local resistance group and drop off our passenger. They'll have enough gas to refuel us. From there we go straight to the Barren Islands."

"Will we have enough fuel to get back to Yakutat?"

"We'll worry about that when the time comes."

Lt Hart gave him an odd look which Brian ignored.

Chief Harris came through the hatch next to the helm.

"Skipper, we received a message from TPN HQ. There's a Jap cruiser with a propulsion problem and she is drifting somewhere south of Montague Island while they're trying to fix it."

"It's alone?"

"Yep. It's the *Amagi*, part of the Alaska Squadron. The rest of the group continued on to Cook Inlet."

"Are they nuts? What if it's blown onto the rocks?"

"They've called for a tug out of Valdez but it's hours away from them."

"We can't get to *Amagi* before the tugboat," Brian said. "However, we *might* get to her before she's repaired. Did TPN tell the other units about this?"

"Yeah, they're all straining their rivets to get there as soon as they can."

"Keep me informed, chief."

"Sure, Bri- uh, captain."

The farther north they traveled the more chop they encountered. The pounding became so overwhelming that Brian reduced speed by ten knots to smooth out the ride.

It wouldn't do to get there and have my crew unfit to fight and the boat damaged. Besides, I have a delivery to make.

The hours passed and one of their new shipmates, Ship's Cook First Class David Ace Fowler, emerged from the tiny galley with hot ham sandwiches and thermos of hot coffee. They all felt lucky that Ace had left his successful cafe in Juneau and made his way over to Angoon to enlist. The Resistance in Juneau had vetted him before welcoming him with open arms. The crew knew him already and felt fortune had smiled on them.

Brian never stopped visually sweeping the horizon. What at first seemed to be a small cloud had grown, and was moving toward them from the west. Everyone already wore life vests.

"Pass the word for Bosun Andrews," Brian said into the comm.

Thirty seconds later the man popped up through the hatch.

"What's up, skipper?"

"Look over there." he nodded to the west.

"Shit, we're in for some bad weather."

"Yeah. Rig lifelines around the boat."

"Aye, aye, Brian, I mean, captain!"

Brian smiled. "Just do it, Clyde."

The seas grew more pronounced and Brian had to reduce speed even more so he wouldn't bounce anyone overboard. The rapidly passing time weighed heavily on him but he knew a beat-up boat and crew were worthless in a battle. He gritted his teeth and pressed onward in the rising seas and fading afternoon.

Stoney Compton

35

IJNS *Amagi*
Gulf of Alaska

"Captain Kodo, our situation is worsening."

Commander Toyo Kodo looked up from the report he was reading. "Explain what you mean, Lieutenant Kizumi."

"There is a weather front moving in from the west southwest. I forecast waves will reach fifteen to twenty meters."

Kodo felt his heart rate increase and he peered through the bridge windows into an impenetrable night.

"Are you sure, lieutenant?"

"I wish I could say it is merely probable, but it is a certainty."

"Thank you, lieutenant. Navigation, what is our status?"

"Captain, our rate of drift toward Montague Island has increased. At out present rate we will go aground in eight hours. If the wind increases it will be sooner."

"Where is the tugboat?"

"It is still three hours away, captain."

Why, in the name of the Emperor, did Admiral Shima leave us out here alone? Does he hate me for a slight I do not remember?

He willed himself to remain calm rather than scream as he desired.

"What is the situation in engineering?"

"The Engineering Officer said they have repaired two of the shaft casings and are applying power to the two starboard screws. If they produce power the quartermaster will have to compensate."

Kodo saw the situation in his mind's eye; the *Amagi* would want to steam in a circle to port. Putting the helm hard over would allow them to steam forward, but drunkenly and not at all as smartly as he desired.

But we could stay off the rocks!

He had no illusions about surviving if the *Amagi* went onto the rocks. The water temperature was barely above freezing and he dare not abandon ship until the last possible moment. He quietly beseeched his ancestors to restore the seaworthiness of his ship else he would be forced to join them.

A captain always went down with his ship.

36

USS Bonefish
Gulf of Alaska

"Captain, the weather is turning to crap," Lieutenant Dunn said, standing in the door to the captain's quarters.

"Thanks, DH," Commander Edge said, instantly awake and sitting up. "I'll be topside in a minute."

As soon as he voided his bladder he grabbed his hat and hurried up the ladder to the conning tower. The boat was rocking from side to side enough to make operations problematical.

"Well, Russell," he yelled over the weather into the ear of the OOD, "I guess that's the end of our heady twenty knots an hour. Let's take her down."

"Lookouts in! Clear the tower! Prepare to dive," Lt Johnson said over the comm.

The bridge watch dropped down the ladder and Captain Edge did a quick survey to ensure nobody was left topside. He slammed and dogged the hatch after him. His heart was racing.

This was their first dive in over twenty years and the new people were even more anxious about it than the original crew.

Here's where we discover if our maintenance was top notch or not.

"Chief of the Boat, take her down! Make our depth fifty feet."

From the first sound of the dive klaxon to the chief's, "Fifty feet, captain, and all stations report smooth running." took twelve minutes.

At fifty feet below the surface of the wind-crazed surface the boat ceased its perpetual rocking and moved smoothly through the depths. The highest speed they could attain was ten knots.

"I hope we get there in time, captain," Lt Russell Johnson said.

"All we can do is give it everything we have, Russ. It is sure a lot quieter with the engines shut down. Keep the same heading, Mr. Johnson. Maximum knots."

"Aye, sir."

After an hour memories surged back and Larry Edge re-experienced a reaction he had first realized over twenty-five years ago.

"Damn this boat stinks when we're buttoned up!"

Chief Motor Machinist's Mate and Chief of the Boat Grant Fuller laughed. "I remember the first time you said that, captain. I'm so thankful we got to smell it again."

"Good point, chief. Hell, I'm already used to it."

Ensign Frank Kern slipped into the control room. "Our batteries are holding up pretty good, skipper. Those two replacements we got out of Juneau are top notch."

"They should be, they cost us enough."

"Did we ever discover who found those for us?" Chief Fuller asked.

"No," Edge said. "I didn't push it. There were so many middlemen on that deal I'm surprised anyone made any money. The TPN handled most of the deal and they love secrecy."

"Maybe that's why we were never discovered," Chief Fuller said.

"It all helped," Captain Edge said. "I'm just thankful we get another chance to take back our country."

Everyone fell silent and Edge knew they were all thinking of the homes and families they had left back in 1944. He felt honored to be among these men, and amazed they still followed his commands.

37

IJN HQ, Juneau, Alaska Prefecture

Admiral Jo Tanaka flipped through the stack of reports with growing anxiety. The total silence from their investigating force at Yakutat had the Sitka detachment in an uproar demanding patrol craft Jo did not possess. The *Genda's* commanding officer suggested destroying the floatplane and patrol boat sitting empty at Yakutat to keep them out of the hands of the insurgency.

The squadron at Sitka refused to authorize that action because they didn't have enough aircraft already and wanted to save the Kawanishi if at all possible. Jo was rapidly coming to the conclusion that saving the patrol plane wasn't in the stars. His stomach lanced with pain and he automatically took another drink of the vile liquid the doctor had prescribed.

His request to GQ in San Francisco had nearly elicited a rebuke. Grand Admiral of the Fleet Nishiawa had all but shouted at him by telephone.

"The Imperial Fleet has suffered grievous losses at San Diego and Long Beach in California! We are trying to assess the damage done there as well as in Anchorage and Fairbanks. Just today we received word that over a dozen small bases along the coast between Oregon and British Columbia have gone silent just as at Yakutat.

"You are in charge of Alaska Prefecture, Admiral Tanaka. Seize control of your area or you will be replaced! We have no spare units to send to you. Soon the Alaska Squadron will return and hopefully make your duties easier!"

Small wonder my stomach rebels.

He pondered the local situation. With the bruising exception of the patrol boat and aircraft being lost, the Juneau area had been quiet. The small community at Tee Harbor was not to be found and the Tokkeitai had no idea who they sought.

The likelihood of the offensive craft being a fully armed PT Boat bordered on the surreal. At any rate, it seemed to have disappeared. Perhaps it was damaged and sank off shore?

He shook his head and hoped the situation would not worsen.

A knock sounded on his office door. He pushed the medicine into a drawer.

"Enter."

Lieutenant Matsuda carried a message flimsy over and lay it on his desk. "This just came in, admiral."

"The squadron *left* the *Amagi* in the Gulf?" Admiral Tanaka said in disbelief. "That is unbelievable negligence!"

"We just received a radio report from *Amagi*, sir. The weather has worsened and their rate of drift is increasing. They request any aid we can offer."

"Does the *Hamiba* have her steam up?"

"Yes, sir. They can leave port within the hour if needed."

"They are to immediately deploy to the aid of the *Amagi*. Once they have rendered all aid required, they are to investigate Yakutat."

"Hai, Admiral Tanaka!" The lieutenant hurried out, shutting the door behind him.

"I just hope we don't need the *Hamiba* here," Jo muttered to himself.

His stomach twinged again.

38

Juneau, Alaska Prefecture

A knock interrupted Dapper Dave Hammond's reverie. He felt grateful for the interruption, the day had been far too quiet to suit him and when that happened he drank too damn much.

"Come in!" he called in his deep voice.

Angus opened the door just enough to stick his head in. "Dave, that crazy lady is here to see you."

"Thanks, Angus. Send her in."

Moments later Sue Ann Freeman came in and closed the door behind her. Dave nodded to the chair on the other side of his desk and she glanced around as she sat.

"Are we alone here?"

"Well, that sounds titillating!" Dave said with a wide grin. "Yes, we are very much alone."

"Have your heard the latest?"

"That covers a lot of ground. The latest about what?"

"The fucking war that has started, Dave! You need to get out more."

"No need, eventually I hear everything right here in the comfort of my well-appointed office."

"Speaking of which, you haven't offered me a drink yet."

"What may I serve you?" he said, swiveling around in his heavy wood chair and opening a cabinet filled with a variety of bottles.

"Some of that lovely scotch you plied me with the last time I was here. Where do you get that, anyway?"

He poured a generous amount in two glasses and sat them on the desk, pushed one over to her.

"That's a business secret, but it *is* excellent scotch. Did you just come by to get a free drink off me or to tell me the war news?"

"Both, for starters."

She told him about the Alaska Squadron, the *Amagi*, the destruction of the Japanese patrol boat and aircraft, and the elimination of the Japanese naval base at Yakutat. He had already heard a great deal of it but didn't announce the fact.

"Their cruiser is adrift and they *left* it? Why the fuck are they in such a hurry to get to Anchorage?"

"I didn't say the squadron was going to Anchorage, Dave." Sue Ann sipped her scotch.

"I must have heard it somewhere else, huh? You didn't come in to gossip about how fucked up the Japs are. What do you want?"

"No need to be rude," she said sweetly. "I'm actually here on official business that I'm sure only you can handle."

He grinned. Whenever she said something like that he had ended up with a great deal of money or other negotiable items.

"I'm all ears."

She pulled a small piece of paper out of her sleeve and glanced down at it.

"We need a minimum of two tons of bunker oil, as much .30 caliber rounds as you can locate, and as many 20mm and 40mm shells as you can produce."

"Why don't you just ask for a goddamn battleship while you're at it?"

"Can you get one?"

"Sue Ann, do you realize how much it would cost to fill the list of stuff you just asked for?"

"Several thousand yen at the least."

"Several *hundred* thousand yen at the very least!"

"Well, that can be arranged. Can you fill the list?"

"I am rarely at a loss for words–"

"Ha! More like *never* at a loss for words!"

"Damn it, Sue Ann, this is serious. Everything you want here is considered military stores. I don't own a supply depot!"

"I'll take your word on that. But, I know you have people in places that *do* have supply depots. In the past you—"

"As you pointed out when you first came in, the fucking war *has* started. My sources were fine with a bit of pilfering here and there in return for money or sex. But now things are *very* different.

"I wouldn't dare ask for any of this list for fear they would arrest me, torture me, and then shoot me. I can't believe you are seriously asking me to do this."

She knocked back the remainder of her scotch and stared into his face as she sat the glass on the desk. Her demeanor had changed from frivolity to matter-of-fact.

"All I'm doing is asking. Nobody's going to shoot you if you say no. You *have* come up with some pretty remarkable things in the past."

"We weren't at war then, we are now."

"I've known you for a long time, *Dapper* Dave, and I know that you are honest to your own set of morals. What I need to know now is are you loyal to the community or to the occupier?"

"That's not fair, Sue Ann!"

"Oh, Dave, when was I *ever* fair? I am blunt, honest, and often outrageous, but fair? I think not. You'll need another venue for your discomfort."

"First you said nobody would shoot me, then you want to know where my loyalties lie. This sounds like a set-up and I'm not a big fan of those things. You could ask a recent customer but he no longer has the ability to answer."

"You mean that Davis person who was a plant for the Kempeitai? We noticed he didn't leave by the front door."

"You're spying on me?"

"No, a friend was following Davis."

"You mess with the Yakuza? I'm impressed."

"He wasn't running from the Yakuza, he was an agent. You did us a favor, I think."

"I'm real big on self preservation, and that hasn't changed. Are you threatening me or not?"

"No, you big dope, I'm not threatening you! We're asking you to join us. Think about it, but please don't take too long to answer, we have a lot on our plate."

She stood and smoothed her dress, pulled her coat tight around her.
"Thanks for the drink, Dave."
"You're welcome. Be careful out there, Sue Ann."

39

USS *Bates* (APD-47)
Gulf of Alaska

3 00 miles southeast of the Barren Islands the storm enveloped the *Bates*. The ship rolled heavily from side to side while groaning up onto a wave crest and then arrowing down into the trough with enough force that green water smashed into her bridge and superstructure.

"Son of a bitch!" Lt Brad Phillips, the XO exclaimed. "I'd forgotten how bad we could have it in heavy weather!"

Captain Maher nodded in agreement and watched the next three tons of seawater engulf them.

"You did pass the word to stay off weather decks, didn't you XO?"

"Yes, captain, I sure as hell did. Should we reduce speed?"

"Was that a question or a suggestion?" Maher said with a grin.

"Um, maybe a bit of both."

"Helm, reduce speed to three-quarters."

"Three-quarters, aye, captain." The engine room telegraph ring carried above the shriek of the wind and pounding water.

The reduction speed lessened the pounding but did little to alleviate the motion of the ship. Some of the new crew experienced sea-sickness they never thought they would have. The violent motion the ship made it impossible for the cooks to make a hot meal so the evening mess consisted of salmon salad sandwiches. A large portion of the crew wasn't hungry any way.

"Skipper! I have an urgent message from TPN for you."

"Thanks, Sparks. Stand by, I may want to answer." Maher quickly read the flimsy and handed it to Phillips. "Suggestions?"

Phillips frowned as he read.

"They want us to go to Yakutat? That's hundreds of miles out of our way and we would never be on station in time to sucker punch the Japanese Alaska Squadron. That's my take, sir, what's yours?"

"I agree with you, XO. They have to make up their minds which is more important, sinking a Jap carrier or securing a Jap plane. Sparks, send 'Your choice, we can do either but not both. Reply soonest.' "

"Aye, aye, captain." Sparks hurried off the bridge.

"I want to kill Japs," Phillips said. "But we'll do whatever you say, skipper."

Maher lowered his voice so only his XO could hear his words.

"You do realize this might be a suicide mission, don't you, Brad?"

"I know the odds of success are daunting, sir, but I don't think they are impossible."

Maher laughed. "You have always been a bit delusional, Brad. I like that about you."

Sparks hurried back onto the bridge.

"Reply, captain."

Maher took the sheets of paper and smiled as he read the first one out loud, "Jap ships first, seaplane second."

Lt Phillips grinned, "Well, they seem to think we're going to get through this."

"Oh, this makes a difference! 'Japanese Destroyer Escort *Hamiba* en route to Yakutat from Juneau.' Now what do we do?" Maher asked.

"Like I mentioned, skipper," Phillips said. "We'll do whatever you say."

40

IJNS *Genda*
Gulf of Alaska

"Captain Mihashi, we have lost sight of all the ships in our group."

"Any word of *Amagi*?"

"No, captain," the OOD said. "But we also have not heard any distress calls."

"Not that we could do a damned thing about it if we did! What is our current position?"

"We are twelve miles southeast of Granite Cape near the Kenai Peninsula, and twenty miles east of Cape St. Hermogenes near Kodiak Island. Right here," he said pointing at the chart.

"Helm, continue steaming in a tight circle. Nav, try to find the rest of our ships. Comm, closely monitor the radio for word from *Amagi*." Captain Mihashi felt livid.

I should have argued with the admiral. Leaving one of your ships is only something you do when you are under attack!

As if summoned by evil spirits, Vice Admiral Shima entered the bridge and came over to look at the chart with the others.

"What is our situation?"

"We are steaming in circles until this storm blows itself out, admiral. We have lost visual contact with our escorts and with the intensity of this storm I greatly fear for *Amagi*." Captain Mihashi said.

"Why have we not entered Cook Inlet, captain?"

"Because these are treacherous waters and our visibility is less than a mile. I will not endanger my ship and the escorts until conditions improve."

Admiral Shima raised his head and gave Captain Mihashi a level look.

"You will follow my orders, captain, or I will have you replaced."

"Admiral, our friendship goes back over a third of a century and I give it high value. However, I feel we have already made a military error in abandoning *Amagi*, and at this moment we are endangering this ship and all of her escorts by remaining so close to land."

"You are not following my orders, captain! I will not endure mutiny no matter how long I have known you!"

Captain Mihashi stepped back from the chart table and yelled, "Place the admiral under arrest and confine him to his cabin."

Two marines carrying weapons moved over to the admiral.

"You dare arrest your superior officer! I will have you beheaded for this!"

"At least my ship will be safe, sir. Take him away."

The marines escorted the admiral off the bridge. The entire bridge watch stared at Captain Mihashi as though he had sprouted wings.

"Attend to your duties! We are in a perilous situation and if every man does not do his duty we will die out here!"

They all immediately went back to their appointed tasks. Tatsuya Mihashi felt drained and unreal. If events didn't exonerate him he would lose his head.

My ship comes first. I will not allow that old man to sacrifice my command for his irrational fixations.

41

IJNS Amagi
Gulf of Alaska

"Captain, we have one shaft operable. Do we have your permission to make revolutions?"

"Yes! Do so at once."

The talker relayed the message and Captain Kodo stepped over to the helmsman.

"Be prepared to keep us off the rocks, we are too close to Montague Island to suit me."

"Hai, captain!"

The *Amagi* shuddered and began to move slowly in the storm. The violent rocking ceased and became more moderate.

"Get us south, away from the island and rocks."

"Hai, captain," the quartermaster said.

"Captain, we have a message coming in from Tugboat 39."

"What do they say?"

"Regrettably unable to achieve your position for minimum of ten hours."

"It is well we didn't really need them," Kodo said bitterly. He felt betrayed by his own navy in general and by Admiral Shima in particular.

How can he be so blind as to abandon a heavy cruiser just so he could keep an arbitrary timetable that rests entirely in his own head? At that moment Captain Kodo realized the admiral must be insane or at least mentally unbalanced. Oddly, the thought made him feel better on one hand and very sad on the other. The Empire of Japan did not lack for suitable senior officers, especially the type of hardliners the admiral represented.

Kodo had long ago discarded the unstated attitude that high rank conferred a god-like mantle on an officer and everyone under him must be willing to make the ultimate sacrifice on his behalf. He had seen too many men of high rank make decisions that not only were not well thought out, but deleterious to the Empire and the service. He gave honor where he felt it was due, and paid lip service to the rest.

The prevailing attitude had come close to wrecking his ship and killing him and his entire command for no viable reason at all. He reined in his anger and consigned it to the secure part of his consciousness that conserved the emotion for future use.

A day will come...

42

Juneau, Alaska Prefecture

Andy King walked into the Juneau Public Library with a sketchpad in one hand and a book in the other.

"Good morning, Miss Phillips, uh, Betsy."

"Good morning, Andrew. I see you're still having trouble with my first name." She smiled.

"Habit. Is there anyone else here?"

"No. Addie is down at the market searching for real coffee."

"I've been hearing some interesting things and need to know if they are true."

"Like what?"

"Tokyo and Berlin?"

"Both gone," Betsy said flatly, her smile had gone flat. "...and good riddance."

"Wow, he was right."

"He?"

"Mr. Kimura, my printmaker sensei. He was the one who told me."

"How did he seem to feel about it?"

"I memorized his statement, 'My heart smiles at the application of so much karma in such a short time.' "

"Well put. The man is also an artist with words. Is that why you came in, to check his statements?"

"He wants to help."

"Help do what?"

"Defeat the 'militaristic regime' that runs half the world."

"Of course there are two of those and together they run nearly *all* of the world, but I take his meaning. Do you think he's sincere?"

"I've given this a lot of thought. I've worked with him for five years now and he's turned me into a pretty good printmaker—"

"I won't argue with that."

"Thank you. I realized immediately that to trust him meant trusting him with my life and the lives of people I care about. He told me he came here to cleanse his soul of the things he did in the army during the war."

"We do get a lot of rain."

Andy smiled and continued, "He has a radio and monitors military channels. During the war I think he was in intelligence. He also knows I am in the resistance, as he puts it, and has known for four years."

"Then he knows a hell of a lot more than that. He also knows he has put his life in your hands. I think I will have a friend give him a visit."

"You're not going to kill him, are you?"

"Not if he is what he claims to be. As you just said, all of our lives might depend on it."

43

IJNS Hamiba
Gulf of Alaska

"Captain Yoshino, the prediction is the storm will get much worse, with no end in sight."

"Lt Uchida, has the crew been ordered to stay off all weather decks?"

"Yes, captain, we passed the word over an hour ago."

The destroyer escort hammered through the waves, the ship spent as much time submerged as above the water. The forty to sixty foot waves went far beyond intimidating, they towered, heart-stilling frightening. Despite the less than warm ambient temperature, every man on the bridge ran with sweat.

When waves lifted the ship high into the storm those with keen vision could see the land mass of Alaska some miles off to starboard. Then the ship would plummet into the trough as the next wave broke over her at mast height and she would roll and swim up into the air again.

"What is the *Amagi's* current situation?" Yoshino asked his bridge talker.

"Captain, the radio room reports that the main antenna has fallen victim to the waves. We are out of contact until they can rig a replacement."

"Tell them I forbid any attempt to do that until the weather breaks. We cannot afford to lose anyone."

"Hai, captain!"

The XO stood next to his captain and said, "Perhaps we should pull into Yakutat first. We can effect repairs as well as investigate the Kawanishi patrol plane."

"Our orders were to attend to the *Amagi* first, but without our radio in operating condition we would have no chance to do anything positive."

"The Kawanishi has a radio, captain. We could then report in to Sitka."

"I commend you for your initiative, Lt Uchida. Change course to Yakutat."

"It is auspicious that we have only the sea to fight," he said.

44

PT-245
Gulf of Alaska

"Keep out far enough to stay off the rocks, John!" LCdr Brian Williams shouted over the roar of ocean and engines. Another massive comber smashed into their port side and rolled the boat to starboard. Both Brian and Lt. Hart were lashed to the deck and had lines running from the cabin to the radar mast behind them.

The rest of the crew were below decks, bracing themselves to keep from breaking bones or suffering concussions. Brian had allowed his XO to spell him at the wheel. They had been at sea for more hours than ever before and between the constant pounding of the boat and the foul weather, everyone was nearing the end of their endurance.

Under normal circumstances they would be less than an hour out of Yakutat. On this day he had no idea. Places look different when a North Pacific storm is slamming into your stern, your foul weather gear is slick with ice, and you are drenched all the way through to the skin.

Brian shivered in the incessant wind and glassed the shore with shaking hands. It had been at least three years since his last visit to his cousin in Yakutat and he hadn't paid all that much attention to the scenery as he had been talking with a number of cousins. He now inwardly cursed himself for his previous inattention.

Though the binoculars he saw a great gust of wind pushing a huge wave toward the shore. It didn't stop but went completely out of sight – into Yakutat Bay.

"There it is! We're there!" He keyed the intercom. "Battle stations, battle stations!"

The crew poured out of the hatch aft of the wheelhouse and through the hatch in the middle of the bridge. All wore their foul weather gear in addition to life jackets and helmets. The engine room reported ready and secure. Chief Harris stuck his head out of the radio room and gave Brian a toothy grin.

"Ready to go, boss!" he shouted.

Brian swung wide around Ocean Cape and motored up toward Monti Passage.

"Raise the stars and stripes!" Brian ordered.

Bosun Andrews, who had long anticipated the order, immediately snapped the flag onto the jackstaff, let it catch in the wind and gave it a quick salute. The flag snapped and popped in the brisk gale and Brian felt warmed by the sight when he looked aft.

"There's the Jap plane!" Seaman First Class Jerry Kohler yelled. "And the patrol boat is just behind it."

They came alongside the long dock and motored past the Japanese sea plane and patrol boat. Two men hurried down the dock and waved them to a mooring spot. Brian returned the wave, then spun the wheel, advanced the port engine and the boat turned in its own length.

He rang for engine shutdown and the storm suddenly dominated all sounds as the engines died away. The two men on the dock had tied the PT-245 down and one jumped up onto the deck and hurried toward Brian.

"Cousin! You made it!"

"Jimmy, it's so good to see you!" Brian and the somewhat taller, sinewy man embraced.

"Damn, Brian, you're a block of wet ice! Let's get you some heat and warm clothes."

"I won't argue with that. John, post a watch and have everyone else come ashore."

Lt John Hart posted one of the new apprentices who had not even seen the weather deck for the entire trip, and the rest of the crew hurried ashore.

One of the men took three steps and fell on his face. He jumped up looking sheepish.

"The dock doesn't move like the boat does, huh?"

They moved into the village and entered a two-story structure with a huge NC in faded paint on its side. From the outside the building looked abandoned, inside was a completely different situation. A large area had been cleared and tables set up with chairs.

Farther back was a large kitchen where three people were working at top speed.

"Supper's almost ready, Brian," Jimmy said. "Your guys can wait here and you and your buddy," he motioned toward John Hart, "can get into some dry clothes."

"Bless you, my cousin. You have thought of everything."

"We saw you coming. We have a guy up on Ocean Cape and he can see for miles, even in this shit." He thumbed toward the wall where the wind could be heard moaning past.

"He's still out there, isn't he?"

"Of course. We keep that post manned twenty-four hours a day. Nobody is going to catch you with your pants down while you're here."

Fifteen minutes later a completely warm and dry LCdr Brian Williams walked back into the common room and gratefully accepted a huge bowl of moose stew. While Juneau had never seen a moose, Yakutat was prime hunting grounds with a very healthy population of the massive animals. His crew were all eating and having an animated conversation with the Yakutat warriors.

"How'd you capture the plane?" Brian asked after several bites.

"It was beautiful, cuz, just beautiful. The Jap marine officer sent a few guys in to check things out. We took all of them out with arrows. Then he sent in three more." Jimmy laughed.

"It was like the guy was on our side! Then he decided to bring all of them in with a big charge. The Jap captain looked like a porcupine in an instant.

"It was like shooting fish in a barrel. Then we pulled off the least bloody tunics and had five of our guys put them on and go limping down the dock supporting an injured man. The air crew poured out to help and our people on the shore took them out with arrows.

"The pilot and copilot showed more initiative than the rest but we got them, too. So now we got this big damn bird and nobody knows how to fly it."

Brian turned his head and yelled, "Lieutenant Hooper, come here, please."

A blonde, wiry man in his late 30s hurried over to them.

"What's up, commander?"

Jimmy looked at Brian with astonished eyes. "*Commander?*"

"Actually, it's Lieutenant Commander. Jimmy Walker, meet Lt. Ben Hooper, who can fly anything with wings."

"That has propellers," Hooper added with a laugh. "Pleased to meet you, Jimmy."

Brian continued, "Jimmy is the colonel in charge of the Yakutat Warriors. His people took out the naval station here as well as the patrol boat, the Imperial Marine contingent, and crew of the plane that brought them all here."

"So I refer to you as Colonel…"

"Jimmy. Just Jimmy. Everyone knows who I am and those titles don't mean shit around here. We all know our jobs and what to do.

"You're going to need an air crew and we have lots of volunteers. That being said, everyone here is pretty much related with everyone else. But you are the commander of that bird out there and what you say goes with no argument. Okay?"

"Sounds sweet to me, Jimmy. Please just call me Ben, like my family does."

"You got it, Ben. Welcome to Yakutat!"

Brian nudged his cousin. "Jimmy, where do we sleep? I am out on my feet. It's been a long damn day."

"Come on, I'll show you."

As they climbed to the second floor where rows of comfortable beds waited, Jimmy said, "We have people on watch both up on the bluff and down here on the dock. Nobody will mess with your boat. Okay?"

"Great. Would you please tell Lt Hart, the skinny white guy who looks bewildered a lot, that I said to secure the deck watch so everyone in the crew can get some sleep."

"Happy to do it. It does my heart good to see you and know that we're really hitting the bastards."

"At least until they hit back."

Stoney Compton

45

Juneau, Alaska Prefecture

Dave Hammond pulled the knit wool hat lower over his eyes and tightened the wide collar of his overcoat around his face. Instead of his usual snappy three-piece-suit he wore a pair of faded coveralls and work boots. It was the best he could do to disguise his identity, being a large man sometimes had its drawbacks.

A new gust of wind blew rain sideways over him, and the damp cold slowly crept into his bones. He rounded the last corner among the random buildings along the waterfront and pushed through a door and out of the weather. The space was marginally warmer than outside but felt wonderful.

Long stacks of shelves went deep into the building with breaks every twenty feet to allow cross access. Due to the presence of no more than ten overhead lights, the place seemed to exist in perpetual shadow.

He pulled his collar away from his face and pushed the cap farther up on his head.

"Anybody here?" he called out in as jovial a tone as he could muster.

He heard the distinctive click of a cocking knob being pulled back on a Type 14 Nambu pistol. He was familiar with the weapon since he currently carried one in his pocket. He left it there.

"Hey! It's Dave Hammond, the charming fellow from the Lucky Lotus!" He had never before realized how difficult it was to sound friendly when terrified. He loathed learning situations.

A stocky Imperial Army sergeant edged out of one of the access points carrying a pistol pointed downward in one hand and a bottle of saki in the other. As the owner of several bars, Dave knew a drunk man when he saw one. Unsettling; drunks could be difficult when it came to reason or anything else.

"Sergeant Mikatsu, my old friend! How good to see you again."

"What do you require from me this visit, fat man?"

"You seem to have started without me. May I have a glass of that wonderful nectar?"

The sergeant didn't move.

"What is it you require?" He lightly and repeatedly bounced the Nambu on his thigh.

"Well, the list is quite long and very expensive. Perhaps I can come back tomorrow and discuss it when you are more amenable to having company."

"Come with me," the sergeant nodded toward the rear of the building where Dave knew the man had his office.

"Of course, lead the way."

The office was in even more disarray than on previous visits. Dave lifted a pile of paper off the visitor's chair and sat them in the middle of an already overloaded desk. He sat down, feigning nonchalance and quickly plotted three different escape routes if this meeting went south.

Sergeant Mikatsu pushed a stack of files and paper off his desk onto the floor and carefully sat the saki bottle in the middle of the cleared area. He opened a drawer, produced two small glasses and ponderously placed one in front of Dave and the other in front of himself. He pulled the cork on the bottle and poured a generous portion for Dave and a smaller one for himself.

You're too late on that count, Dave thought.

"To the Emperor!" Sergeant Mikatsu held his glass high and Dave quickly stood, grabbed his own glass and matched the sergeant's stance.

"To the Emperor," Dave said solemnly.

They both threw back their drinks and the sergeant dropped into his chair. As he reached over and filled Dave's glass again, he said, "Please to sit, my friend David."

Dave sat and nodded politely when his glass filled. Again the sergeant only poured half as much in his own glass.

"What items do you require?"

"I wish to point out that I am making this inquiry for a different party, not for myself."

"You always say that. Tell me what you want."

"Two tons of bunker oil." Dave closely watched the man's face.

"Is that all?"

"Uh, as many .30 caliber rounds as you can produce, and as many 20mm and 40mm shells as you can provide."

"So you are part of the resistance to ask for these things?"

"Not me. I belong to the Kingdom of Dave Hammond the Wise. I take no sides, I merely try to be a paid factor for business arrangements that might not fare well in public. I have expressed all of this to you many times."

"But this tells me you have connections with the resistance, which is a vital bargaining point."

Dave began to suspect the sergeant wasn't as sloshed as he previously thought.

"Do the politics of my client jeopardize the possibility of an arrangement?"

"Drink your saki."

Dave drank even though he didn't want to. He was beginning to feel the effects of the liquor and he wanted to maintain a clear head.

"If I could provide these items, and more, what sort of a deal could you make for me?"

"I have access to a great deal of yen–"

"I require more than yen this time."

"Tell me what you need and I will see what I can do."

"I must be hidden from the authorities. They are coming to audit my accounts in two days. If they do that I will be shot."

"Tell me, Sergeant Mikatsu, what all do you have in here?"

"A great deal. There are more warehouses besides this one. I am feeling very generous only as long as my largess is reciprocated."

"I think I can guarantee that," Dave said, rubbing his mental hands and feeling blessed.

46

IJNS *Hamiba*
Gulf of Alaska

"Captain Yoshino, radar shows Yakutat Bay approximately nine miles ahead."

"Thank you, Lt Uchida. Reduce speed and cross in front of the bay. I want people searching the area with binoculars, understood?"

"Hai, captain!"

He went over to the chart table and studied Yakutat Bay. They would have to swing wide around Ocean Cape and slowly come into Monti Bay. The bottom shelved quickly in spots and he didn't want to run aground.

Lt Niwa, the navigation officer, silently studied the chart with his captain.

"We cannot leave this place in a hurry, captain."

"You are correct, lieutenant. Make sure you know which way to go if urgency becomes an issue."

"Yes, sir."

The ship rolled heavily to starboard before coming upright again.

"This area has inordinately large swells, captain. The closer to shore we get the more pronounced they will become."

"Stand out from the headland, quartermaster. Cross the bay and then swing back on the heading the navigation officer will supply you."

"Hai, captain."

"XO, sound battle quarters."

The rapid gong rang out and men rushed to their battle stations. Those manning weapons on decks open to the weather bundled themselves in the warmest clothing they owned or could borrow. As the *Hamiba* turned into the brunt of the storm to come about, all hands huddled behind blast shields and heavy weapons as the gun crews were drenched in frigid saltwater.

At the head of Yakutat Bay was the aptly named Disenchantment Bay where the Hubbard Glacier reigned. Due to the glacier, the waters of Yakutat Bay were but a few degrees above freezing. The saltwater inundating the *Hamiba* wasn't any warmer.

The gun crews already shivered in cold agony as the ship entered the large bay.

On the bridge, Captain Yoshino could see the Kawanishi tied to the dock. He also thought he could see a patrol boat, perhaps two patrol boats behind it and closer to the shore. He wondered at the lack of inhabitants.

"Mind the shoals, this is a tricky harbor." The last time he had brought the *Hamiba* into Yakutat the weather has been fair and the seas calm. Even this far inside the bay the wind and rough water made navigation difficult.

"Dismiss battle stations. Line handlers muster on deck. I want two squads of marines on deck in full battle dress." Captain Yoshino wanted to be ready for anything.

47

Juneau, Alaska Prefecture

"James, we think it's time to mobilize."

"Who would *we* be, Amelia, and what could I do about it?"

"The SEAPA War Council."

"*You're* a member of the Southeast Alaska Peoples Army? Since when?"

"Since I was twelve years old. Long before I met and married you."

"You never told me! Why not?"

"When you first came to town and joined SEAPA we weren't sure if you wasn't a spy, or a plant. So we watched you. Then you and I met and when you asked me out it seemed a good way to see what you were all about.

"Neither SEAPA nor I were disappointed. I planned to tell you when we were married, but the War Council asked me not to, they didn't want any extra worries on your head. I'm glad that I agreed.

"You have had more than enough crap to shovel up there at the A-J. You didn't need to be worrying about me doing my part for the resistance. Now it is time to pull all of SEAPA's parts together and openly attack the Japanese."

"Well, I am a captain in the rangers," he said. "What's your rank?"

"What does it matter? What does matter is that we need to find a lot of people in a very short time. We think you are the key to that problem."

"What is your rank?" he asked flatly.

"I think it's major, I never really cared one way or the other. Now, do you want to know why you're the key?"

"A major! Are you keeping any other secrets from me?"

"Dammit, James, you have nothing to be upset about! We have all lived under the fucking Japs for over two decades and we are all doing our bit to change that. If you're going to fixate on something as unimportant as this, you might *not* be the person we need!"

He took a deep breath. "Okay, why am I the key?"

"You have an army working for you."

"The Chinese slaves? They are so beaten down they won't even help one another. Why do you think they would help us?"

"Because they *are* slaves. They know they will work in that mine until they die unless they get a chance for freedom."

"They won't fight for us!"

"Have you *asked* them?"

"Of course not."

"You *need* to, today. Everything is coming unglued in Alaska Territory and we might have under a week to field an army."

"Amelia, is this an order?"

"Um, it could be interpreted that way."

"Just to be clear, you have shaken my trust in you."

"James, I have *never* lied to you. I have not shared some truths but that was part of my position description. There are six other people who know how I fit into SEAPA and that's it.

"If you don't know something, you can't tell the Japs about it under torture. I didn't know you were a ranger captain until last week, and I sure as hell didn't hear it from you!"

He grinned. "Looks like we're both good at our jobs. I need at least a day to sound people out. I can't promise an army if they have no desire to serve."

"Are we okay?" she asked.

"Sure, come here."

They hugged tightly.

She whispered in his ear, "Now that I think about it, I believe they promoted me to lieutenant colonel last year."

He started laughing.

48

IJNS *Genda*
Gulf of Alaska

"Do we have any indication when this weather will abate?"

"No, captain, all indications show it lasting for at least another week. This is normal for this part of Alaska at this time of the year."

Captain Mihashi was at a loss. The admiral had brought the entire squadron into an untenable situation and would have exacerbated it by going into Cook Inlet. The squadron now steamed in circles to safely weather the storm and not run aground.

What should I do? Shelling Anchorage offers few benefits and many drawbacks. What good would it do in the long run?

As he pondered his situation he realized he faced a two-pronged threat. If the Imperial Navy agreed with Admiral Shima he would face execution either by his own hand or that of another. If the navy upheld his decision that the squadron was facing extreme threat for no viable reason he would be retained.

However, he had to do something right now to save the squadron.

"Where did my meteorologist go? I need him!"

In moments the weather officer reappeared on the bridge.

"Captain?"

"Would the weather be better in Cook Inlet than out here in the gulf?"

"It wouldn't be any worse. The main thrust of the weather would be deflected by Kodiak Island and the Alaska Peninsula, which would have a moderating effect inside the inlet. I must caution you, captain, it would not be calm by any means."

"Thank you, lieutenant. Helm, make for Cook Inlet. Notify the squadron."

Orders were passed and the carrier turned nearly into the storm. Wind and water raked over the flight deck. The sea alternately dropped away from the hull and then rushed back to inundate all weather decks.

Green water rolled down the flight deck high enough to engulf the mobile crane in its entirety.

"I have never before seen such weather at sea!" The XO said. "Will we still attack Anchorage, captain?"

"No. It would like strafing Hiroshima in order to kill rats. Anchorage has been a Japanese city for over twenty years. We cannot kill our own people."

"What about the resistance? Do we just let them take the city?"

"In my opinion what is needed is ten thousand Imperial Marines or soldiers. This will be a land war, not a sea war."

"There aren't that many Imperial Marines in all of Alaska Prefecture. Are they available in the Pacific States or Japan herself?"

"The largest army and marine bases in the Empire were both on the edge of Tokyo."

"So unfortunate in so many ways," murmured Lieutenant Commander Kanegasaki.

49

Yakutat, Alaska Prefecture

"That's not one of ours!" Jimmy Walker said, peering through his binoculars from the roof of the two-story Northern Commercial building.

"The guys in Angoon told me we had a DE that would be coming north," Brian said. "Are you sure that isn't the one?"

Jimmy pushed the binoculars into Brian's hands. "Did they say they'd have Imperial Marines on it, too?"

"Shit! You're right," Brian said watching the marines lining up with difficulty on the rolling deck. "We've only got ten minutes to do something."

Jimmy leaned over the edge of the roof and shouted down, "Crews, man your boats! Warriors, man your harbor defense positions!"

Brian heard his cousin even though he already neared the bottom of the second set of stairs. Grateful that he had put on his foul weather gear before coming out to look at the announced ship, he sprinted for the PT-245. When he arrived, gasping for breath and flagging, he noted with pride his crew was already aboard and clearing for action.

The Packard engines started up one after the other and he knew the exhaust could be seen by anyone who cared to look; the cat was no doubt out of the bag. Still low on crew members according to the US Navy, they had picked up six new people in Angoon. The fishing fleet was heavily populated with former Navy and Coast Guard sailors itching to hit back.

Brian scrambled aboard and yelled, "Cast off all lines! Battle stations!"

Chief Foster, already clearing the breech on the 40mm, grinned at him through the wind and rain. "Where else would we be, skipper?"

"Force of habit," Brian said with a laugh. "Ben," he called to the new 2nd class Torpedoman's Mate, "how fast do we have to be going to launch a fish?"

"You never fired one, skipper?"

"How'd you know?"

"You have Mark-18 electric torpedoes. Just arm them, dump them in the water and they run straight ahead. You get me out to where I can see the side of that ship and I'll hit it."

"You have a deal!" Brian said and pushed the throttle to full speed.

As the PT-245's screws dug into the water at maximum revolutions, the bow rose and they tore away from the dock and into the storm.

"All guns fire as you bear!"

"Aye, aye, skipper!" Chief Foster yelled. "Did you hear that, Doty?"

"Sure did, chief!" the new 3rd class gunner's mate said with a wide grin as he swung the starboard 20mm around.

The Japanese ship had slowed to thread its way past the shelving bottom. People on the fly bridge pointed at the PT-245 and a klaxon sounded. By that time Brian had turned hard to starboard and was heading straight for the ship.

"Let them have it! Fire the torpedo!" he shrieked.

Roy Doty released the cradle holding the torpedo. It rolled off the side of the boat and instantly raced straight ahead. The two 20mm mounts and the 40mm bofors fired at the bridge and anywhere else sailors or marines could be seen. Brian spun the wheel to port and raced past the stern of the destroyer escort as .50 caliber rounds snapped over their heads and thudded into the side of the boat.

The torpedo hit aft of the bridge and three feet below the waterline of the DE. Three hundred pounds of TNT exploded, causing the ship to rise briefly in the middle as if going over a bump before a huge explosion tore the ship in half.

"Christ almighty, skipper, we hit the fuel tanks!" Doty screamed in delight.

Fuel from the ship tried to burn on the surface but the storm scattered it and drenched the flames. The aft part of the ship, driven by the still-turning screws, quickly filled with water and went to the bottom 27 fathoms below. Sailors and marines leaped off the forward portion of the ship as it tilted back and rolled over to port.

The water around the stricken DE teemed with survivors trying to grab anything that floated, including each other. The storm drove a succession of huge waves in from the gulf and with every wave more of the survivors disappeared. The bow of the ship slipped under the water and some of the survivors were sucked beneath the surface.

Brian made a hard turn to starboard, came back toward the scene and idled back the Packards.

"Save any that you can!" he yelled.

His men grabbed life rings and tossed a few out.

"Put her in neutral, skipper, I got a live one!" Chief Foster yelled.

"I got one!" Hooper shouted.

Lt Hart came out of the forward hatch leading to the crew quarters.

"Captain, we still have hull integrity, but we also have a casualty."

"Who and how bad?"

"New seaman, name of Quinn. Took a .50 caliber round through the head."

"It's been so crazy that I don't remember him at all. He certainly didn't suffer."

"No, sir. I have a couple of the fellows cleaning up and putting him in a mattress cover."

"Good work, John, thanks."

The crew continued pulling drenched and freezing Japanese sailors out of the water. The few marines still alive refused any help and stubbornly swam for shore over an eighth of a mile away. None made it.

"I thought that shit went out of fashion when the war ended," Brian said, watching the marines struggle toward shore.

"Bushido," John said, "which I think is more bullshit than anything else."

Brian abruptly started shaking and had difficulty standing up.

"You okay, shipper?" Hart asked.

"We sank a destroyer escort! I really thought we were going to die, every damn one of us."

"I think most of us were on the same page with you, sir."

"You were definitely on the same boat! Get us back to the dock so we can offload these prisoners."

50

Juneau, Alaska Prefecture

D ave Hammond hurried through the door of the Juneau Public Library and locked it behind him.

"What are you doing, Mr. Hammond?" Betsy asked, rising to her feet.

"Are we alone in here?"

"Yes, but–"

"You need to find ten thousand square feet of storage and at least twenty able bodied men to help me, right now!"

She had never seen him this agitated before. He always maintained an attitude of amused superiority.

"I would do this, why?"

"I have filled Sue Ann's list and more."

"How much more?"

"*Three* Imperial Japanese Navy warehouses full of ammunition, uniforms, gear of all sorts, and *twelve* fucking Mark-14 torpedoes!"

She wanted to ask how, and who, and other questions that didn't matter now.

"Did you have to kill anyone, Dave?"

"Not yet, Betsy. We have about thirty hours to do all this and you're burning daylight."

"Where do you want the men?"

"Warehouse 117 down by Thane Road. Tell them to come down as unobtrusively as they can. The Japs aren't smart but they are observant."

"Twenty men?"

"Thirty would be better. And, Betsy, you are trusting every damn one of them with your life, do you understand?"

"I'd already figured that part out. I have to know, what is this going to cost us?"

"One hundred thousand yen and safe passage out of here for one man."

"Japanese?"

"Yes."

"We can do that. Now go unlock the front door and get out of here."

She locked the door behind him and grabbed her hat and coat before easing out of the back door. The street light didn't illuminate this part of the building and she tried not to use it unless the situation was important.

Twelve torpedoes! Where the hell am I going to hide twelve torpedoes, and how are we going to move them?

Her mind seethed with possibilities and schemes. She hurried over to the home of James Flanagan and knocked on the door, three quick raps, a pause, and two more.

The door opened and Amelia Flanagan snapped, "In, quick!"

"Leave the light off, Amelia," Betsy said. "Is James home or at work?"

"Work."

"Damn! I need someone trustworthy who can gather men."

Amelia smiled oddly. "Please follow me."

Betsy trailed her up the steps to the second floor where Amelia tapped on a bedroom door.

"May I come in?"

A muffled answer and Amelia opened the door and beckoned Betsy inside.

"Joe Coffey! I thought the Japs had taken you." Her heart suddenly beat faster, she had thought him dead.

"Hi, Betsy. They did, that's why my complexion is so varied."

She finally noticed the massive bruising.

"Oh, my God, Joe." She felt like weeping. "How did you endure it?"

"Mostly by ignoring them. What do you need?"

"Twenty to thirty people we can trust." She explained the situation and watched their faces as she talked. Both immediately frowned in concentration and she was overjoyed she had them behind her.

"There are about twenty miles of old shafts and adits that nobody ever goes near," Joe said, "especially the Japs."

"How would we get the torpedoes up to the mine?" Betsy asked.

"I'm not talking about the A-J, I'm talking about Thane."

"That's just as high on the fooking mountain as the A-J!" Amelia said and immediately blushed.

"But we put in a hoist to bring down mining carts and such to use in the A-J," Joe said. "It could easily handle torpedoes and whatever else you have."

"I think torpedoes are a hell of a lot heavier than a mining cart," Amelia said.

"At least we can try that. Maybe we'll come up with some other solution by then."

"Excellent!" Betsy said. "What about people?"

"They'll all be there in an hour. Now get back to the library, you've done your part."

Stoney Compton

51

A-J Mine
Juneau, Alaska Prefecture

James Flanagan slowly moved past his miners, all hard at work. He looked for the ones who helped or directed others even though their job did not demand those actions. Finally he found one man who seemed to have eyes in the back of his head.

The small, muscular man looked a bit different from most of the other conscripts and not only did his own job but helped others do theirs. James was impressed by the fellow and wondered why he had never noticed him before.

Probably because I try not to really look at any of them. After watching from a distance for twenty minutes, he approached the adit and motioned for the man to follow. Without hesitation the man followed James down to an adit that opened on a depleted bay, they went inside.

"How well do you speak English?"

"Quite well, actually." A hint of British accent flavored his words.

"What is your name?"

"Ajai Terbish."

"What do the others call you?"

"Terbish, that is my name."

"That doesn't sound Chinese."

"It's not Chinese, it is Mongol, as I am."

"Okay, Terbish, I have a question for you that I don't ever want the Japs to know about."

"I rarely spend time with Japs," he said with a wide, healthy grin.

James laughed. "Yeah, me neither."

"Your question, boss?"

"How many of the blokes in this mine would fight the Japs if they thought they had a chance of winning?"

The open, friendly face went hard in an instant. "*All* of us!"

The vehemence in the man's tone impressed James.

"You know that for a fact?"

"Yes. It is the topic of much conversation when we work and when we eat the fish and rice they feed us. We have heard that round eyes are killing Japs, is this so?"

"In some places, yeah."

"Here in Juneau also?"

"How did you know that?"

"There is nothing else to do except talk or complain. New information passes swiftly. Are you going to kill Japs?"

"How did you come to be working here?"

"I was a government worker in a small settlement near the border of Nepal. The Japanese came in the dark of night and took us all away. I have not seen my wife and daughters since."

"How long ago was that?"

"Four years in your next month of October. Do not doubt me, I live only to find my family and kill Japanese. If you can help me do that I will be your friend forever."

"How many are in your barracks?"

"Three hundred, but I only know the one hundred and fifty on my shift."

"I need you to organize the whole barracks into squads of twenty men each. Pick squad leaders who show initiative and can speak English. The English is secondary but a definite plus. Make sure everyone you enlist will actually fight. You've got twenty-four hours, okay?"

"Okay, boss."

"That's another thing. My name is James Flanagan. Call me James or captain. I'm finished with being your boss."

"Thank you, James. Everyone in that barracks will fight to the death rather than work themselves to death in this frigid mine."

"Where did you go to school?"

"In Katmandu. My favorite professor was an old Englishman who had been a paratrooper in the Great Pacific War. Some day I want to find a Guinness and drink it in his honor."

James grinned. "Guinness is good for you!"

Stoney Compton

52

USS Bonefish
Gulf of Alaska

#

"Are you sure we're twenty feet down, chief?"

"Yes, captain. That's a bitch of a storm up there but our batteries need charging. They all need to be replaced but the supply depot seems to have run out."

Captain Edge smiled at the grim humor and braced himself against the rocking of the boat. They had to be close enough to the surface to effectively use the snorkels for the diesel engines to operate, yet as deep as possible to avoid the heavy weather. The hammering diesels deafened the men in the engine rooms and seemed loud everywhere else in the boat.

Cdr Lawrence Edge turned to the plot table. "What's our location, Russell?"

"Near as I can figure, we're within two hundred miles of the Barren Islands, skipper."

Radioman 1st class John Johnson, "John-John" to the crew, turned one his stool and said, "We're getting a message from the TPN, sir."

"Let me know when you have the full text."

"I wonder what's up now?" Chief Johnson said. "Maybe the Japs gave up on attacking Anchorage."

"That's not going to stop *us* from attacking *them*," Edge said.

"Here you are, skipper," John-John said holding out a flimsy.

Edge read it quickly and then stepped to the address system. "Attention all hands, attention all hands, this is the captain. We have just received word that the Japanese cruiser *Amagi*, part of the Alaska Squadron, has suffered major mechanical problems and is underpowered near Montague Island.

"Here's the real kicker, the rest of the squadron has continued on without her. She is currently alone and without aid. We're going to go help her find her way to the bottom."

Excited shouts and whistles could he heard over the diesel racket.

"I wonder who her skipper pissed off to get abandoned like that," Chief Johnson said with a grin.

"The best part is that we only have to change our heading a few degrees to make this date." Edge marked a new position on the chart. "We're a day away."

53

USS Bates
Gulf of Alaska

"Jeff, can you give me an idea of when this storm will peter out?"

"Captain, these things can go on for months in these waters." Lt Brown glanced at his charts and notes. "All I can tell you is the wind velocity has dropped about ten knots over the past eight hours. Other than that conditions are remaining static."

"So the *Bates* in Yakutat Bay would be like floating a thimble in a wringer washing machine?"

Lt Jeff Brown grinned. "That's a good analogy, skipper."

The loudspeaker clicked on.

"Captain to the bridge. Captain to the bridge."

Within moments Captain Maher hurried onto the bridge.

"What's up, Mr. Phillips?"

"We just received a message from TPN HQ. The Yakutat situation is under control, captain."

"How? Wasn't there a Jap DE headed there?"

"You have to read this, sir." The XO handed him a long message.

Maher read it through three times to make sure the communication was as wonderful as the first time.

"This is incredible! Boats, make an all hands call."

"Aye, aye, captain."

When the bosun finished, Maher took the handset.

"It is with great admiration and appreciation that I report to you of the sinking of the IJNS *Hamiba*, a destroyer escort of the same class as our ship, by a PT Boat in Yakutat Bay earlier today. The PT suffered one fatality and the *Hamiba* lost eighty per cent of her crew. Three cheers for PT-245!"

The cheers rang through the ship and muted the raging storm for a full minute. Once they died down, Maher continued.

"Therefore we will continue on our way to Montague Island where the cruiser *Amagi* is currently effecting repairs to her propulsion system and has been left alone by the Alaska Squadron. Once the *Amagi* is on the bottom we will engage the rest of the squadron. We can do this, shipmates!"

He hung up the handset to the continued cheers of his crew.

God, I hope I'm right!

54

IJNS *Genda*
Gulf of Alaska

For hours, Vice Admiral Kiyohide Shima pondered on what he was compelled to do next. At first he thought seppuku was the only honorable avenue left to him. On further thought, he decided that he was the person wronged and it should be Captain Tatsuya Mihashi who must atone for his transgressions.

With nearly fifty years of service to the Empire, he had seen all sorts. Tatsuya Mihashi was nothing new, just another subordinate willing to sacrifice a more skilled warrior in order to advance their star.

I will not allow it, he decided.

He went to his small library and pulled down a volume extolling the wisdom and exceptional military prowess of Admiral Togo during the Russo-Japanese War. He flipped open the cover and pulled the Type 94 Nambu pistol from its nest in the carefully hollowed out pages of the book. It held a full clip of six rounds.

I must be judicious in my targets and not dishonor the Emperor.

He slid the pistol into his pocket, picked up a brass paperweight and rapped on the door to his quarters. In less than a second the Imperial Marine guard opened the door.

"Is there a problem, admiral?"

"That noise, what is it?" He pointed across the cabin.

The marine stepped in with his head cocked and the admiral hit him on the back of the head where the skull joins the spine. The guard dropped in a heap and the admiral dropped the paperweight on him. He pulled out the pistol and operated the slide to chamber a round. Shutting the door behind him, Admiral Shima walked toward the doorway leading to the bridge, where he hoped to find the captain.

* * *

Captain Tatsuya Mihashi decided to change his sweat-sodden shirt for a fresh one and opened the door to the small passageway leading to his day cabin and the admiral's quarters. He stopped in disbelief when he saw the admiral who immediately raised the pistol in his hand and fired. As soon as he saw the gun Mihashi jumped to the side and slammed the door shut.

Unfortunately, before the door closed the round went through the opening and hit the duty talker in the back of the head, killing him instantly. The two marines on duty simultaneously raised their rifles and pointed at the door. Captain Mihashi nodded in approval and swung the door open.

"Drop the gun admiral, we have you covered!"

In response the admiral shot the first marine and the second marine shot the admiral. The wounded marine fell and scrambled behind the steel chart table cabinet. The admiral fell over backward, dead before he hit the deck.

The marine holding the smoking rifle quickly went from jubilant to anguished.

"Captain, I had no choice! He shot the sailor and Corporal Wanatabe..."

"You are to be commended for your quick thinking, Private Bando. You are correct; you had no choice in this matter."

Medics summoned by the OOD collected the two bodies and helped Corporal Wanatabe to the sick bay. Within ten minutes three non-rated men had the bridge cleaned of blood and brains.

Captain Mihashi slowly walked over to his XO, who had been sitting on a stool in the back to watch the OOD to assess his worthiness as a bridge officer.

"Are you in good spirits, captain? It is not every day that a superior tries to kill you."

"He dishonored himself. Rather than committing seppuku he wasted another life. Where is the honor in that?

"When this damn storm finishes with us I want to take the squadron back to Juneau," he said in a low tone. "We are going about this all wrong. With the loss of Tokyo and most of the upper echelon of both services, we need to make allies out of the Americans, not subjects. We *are* at war with the Reich."

He looked over at his XO's face. "Does that shock you? Do you think me a traitor?"

"Personally, I agree with your assessment. I doubt you will find many who agree in Juneau."

"There are a few of like mind, perhaps soon there will be more. The world is changing."

Stoney Compton

55

IJN HQ
Juneau, Alaska Prefecture

#

"Admiral, we have not been able to establish communications with the *Hamiba*. Our last message from her said she was thirty miles off the coast."

"Thank you." The signals clerk left and Admiral Jo Tanaka rubbed his eyes and then bent his back until the spine cracked audibly.

Commander Hokama, the commander of the air wing, and Commander Sunnichi, commander of the patrol boat fleet both sat in the admiral's office.

"I cannot believe that the *Hamiba* sank in the storm," Sunnichi said. "The ship was in good operating order."

"It was also nearly thirty years old," Hokama said. "That is the perfect age for a woman but very old for an active man of war."

"*Amagi's* last report said she was underway using one screw, which will prevent her from going on the rocks," Tanaka said, staring out at the storm lashing the city. "I still do not understand why Admiral Shima abandoned her."

"He has come to see himself as a near deity," Hokama said, anger shading his words. "He believes that he can do no wrong and anyone who does not agree with his views is a traitor. He had a friend of mine dismissed from the navy for no reason other than his own vanity. My friend committed seppuku."

193

"Was that Commander Toshiro?" Tanaka asked.

"Hai."

Two quick knocks sounded on the door, and the signals clerk stepped into the room, handed Admiral Tanaka a long message, and hurried out again.

"Must be a busy day," Sunnichi said. "I hope this one has better news."

"We were just discussing this situation," Tanaka said. He then read them the long message from Captain Mihashi about the incredible actions of Admiral Shima.

Silence reigned in the room for many minutes when he finished.

"I want to give that marine a medal," Hokama said with a snort.

"That makes you commander of all Imperial Navy units in Alaska Prefecture, Admiral Tanaka," Commander Sunnichi noted. "At this moment I would not trade you positions, sir, your chenbâpotto_{stet} is overflowing."

"Indeed, it is well we have the sewer now."

56

SEAPA HQ
Juneau, Alaska Prefecture

"We have a great deal to cover," Betsy Phillips said. "So let's get to it."

The group occupied a room on the third floor of the Sisters of St. Anne Hospital which commanded an excellent view of Juneau, Gastineau Channel, and Douglas Island.

Andy King sat where he could see any movement on the street in front of the building and still be part of the meeting. Jerry Tanaka sat near the door. As the only flawless speaker of Japanese, he would intercept any inquisitive official who might wander by.

Addy Johnson sat poised to take notes. She not only knew shorthand but also spoke perfect Tlingit. She was the only one who could read her meeting minutes. Next to her sat Sue Ann Freeman, SEAPA's supply chief. She bordered on magical in the proscribed items she could produce on short notice.

Joe Coffey cleared his throat. "The Japs are dangerously agitated since the PT Boat incident. They know we are out here but they don't even know our name, let alone our members."

"How did you keep from spilling your guts, Joe?" Dr. Anderson asked in an offhand manner. "You thought you were going to die, right?"

"Yep. And that's why I wouldn't tell the bastards anything, I figured it wouldn't make any difference in what they did to me."

"Why did they release you?" Sue Ann asked.

"I am as bewildered as you are on that one," Joe said looking around the group.

"I think I might have the answer to that one," Jerry Tanaka said. He immediately had everyone's attention. "I sometimes drink saki with a Commander Nagano of the Tokkeitai. After his third cup he becomes loquacious and since he is full of himself his mouth spills more than his hand."

Betsy grinned. She loved listening to Jerry even when they were in grade school together. His viewpoint always bordered on unique.

"It seems that when Admiral Kato dissected himself, his chief of staff, Captain Tanaka, was made admiral in his place. The new admiral was in the war as a very junior, undertrained officer and does not hold the rigid militaristic tenets his superiors do. According to Nagano, the admiral thinks we have all wearied of the stick and deserve more carrot.

"Nagano was ready to take your head off, Joe. The admiral told him to release you. I think that is definitely a 'saved by the bell' situation. You are a lucky man."

Betsy hadn't realized an air of tension existed until it abruptly dissipated.

"We need some place to hide a bunch of torpedoes!" Sue Ann blurted.

"Torpedoes!" Andy King said. "Where the hell did you get torpedoes?"

"From the Japs," she said smugly. "One of our people had the good fortune to encounter a Jap supply sergeant who needed money and a way out of town. In return we had twelve hours to clean out three warehouses down past the sawmill."

Betsy almost told them Dave's name but decided the situation could still turn against them and the less people knew the less they could tell a potential interrogator.

"How many torpedoes and what model?" Jerry asked.

"Twelve Mark 14s. We were going to hide them in the old Thane Mine but the lift broke."

"I know where we can hide them, and it would be perfect for transferring to a ship when the time comes." Jerry all but beamed.

"Please enlighten us," Dr. Anderson said drily.

"In the cold storage building. Most of it is empty, since the spring runs are a long way off and the stock on hand is transferred to the Empire almost as soon as it's frozen. We have lockable rooms in there that have been empty for months."

"That's perfect!" Sue Ann said. "Joe, have the guys stop carrying stuff up the damn mountain, we'll put it all in with the torpedoes."

"Which sergeant?" Jerry asked.

"Mikatsu," Sue Ann said. "Do you know him?"

"Yeah, he gambles too much and he isn't good at it. Did you get him out?"

"Yes, we did. We also took possession of old U.S. Army rifles left over from the war. The boxes were even moldy but the rifles all look pretty good."

"I've got the people to carry them," Amelia said. "Well, James does. He has recruited all of the Chinese conscripts in the mine."

"They'll fight?" Jerry asked. "According to Nagano they put up minimal resistance when they were rounded up in China."

"Wouldn't you give up if someone was pointing a gun at your wife and kids?" Amelia snapped. "Sorry, I didn't mean to be rude. As James has discovered, they all would rather die fighting than die mining, and that's the only way they get out of the A-J and we all know it."

"When we win this war," Andy said, "what becomes of the Chinese? Do we send them back to China?"

"The Japs would love that!" Sue Ann said. "Here are your slaves back, we're done with them."

"That's not what I meant," Andy said. "But you do raise a good point, they have nowhere else to go, do they?"

"They are hard workers," Joe said. "They know they are somewhere below donkeys on the Japanese social ladder, and they know they can be killed on a whim. That would sure as hell make *me* angry if I was one of them."

Betsy rang a small bell. "Okay, we need to make a couple of alternate plans. One is predicated on the success of our naval assault on the Alaska Squadron. The other is predicated on the failure of that assault.

"Either way, we need to have a plan to mobilize every fighter we can, and I don't care where their parents were born. What are your thoughts?"

Stoney Compton

57

IJNS *Amagi*
Gulf of Alaska

"Captain Kodo, the weather appears to be less intense," the OOD said as the captain entered the bridge.

"What is the state of the repairs?"

"Engineering has replaced two more of the damaged shafts and is working on the remaining one that came apart initially. Some of the sheathing in the shaft alleys is also being replaced."

"When can I have my ship moving again?"

"Lieutenant Kizumi says within the next two watches, captain."

"That is gratifying to hear. No captain of a warship wants his ship sitting in one place for more time than is absolutely necessary." He stared out the windscreen at the heaving sea and parallel rain. "Is the rain thickening?"

"The watch reports mixed rain and snow, captain."

"If it gets any colder we will have ice to contend with. I hate icy decks!"

"Port watch reports something in the water headed our way!"

Captain Kodo ran to the port wing and stared where the man was pointing.

"Full speed, hard to starboard! That's a torpedo! Battle stations!"

The single screw went to full revolutions and the quartermaster steered hard to starboard as the klaxon sounded. The ship inched forward, barely leaving a wake. A single gun mount fired at the rapidly closing torpedo.

"There are two more!" the bridge watch screamed.

Captain Kodo stared at the speeding weapons, willing his ship to clear their paths and knowing it wouldn't. Rain and snow pushed by a hard wind stung his skin and he concentrated on the Zen of the feeling as it was the only part of this surrealist moment he actually felt physically. Tears mixed with the icy rain on his face.

The first torpedo hit just abaft the bridge and the immediate explosion made the whole ship shudder. Men on the main deck were knocked off their feet. The second torpedo hit the hull between the stacks and destroyed the aft boiler room. The third torpedo hit the stern, less than fifteen feet from the fantail.

The third explosion destroyed the shaft alleys as well as the men working on them. The Amagi immediately began to list to port.

Kodo knew his ship was doomed. "Abandon ship! Lower life boats and deploy the rafts! Radio, get our location out to the rest of the squadron, your life could depend on it!"

Chaos spread over the ship. Most of the sailors had never heard a shot fired in anger and believed their ship to be invulnerable. Now they panicked, many dooming themselves. The vaunted discipline of the Imperial Japanese Navy crumbled and broke when it was most desperately needed.

"Captain, you must come with me!" the XO shouted.

Kodo shook his head. "I will be the last man off. Save yourself, that is an order!"

The Amagi rolled to port another twenty degrees. Men leaped off the side and began swimming into the storm. The 39° water quickly sapped their strength and warmth, bringing rapid hypothermia and certain death.

On the bridge, Kodo wept bitterly. He had done everything he could and yet this was the result. His ancestors had abandoned him, his ashes would not be enshrined at Yasukuni. He briefly considered shooting himself but decided it an unworthy demise for a naval officer.

He would go down with his ship.

58

INJ HQ
Juneau, Alaska Prefecture

"How many men do we have here in Juneau?" Admiral Tanaka asked.

"In the headquarters building we have about forty to fifty," Commander Ito said. "In the barracks we have sixty Imperial Marines and forty Imperial Army soldiers. The soldiers run the day operations of the port and the marines provide security. I have no idea how many Tokkeitai and Kempeitai operatives we have since that is a state secret."

"If we are attacked this afternoon, how many men could we put on the lines?"

"Approximately one hundred and fifty, admiral."

"I want you to plan an orderly withdrawal of all personnel here by order of the Empire. This action must be able to be effected in a matter of hours and be complete."

"Admiral Tanaka, this borders on defeatist—"

"*You* may remain if you wish, Mr. Ito. I want this plan on my desk in four hours. Do you understand me, commander?"

"Hai, Admiral Tanaka! It shall be done."

The signals yeoman walked through the open door of this office, bowed, and laid a message on his desk before hurrying out.

Jo picked up the message and learned of the sinking of the heavy cruiser *Amagi*.

Oh my personal gods, the Reich has attacked us!

He bolted out into the main office.

"Has headquarters in San Francisco been notified of this disaster?"

"Yes, admiral. As yet we have received no reply."

The latest intelligence about the German Navy indicated they possessed submarines that could travel around the world without the need to surface. It seemed science fictional to him but he also knew the Reich possessed aircraft capable of flying from Europe to America in less than four hours. When it came to threats from the Reich, nothing could be dismissed out of hand.

"Send a message asking for clarification of relations with the Reich. Are we at war or not?"

"Hai, admiral!"

If a Nazi sub is at large in the North Pacific..., he could not finish the thought, else he would weep.

59

A-J Mine
Juneau, Alaska Prefecture

"Do you trust these men?" James Flanagan asked.

Terbish looked him in the eyes and said, "With my life and yours."

Flanagan laughed. "Don't be too free with mine, thank you very much!"

The fifteen squad leaders in the abandoned stope were all undeniably Asians, but there were differences between them. He wondered how widespread in distance their origins might be.

"Do you know who I am?" he asked the men.

All responded at once, "Boss!"

James gave Terbish a frown and the man shrugged. "They didn't believe me, captain. You tell them."

"Right. We are all now fighting the Japanese. I am *not* your boss, I am your captain. Call me *James* or *captain*, okay?"

The tallest man in the group held up his hand.

"Yes. What is it?"

"Does not *boss* mean the same as *captain*?"

"What is your name?" James asked.

"Chan Lo."

"You are a very intelligent man, Chan Lo. From here on you are the second in command under Terbish. To answer your question, both titles demand respect and compliance, but *boss* in our case indicates that you have no choice in what you do. Whereas *captain* means you have agreed to follow my orders. Do you see the difference?"

"Either way, you are the boss, no?"

"Shit, I give up. Yes, either way I am in command. Do you want to be here or not?"

"No, boss, I want to be home in China. But I *am* here and I want to kill Japs, so I will call you *captain*."

"Any other questions?" James asked quickly.

They all stared at him waiting for answers or instruction. He felt overwhelmed but exhilarated at the same time.

"All right then, here's what we're going to do."

He gave each squad leader instructions on what part that they would play in the plan the war council had given him. Waiting for the command to execute would be the hardest part for all of them. Even he wanted to go start killing uniformed Japanese.

"Oh, yeah, this is very important. We only kill Japanese who are wearing a uniform, is that understood?"

"Are not all Japanese our enemy?" Chan Lo asked, perplexity furrowing his face.

"No. We have many Japanese citizens here in Juneau who have been here for decades before the Great Pacific War even started. They are helping us fight the Empire just as you are. If they are dressed in clothes like I am wearing, they are friends. Okay?"

"What is a uniform?" one of the squad leaders asked.

"What Sergeant Ando and Private Shimono wears. Clothing like that. It looks much the same with differences here and here." He touched his shoulders and upper arm.

"This is very confusing," Chan Lo said, "but we will try to do as you say."

"I damn well can't ask for more than that!"

60

USS Bonefish
Gulf of Alaska

The atmosphere in the sub had never been lighter. Captain Edge knew he now had a completely unified crew. Everyone had done their duty and played an important role in the first victory the *Bonefish* had enjoyed since 1945.

The surface still roiled with the incessant storm that now blew more snow than rain horizontally. There had been no question of surfacing to pick up survivors. The weather conditions would have put his crew in harm's way and they did not have room for enemy prisoners aboard *Bonefish*.

Edge had come to terms with the inhumanity of submarine warfare while still in OCS. The equation was simple; war was all about eliminating the other guy's military until they stopped fighting you. He and his crew had never surrendered and he knew they never would.

As he had many times in the past, he wondered if there were any other submariners out there hiding their boats and biding their time. He hoped so. It would be a lonely world if they were the only American sub crew.

"Skipper, sonar has a reading southeast of us," Lt Abel said. "It's on the same heading we are."

"That has to either be the *Bates* or a Jap ship maintaining radio silence."

"Why would they maintain silence, sir? They think they own the Pacific."

"That's a good point, Don. Have sonar ping them with the letter 'V' in Morse."

"Aye, aye, sir."

Everyone listened closely but only those with excellent hearing heard the same sequence hit the sub's hull a minute or two later. More pings followed. Seaman First Class Fred Vincent was the duty sonar man.

"They're sending Morse back in pings, captain. B, A, T, E, S!"

Applause broke out.

"Chief of the Boat, bring us up to twenty feet and raise the radio mast."

"Twenty feet, aye, sir."

Within ten minutes the radio mast rose above the water and Radioman Johnny Hackstaff asked, "Frequency, skipper?"

"UHF, John."

"You got it, skipper."

"*Bates*, this is the *Bonefish*, do you read?"

"*Bates* here, *Bonefish*. Good to hear you. This is Lieutenant Commander Eric Maher, commanding."

"Pleased to meet you, Captain Maher. This is Lieutenant Commander Lawrence Edge, commanding."

"So where is our crippled Jap cruiser?"

"On the bottom, sir. For about three hours now."

"Well done, Captain Edge!"

"It made our day rather memorable," he said with a chuckle.

"Any sightings of the rest of the Alaska Squadron?"

"Not yet. It either went up to Cook Inlet to raise hell in Anchorage or went in to avoid some of this heavy weather. Either way, they have to return this way to get back to Juneau."

"Do you have a chart in front of you?" Maher asked.

"Always."

"Okay, how about we do it this way…"

For ten minutes they conferred and finally agreed on a plan of action.

"If our tough little PT Boat shows up I'll tell him we need them closest to the mainland." Maher said.

"Sounds great. I look forward to meeting you in person, captain."

"As do I, I want to buy you a drink for putting the *Amagi* on the bottom."

Both ships signed off and the *Bonefish* went back to ten fathoms as they resumed their vector for attack.

61

Imperial Headquarters, San Francisco, Pacific States

G rand Admiral Nishiawa and General Hokita stood in the bemedaled glory of their best dress uniforms and held a salute as the massive, four-engined Mitsubishi and six fighters roared out of New West Airport enroute to the Empire. In the distance they could hear artillery and air strikes. They knew the air strikes were theirs, but they weren't sure about the artillery.

"I believe the Emperor and Prime Minister will be much safer in the new capital at Osaka," Hokita said as they ended their salutes. "What is the navy's status this interesting morning?"

"We have lost two of our carriers and an alarming number of other fighting ships," Nishiawa said guardedly. "Our fleet never rebuilt after the Great Pacific War, you know."

"What about all of the vessels you inherited from the American navy? There were thousands..."

"May I share a bottle of saki with you in the Jade Palace, general? We can speak about this in a more secure location."

Hokita glanced around at the growing numbers of civilians and military personnel in transit now that high security had been lifted from the terminal wing. Some civilians watched them with obvious interest.

"Thank you, admiral, I agree with your sentiment."

Ensconced in a secure booth in the Jade Palace, one of the more elegant inn-like establishments the airport offered, both men relaxed.

"The American navy scuttled most of their ships rather than hand them over to the Empire. Every captain we apprehended who did so lost his head for his actions. Of course that did not bring any of the ships back but examples were made."

"Rightly so," Hokita said, sipping his saki.

"The ships they could not sink were those in dry dock or still being built. Our newest carrier, the *Genda*, was completed after the war. It is the lead ship of the Alaska Squadron and one of only three carriers we now possess."

"I have heard nothing of the results from that squadron, was it not going to reconnoiter Anchorage and Fairbanks?"

"That was their task, yes. The insurgents in Fairbanks shot down all four of the jets sent to that place, we received no real intelligence as a result."

"What about Anchorage?"

"The recon flight was recalled. Vice Admiral Shima felt it was too dangerous to send aircraft." Nishiawa coughed into his hand. "So he ordered the squadron to Cook Inlet to strike Anchorage with naval guns as well as aircraft."

General Hokita nearly choked on his drink. "What! Is the man insane?"

"That proved to be the unfortunate truth." He then related the message sent by Captain Mihashi.

"By our ancient gods, we are fighting our own people and the insurgents at the same time."

"Not to mention the Reich," Nishiawa noted. "I realize they are having just as much trouble with their Americans as we are with ours, but that does not lessen the fact that we are at war with them."

"I thought being transferred here would be a plum to enjoy in my senior years," Hokita said. "Now the plum has soured and I fear for the Empire's fate in this place."

"It is auspicious that they have us battle-hardened veterans to keep the situation from disaster."

Both men laughed.

Hokita shook his head and in a rueful tone said, "Some of my subordinates are so completely ignorant—"

The booth door slid open and an elegant young woman of mixed nationality dressed in a classic kimono and carrying a tray holding a fresh bottle of saki and clean glasses entered, bowed, and slid the door shut behind her.

"What is this?" Hokita said. "We didn't order this."

"A gift from loyal subjects, general, admiral," she said bowing to both men. She sat the tray on the table between them, showing ample cleavage, smiled, and stood up. Neither man had stopped staring at her.

"I would give much to see beneath that kimono," Nishiawa said thickly.

She cocked her head and smiled. "I think that would be appropriate." She untied her obi and let it fall to the floor.

Both men grinned as the kimono swung open revealing her long legs, generous breasts, and a curious belt of boxes around her middle.

"What is that?" Hokita asked.

"Press this button, it will show you your fate," she said sweetly. She closed her eyes and her lower lip trembled.

Grinning, Hokita reached over and touched a button on the top of one box.

The resulting blast atomized the three of them as well as destroying the majority of the Jade Palace. In the distance the explosions intensified as alarms howled inside the massive airport terminal.

Stoney Compton

62

IJN HQ
Juneau, Alaska Prefecture

Admiral Jo Tanaka studied the all too brief report on his desk. In the past he had not worried about the number of personnel stationed here. The Alaska Squadron and the air base at Sitka were always within comfortable reach if a problem occurred.

The situation had changed dramatically in the past three days. Reports of losses in Yakutat and in the Gulf of Alaska had reduced his options most alarmingly. Here in Juneau an investigation of a corrupt supply sergeant revealed the loss of the contents of three warehouses of military stores, one of them full of munitions.

The *Amagi* and the *Hamiba* were both on the bottom of the Gulf of Alaska. Admiral Shima had gone insane and was now dead after killing an innocent sailor. All of this was now *his* problem. His stomach twinged painfully.

His telephone buzzed and he picked up the receiver.

"Yes. Send him in." He replaced the receiver and looked up at the door. It swung open and an Imperial Marine colonel bowed from the waist before marching into the office. Jo sighed inwardly.

"Admiral Tanaka, I must speak with you."

"It seems to me that you are doing just that, colonel. Please be seated."

The colonel sat at attention as if he were a naval cadet. Another inward sigh.

"What is on your mind, Colonel Hiraki?"

"Our situation here in Alaska Prefecture leaves much to be desired. We are understaffed, undermanned, and possess inadequate material to keep the population subdued if an uprising should occur."

"Colonel, the uprising has already started. Everything you just told me has been eating at my guts for two weeks. Do you have any insights or solutions to offer or are you here to cover your political ass?"

"Admiral, that is very offensive!"

"What is it you want of me, colonel? I am a very busy man."

"I, I only wished to make the situation from my point of view known to you, admiral. I meant no disrespect."

"How many effectives do you currently have?"

"Sixty, admiral. An even hundred if you count the Army personnel."

"Do you have any idea how many insurgents there are in the area?"

"Surely no more than thirty, sir. Most of the locals are hard working laborers and craftsmen, not radicals."

"Mobilize all of your men, including the Army personnel. Place squads at every possible entrance into this compound and send two squads up to the administration building and escort every clerk and functionary to this building. Do you understand my orders?"

"Hai, admiral!" Hiraki shot to his feet and saluted.

Jo returned the salute. "Then do it."

What is the term I heard the other day? He thought. *Oh yes; we're fucked.*

63

PT-245
Gulf of Alaska

"Why couldn't we wait for the storm to lighten up, skipper?"

"Because there's going to be a battle soon and we need to be there for it, Mr. Hart."

"We're going to be a fast moving iceberg by the time we arrive," he said, shivering in the constant blast of frigid air whipping around the windscreen.

Brian knew his XO had a point. Ice was forming on all metal parts of the boat and the deck was dangerously slippery with slush. He felt as if they had traveled back in time to the fight for the Aleutians.

Except we didn't have adequate cold weather gear then. God that was cold campaign!

"Why don't you go below and spell me in about an hour. We'll do one hour on and one hour off just like the lookout."

"How long have you been out here, Brian?"

"Long enough to freeze my nuts off," he said with a laugh. "Don't worry, Tlingits are used to this stuff."

"See you in an hour, skipper." Hart went down through the hatch into the officer's quarters. Brian peered ahead to make sure there was open seaway in front of them then pulled his head back behind the windscreen.

You can tell they designed these boats for the South Pacific!

They had been so busy getting the boat ready for this patrol that he hadn't had time to really get to know the new guys, but they all seemed to be fitting in. He knew that Chief Foster was teaching his two new gunner's mates the fine art of field stripping the .50 caliber machine guns using the spare he kept below deck. JW wanted his men to be able to tear the thing down and put it back together blindfolded. They weren't quite there yet.

Nor are we, he thought, peering over the windscreen again.

From Yakutat it was a fifteen hour run to where they hoped to ambush the Japs east of the Barren Islands. The boat had a three-thousand gallon fuel tank capacity and at their top speed of forty-five knots went through 500 gallons in an hour. Since they could go farther at a lower speed, he kept it down to twenty knots, despite having ten 55-gallon drums of fuel securely tied to the deck between the fore and aft torpedo mounts.

If they ran into trouble all the drums could be rolled off the sides into the sea.

It would have to be a matter of life or death before I would jettison that much fuel.

PT Boats always provided a bumpy ride. In these conditions it scaled up to brutal. His legs ached from the cold and constant shifts in bracing against the bouncing deck.

The door to the crew's quarters opened and Chief Harris came on deck.

"What's up, chief?"

"I've got some radio traffic I want you to hear, skipper."

"Give me a minute or two."

Harris disappeared back into the charthouse and Brian stomped his foot three times on the hatch to the wardroom. The hatch immediately opened and Lt Hart peered out.

"Has an hour passed already?"

"Pretty close, John. Chief Harris has something on the radio he wants me to hear."

"Give me a minute." The hatch closed. After five minutes Lt Hart came up on deck more bundled up than previously.

"You have the conn, Mr. Hart."

"I have the conn, aye, captain."

Brian stepped down into the welcoming warmth of the radio shack. Little more than a cubby hole off to one side of the steep ladder descending into the crew quarters and galley, it offered Chief Harris a small stool and two small windows facing starboard. Today the window covers were dogged shut as added insulation against the cold.

"What do you have, chief?"

"Put these on," he said handing him headset.

Brian always felt like his head was in a clamp when he wore these things. Today he instantly forgot any discomfort as he heard, "...three DDs and a DE...", "...r word on move..."

He pulled the headset off.

"Why's it breaking up, chief?"

"The storm. They're somewhere between fifteen and twenty miles away and this is UHF, basically line-of-sight radio. If they broadcast on a different band we would be able to hear them clearly, but so would the Japs."

"So we can't *see* that far?"

"We go into a trough or they go into a trough and the radio waves get swallowed by the sea."

"Oh, of course. I wonder if they're ahead of us or behind us. But, the thing is, they're out there!"

The two men grinned at each other and shook hands.

"Keep monitoring.When you think they're close enough for an intelligent conversation, let me know."

"Aye, aye, skipper."

Brian went back on deck, thoroughly warmed from the heart on out.

Stoney Compton

64

A-J Mine
Juneau, Alaska Prefecture

"Why are these men standing around idle?" Sergeant Ando demanded in an outraged tone as he quickly surveyed the dozen Chinese standing in the main adit.

"It's called a *break*, sergeant. That's when the workers stop for ten to twenty minutes and rest."

The sergeant looked at the private with him in mock surprise.

"Did *you* permit this lack of activity to take place, Private Shimono?" He looked back to James Flanagan as he waited for his answer.

The private maintained his rigid discipline. "No, Sergeant Ando, I did not."

"Then *who* authorized this new concept, Mr. Flanagan?"

"I did, sergeant." He watched the anger immediately cloud the sergeant's face and felt surprisingly light hearted about the events about to unfold. "Actually in English, there are many definitions of the word *break*. The one we are using today is the term involving an uprising of prisoners."

A flash of surprise washed over Sergeant Ando's face and Private Shimono began to unlimber his machine gun. Two of the Chinese workers hit both men in the back of the head with the steel bars used to move gold ore. Their heads cracked like eggs and both were dead before they landed face down on the rock floor.

"How many more Japs are there in the mine, boss?" Chan Lo asked.

"Two at the entrance, one at the colonel's office and the colonel himself."

"I have never seen the colonel, boss," Terbish said. "May I kill him?"

"No, he's mine. But you and the others may eliminate the guards at the mine entrance."

"What about the colonel's guard?" Chan Lo asked.

"I'll handle him, too," James said with a terrible grin.

The guard outside the office door stared unsmiling at him as he nonchalantly walked up. The private kept his machine gun at port arms and said, "What are you doing here? You have not been summoned."

"I need to see the colonel, it's important." He stepped closer to the guard, his right hand down at his side.

The guard raised his head in order to look down his nose at James, which is when James swung his skinning knife, blade down and sharp edge out, swiftly around and cut the man's throat. He caught the machine gun with his left hand when it fell from the guard's suddenly nerveless fingers. He bent down and wiped the blade on the soldier's tunic and slipped it back into the sheath.

He examined the machine gun, found the safety and decided it was off. With the gun in his left hand he opened the door with his right, pushed it open, and realized nobody sat behind the desk. James reached down, grabbed the dead private with his right hand, and threw him through the door.

The glistening blade of a samurai sword swished down and decapitated the corpse. James saw Colonel Hirota's head and squeezed the trigger on the machine gun. The safety was on. Hirota instantly realized his error and pulled back out of the doorway.

James angrily flicked off the safety and made himself hesitate. His Scot's temper, far too easy to ignite, had worked against him in the past. His life was on the line here.

"Come in, Mr. Flanagan, and meet my sword!" Hirota yelled.

"I don't have to, you egotistical asshole! All of your guards are dead, your former slaves are armed and marching on the Jap garrison which is badly outnumbered. You can sit in there and rot."

James quickly stepped back from the doorway as quietly as possible. As he mentally predicted, Hirota jumped into the doorway with the blade flashing in every direction possible. James admired the man's deft handling of the sword for a moment and then shot him five times.

One of the shots hit the sword and snapped it in half.

Shit, I always wanted one of those things!

From both sides of the hallway Chinese men carrying picks, iron bars, and a few machine guns ghosted up. They wanted to look at the man who had ruled their lives without even looking at them. One of the Chinese undid his rude trousers and urinated on the dead colonel.

"Okay, lads, let's go kill some sons of the Empire!"

Stoney Compton

65

IJNS *Genda*
Southern Cook Inlet

C aptain Tatsuya Mihashi was in a quandary. The weather had moderated to the point he felt the squadron could navigate safely in restricted waters. He wasn't sure which way to go.

The Emperor wanted information about Anchorage and Fairbanks but he wasn't sure the Emperor wanted them to bombard what was essentially a Japanese city. However, he knew they were close enough to do a single reconnaissance flight over the city and he ordered the "camera plane" to be readied.

The morning had dawned clear and very windy, but nothing Imperial Japanese Naval Aviation couldn't handle. Keeping south of Kachemak Bay, they launched the aircraft. Captain Mihashi remained on the bridge and had the communications between ship and plane put on the bridge speaker.

"This is Voyeur One, I'm passing over Kenai, all cameras rolling."

The Operations Officer and the pilot had named the mission. Captain Mihashi thought it amusing and clever, he didn't care what anyone else thought.

"Anchorage dead ahead. I just saw an artillery emplacement on the south side of Turnagain Arm. Could it have been one of ours?"

Captain Mihashi turned to the OOD. "Have someone check with the Army and get a location of all of their artillery emplacements in Cook Inlet."

"Aye, aye, captain!" The ensign passed the task to one of the bridge watch and the man hurried toward the radio room.

"First pass complete! No hostilities noted. I will fly up to the mountain and loop back over the other portion of Anchorage on my way to the ship."

Mihashi knew the pilot referred to Denali. Early in the occupation a delegation of Athabascan Indians had petitioned the officer in charge of Southeast Alaska Prefecture to do away with the name the whites had labeled it. He had agreed at once.

The Japanese understand the significance of a great mountain, Mihashi thought.

"Passed Eagle River and planning to pass over the southern end of Anchorage. *Genda!* They have just launched two missiles at me. Going to afterburner to outrun."

"All eyes on the sky, we should see him soon!" Mihashi ordered.

The Fuji roared over the ship two minutes later. The missiles had self destructed or fell into the inlet before they reached the squadron. Five minutes later the pilot made a perfect landing on the carrier.

"So what can we see?" Mihashi asked as he entered the photo lab.

"We're still souping the film, captain," Chief Photographer's Mate Asumi said. "As soon as we have a negative, we will burn large images of the entire area and then fit them together."

"How long will that take, chief?"

"At least a half hour, sir."

"I'll come back then."

66

Homer, Alaska Prefecture

"What the fuck are they doing down there, having fucking tea?" Marion Matthews all but spat as she lowered the heavy binoculars and handed them to Barney Benson.

Barney patiently raised the binoculars and watched the Japanese, it was his turn for the next half hour.

Mike Armstrong grinned at Marion. "You never talk like that in the library."

"That's because I'm in charge and everything goes my way. The Japs came into the inlet like gangbusters and proceed to sit on their asses for three days."

"The weather *was* pretty bad." Mayor Orin Beeder pointed out.

"They just did an over flight, so what's holding the little bastards up?"

Mike tried to hide his grin. He had never seen Marion this wrought up before and he really wanted to laugh.

"Maybe something changed in their command structure," Arnie Weimer said. "Maybe they are deciding what to do next and they needed current information before they put all their assets in the game."

Mike's eyebrows rose and despite himself, felt impressed. "I think you might have something there, Arnie. They have no idea what's happened up there."

"Neither do we," Orin said. "I wish we could tap into their phone line."

"We don't dare try to find their communications band," Arnie said. "All their ships carry radio location equipment. They'd nail us in less time than it takes to explain."

"Fuck that!" Marion said, glowering at everyone in the room.

"They're moving!" Barney blurted. "They're going north to Anchorage!"

"As soon as they pass the headland and can no longer see us here, get the operation moving as fast as possible!" Orin said.

God, I hope this works, Mike thought.

67

Juneau, Alaska Prefecture

The Chinese maintained great discipline as they left the mine and followed James Flanagan down the hill toward the waterfront. The week of rain and wind had abated to a large degree but water still fell from the sky.

They arrived at a windowless warehouse and James pointed them through the door. Inside they met a smiling man who said, "I want all squad leaders right here."

Once everyone had entered the warehouse, the door shut, and the word passed around. Finally Joe Coffey had all the squad leaders in front of him.

"I want two squad leaders to take their men and go with this man, the next two and their people go with this man, the..."

Each instructor-guide took the Chinese over to a preplanned spot and handed out an M-1 Garand to each man along with a pouch of ten 8-round clips. Slowly, carefully, each instructor went over the nomenclature and operation of the weapons. The instructors waited patiently while the squad leaders translated the information to every man in his squad.

At random the instructors would pick one of the non-English speaking Chinese and ask them questions about what they had just learned. The accuracy was amazing. Each man was taught to aim carefully and then squeeze the trigger.

"I wish we could put them on a firing range for a day," Big Bill Thompson said. "This is a quick bunch, I hope they pick up shooting live ammo as well as they did this part."

When two squads were directed over to Kijan Kimura, they all stopped and glared at him. James Flanagan hurried over to the group.

"This is a good man, an old friend. He once served in the Japanese Army but no longer. We all trust him."

The Chinese recruits listened as Kimura explained the weapon, but not one of them smiled at him. He didn't seem to mind. Jerry Tanaka wandered up and added some information and the Chinese became agitated.

"Are you doing this to play with their emotions?" James said as he came up behind Jerry.

"No. At least I don't think I am."

"They hate Japs and don't fully realize you are an Alaskan of high repute."

"Tell them I didn't mean to cause alarm. I apologize."

"Maybe I'm the one spreading alarm. They need to get used to you and Kijan—"

"And the rest of my family." Jerry smiled. "I'll get out of the way, I'm disrupting their studies."

By now all of the Chinese recruits looked to be proficient with their weapons, at least in handling them.

James pulled a small bell from his pocket and rang atone. All eyes in the large room fastened on him.

"We're going to feed everyone now and give our new people bedding. It is safer to remain in here than to go out where there might be enemy eyes. Any question?"

The squad leaders interpreted his words and many conversations in Chinese followed. One of the squad leaders raised his hand.

James pointed at him. "What's your name, sir?"

"Chin Hoa, boss. They want to know when they can kill Japs."

"Soon, probably tomorrow."

68

Battle of Cook Inlet I

"I don't see anything over there, captain," Ensign Fukita said, continuing to peer through his binoculars.

"According to the intelligence section on the *Genda*, there is artillery entrenched on Point Possession. Look more closely," Captain Hiroshi ordered. He was scanning the same location. At ten miles out from the point and moving at five knots, he felt the IJNS *Sagiri* was relatively safe form shore batteries.

The old destroyer navigated in a constant state of repair and he wanted nothing to do with high speed turns or enemy action. He wasn't even sure they wouldn't pop rivets if they fired one of the 5"/38 turrets. Built in 1944 by the Americans, the destroyer was almost as old as he was.

"It is unfortunate they cannot send us a copy of the aerial photo," Ensign Fukita said, still glassing the point.

"The photo intelligence people said it was well entrenched," Hiroshi muttered, beginning to wonder if the *Genda* was correct about this seemingly phantom weapon. "Helm, take us farther north and circle back on this side of Fire Island."

"Hai, captain!"

The *Sagiri* picked up speed at the same moment both officers saw the muzzle flash of a large bore weapon.

"All ahead full!" Captain Hiroshi shouted. "Incoming fire!"

* * *

The high explosive round easily penetrated the steel of the bridge before exploding. The entire bridge watch ceased to exist and the executive officer, Lt Ano, took command in the after steering room.

"Do we have radar?" he yelled into the sound-powered phone. "Return fire, all mounts! Sonar, give me readings." He heard two mounts return fire and held a brief hope they might get out of this.

The ship rocked violently to port as another round smashed through the armor plating and destroyed the aft boiler room. Cold seawater poured through the ruptured hull and after a few moments the boilers spontaneously fractured, killing what few sailors remained alive in the space.

The *Sagiri* rolled to starboard and didn't stop. She turned turtle and in less than four minutes sank in ten fathoms of water.

* * *

"My God, we got the bastard!" SSgt Heupel yelled. "We actually sank a Jap ship!"

"Get the hell out of here!" Lt Adams shouted. "They're gonna blow this fucker to smithereens!"

"Who is, lieutenant?" Private Ogden said. "We just sank it!"

"That!" Adams pointed down channel.

Another destroyer was headed toward them at full speed and a third ship followed in the distance.

"Holy shit! How we gonna get Long Tom out of here?"

"We aren't, private," SSgt Heupel snapped, "unless you can carry it in your pocket."

The lieutenant already ran down the path they had made in order to build the position, the sergeant was close behind him.

Private Ogden patted the 105mm fondly, it had been part of his life from earliest memory and he felt he was abandoning an old friend. Then he ran for his life.

✳ ✳ ✳

Steaming at full speed, the IJNS *Hayashimo*, a sister ship of the late *Sagiri*, closed on the location and began firing all of her 5 inch/38 caliber guns at the artillery emplacement. After two ranging shots they put three rounds into the position and were elated when the site erupted with pieces of artillery flying in the air.

"Excellent shooting!" Captain Iwata exclaimed. "We have punished the rebels severely."

"Captain, the *Genda* is launching aircraft to assess the damage," the radioman said.

"Acknowledged. Be sure to report their findings immediately. Helm, take us closer to Fire Island."

"Hai, captain."

Lt Nakano, the executive officer, stepped next to his captain. "Sir, if the rebels had artillery on that point they could easily have artillery on this island."

"There was no mention of seeing anything on the images taken by the recon jet, lieutenant."

"Just because they didn't see it, doesn't mean there isn't an emplacement there, sir."

"I commend you on worrying about the ship as much as you do about the crew, lieutenant. However, in this case I feel we are in little danger. Those high resolution aircraft cameras rarely miss anything."

"Just one word, sir, and then I will cease my entreaties."

"And that word is?"

"*Camouflage*, Captain Iwata."

"That is an excellent point. We shall see if it is indeed the case."

✳ ✳ ✳

"They are moving toward us, Captain Kynell!"

"Don't pull the lanyard until I tell you to, Sergeant Olsen." Kynell avidly watched the Japanese destroyer though his Zeiss binoculars. He had lost hope that he would ever again direct firepower on a Japanese position, and here one was steaming toward him seemingly without a care in the world.

They should have more closely studied that other huge empire, the Romans!

"What we're seeing here is a defiant act of pure hubris, Sergeant Olsen. Pure hubris."

"Yes, sir."

"Aircraft!" Corporal Pfeiffer snapped. "It's a Fuji loaded with armament."

"That changes the situation," Kynell said, shifting his attention to the jet growing larger in his binoculars every second. "Everyone stay well under cover."

The jet shrieked over them and curved over Anchorage as if daring something to come out and fight.

"I hope they don't waste the SAMs this time," Kynell said. "We're almost out of them."

The jet circled over the city twice before streaking away to the south where its carrier waited. The destroyer had moved closer to Fire Island. They could not miss at this distance.

"There's another ship coming up behind this one," Pfeiffer said. "Looks like a destroyer escort."

"That leaves one destroyer protecting the *Genda*," Kynell said with relish. "The only word that comes to mind is 'auspicious'," he said with a laugh. He lifted the binoculars to his face again.

❊ ❊ ❊

"Captain, we are being hailed by the *Sakura*."

"What do they want?" Captain Iwata said.

"They remind us that the captain of the *Genda* said not to approach the landforms too closely if resistance was encountered. As was evidenced back at Point Possession, sir."

"Is that what they said or are you editorializing, Petty Officer Kenobe?"

"The captain of the *Sakura* put that in his message, captain."

"Reply to the *Sakura* that I am content in my examination of potential resistance strong points."

And the captain of the Genda *can do as he wishes, I am captain of this vessel!*

"The starboard lookout reports flashes of light on the island, captain!"

"What sort of flashes?"

"He said they appeared to be light glinting off binoculars."

"Hard turn to port, helm! Get us out of here!"

"Hai, captain!"

The XO regarded his captain with a look of awe mixed with concern.

"Your thoughts, captain?"

"Okura has the best eyes on this ship. Coupled with your warning of camouflage, if he saw binoculars that means there is at minimum an artillery emplacement there. It is prudent to put distance between us and the threat. I have no desire to swim in these waters."

"*Genda* asks your intentions, captain," Petty Officer Kenobe said.

"Tell them we suspect rebel emplacements on fire Island and request an airstrike. Get the coordinates from Petty Officer Okura."

* * *

"Where the fuck are they going?" Kynell all but howled.

"Captain, there are three Fuji fighters headed our way!" Pfeiffer said. "I suggest we all take cover."

They all hurried into the bunker where the duty crew slept. The doors, made of heavy steel, swung shut with a satisfying clang and they bolted them.

The Earth heaved and explosions resonated through the suddenly flimsy structure.

I had to bring up hubris, didn't I? Kynell thought as the metal bunker absorbed more and more punishment.

Stoney Compton

69

Battle of Cook Inlet II

The farther from Anchorage they moved, the better Captain Iwata felt. Behind them, jet fighters from the *Genda* were still bombing and strafing Fire Island.

"Lieutenant Nakano, ensure only one of the watch is observing the air arm in action. The rest need to be attending to their duties."

"Yes, captain." The XO moved around the bridge and found no one to instruct. He detailed petty officer Okura to monitor the events on Fire Island. Passing the sonar operator he whispered, "Be very diligent, these are shallow waters for a sea-going vessel."

"Hai, lieutenant!"

"I do not like the way the inlet narrows up there," Captain Iwata said. "Pay extreme scrutiny to those points."

The XO glanced at the their chart. "They are known as East Foreland and West Foreland, captain. The channel is ten miles wide at this place. There are roads on the east side of the inlet, but not on the west side."

"There were no roads to Possession Point, either," the captain said with a growl. "Carefully observe both sides."

"Hai, captain." After a moment of thought, the XO went over to Okura and instructed him to observe the western point as they approached. Fire Island was now so distant they could only be sure of its location by the columns of smoke rising from it.

"Reduce speed to ten knots," Iwata ordered. "These are tricky waters and we would lose much face if we hit a rock."

"Nor do we want to meet Ryûjin any time soon," the XO said with a smile.

Captain Iwata swung around and glared at Nakano.

"Do *not* mock the gods!"

Nakano bowed, instantly contrite. "My apologies, captain, I was attempting to lighten the mood."

"Attend to your duties, lieutenant!"

The *Hayashimo* moved into the narrowest portion of the inlet.

❋ ❋ ❋

Keeping as far back in the covered western emplacement as possible, Lieutenant Baxter studied the Japanese destroyer through his binoculars. He wasn't sure what happened at Fire Island but something spooked the little bastards and he feared he had seen the last of Captain Kynell and his men. Baxter knew they would probably get off three or four rounds before they had to abandon this position or die.

I'm glad we're not the only ones out here, maybe we'll confuse them long enough to sink their ass.

"Be ready to pull that lanyard when we see the signal, Rick."

"I'm on it, Dave, uh, lieutenant."

The gun servers, the two beefy Schmidt brothers who loved to blow things up, both snickered.

Dave Baxter smiled. They might all be dead in a few minutes but they would go down fighting.

❋ ❋ ❋

Captain Hollar thought the lead ship should be attacked prior to it steaming directly between his and Baxter's emplacements. Wingate could wait his turn and Leonard Hollar had no doubts his friend would get his chance. Behind him, Sergeant Jeff Richardson waited with a flare gun at the ready.

Privates Liston and Babcock were ready to reload the 105 as soon as the breech ejected the casing. For once they were quiet, eagerly anticipating action.

Hollar fixed his binoculars on a spot across the inlet. When the bow of the destroyer blocked his view he snapped, "Flare! Open fire!"

The flare burned into the sky and 105mm fire erupted from both sides of the inlet. The Japanese ship was caught in a crossfire but immediately returned in kind. Hollar's first round hit the bridge and he felt a thrill of elation flash through him.

Baxter's first round smashed into the hull between the stacks in an effort to kill the ship's propulsion. Hollar's second round smashed into the forward gun mount that was swiveling to fire on him. The second gun mount fired and the round went over their heads.

He knew they wouldn't miss next time.

"Get the second mount!" he screamed.

Richardson corrected the aim and pulled the lanyard. The round hit the front of the mount and penetrated. The mount blew completely off the ship.

The DE behind the wounded destroyer fired.

An explosion rocked them, knocking Hollar to the ground and throwing dirt and rock like shrapnel. He scrambled to his feet and looked at his crew. Richardson rubbed blood from his eyes and Liston stood wide-eyed, staring at Hollar in confusion. Babcock's corpse sat on the ground, the head completely missing, and the body fell over shooting blood from the severed neck into the ground.

"Load!" Hollar bellowed.

Liston bent down and tried to lift a fresh round off the small stack. Hollar started to help and noticed the barrel of the howitzer had been massively dented.

"Get the fuck out of here, now! We've done what we can."

They ran for the bunker behind the emplacement. The shriek of a Fuji fighter whipped over them and its ordnance hit the maimed 105, blowing it to pieces that cut down its gun crew like bloody grain.

✻ ✻ ✻

237

Baxter got off a fourth round and knew the destroyer would soon rest on the bottom, but it still possessed a lethal bite. Two Fuji fighters circled overhead looking for targets. He wondered to where the third had disappeared.

"Aim for the gun mounts, Rick!" Baxter pulled the flare gun from its holster and fired it to the south. They needed help and damn fast.

✳ ✳ ✳

Petty Officer Okura pulled himself off the blood-filled deck and peered around. He was the only living thing on the bridge and the deck tilted hard to starboard. Another explosion rocked the ship and he heard men scream.

Acrid smoke filled the space and he saw Captain Iwata's contorted face frozen in a grimace. He pushed himself to his feet and hobbled toward the gun mounts forward. Both 5"/38s were ripped and filled with flames. The 40mm mounts were scrap and blood.

A hatch opened forward and three oil-covered engine room ratings raced across the deck and threw themselves into the water. Okura shook his head in derision, most Japanese sailors couldn't swim. At that point the ship blew into two sections.

The water seemed to rush up to grab the shattered remains of the bridge and he wondered how painful it was to drown.

70

Imperial Headquarters, San Francisco, Pacific States

"Admiral Hara, we have a dispatch from Alaska Prefecture."

He held out his hand. It had to be of utmost importance or someone else would have made a decision by now. A quick read informed him of the loss of more Japanese ships in the North Pacific. A Nazi submarine was suspected in the loss of one of the ships, a cruiser.

"I want to meet with my top staff in five minutes," he said to his aide.

The aide, a full captain, bowed from the waist and hurried out of the admiral's office. Tameichi Hara felt all of his fifty six years of service to the Emperor. The weariness of his soul would no doubt have driven him to seppuku had he not been a Christian.

His faith had directed his actions and tempered his actions even as a junior officer. He was the only destroyer commander to survive the entire Great Pacific War. Newspapers called him the "Unsinkable Captain".

He rose to his feet and quickly walked into the adjoining conference room. A vice admiral, a rear admiral, and a general of Imperial Marines all stood at attention when he opened the door. Hara turned to his aide and said, "I will ring if I require your assistance. Contact General Kozuki and ask him to come to my office in an hour about an urgent matter."

"At once, admiral." Hara shut the door between them.

"Be seated, gentlemen." He remained standing and when they had all settled into their chairs, said, "I fear we are in an active shooting war with the Reich." He read them the dispatch about the sinking of the *Amagi.*

"Submarines in the Gulf of Alaska?" Vice Admiral Sochi said in a wondering tone. "Why would they be clear up there when there are more targets in California and Hawaii?"

"There seems to be no understandable rationale to this act," Admiral Hara said with a nod. "Unless they are trying to antagonize us into doing something rash in return. They obviously don't know me."

"You *are* new on the job," Vice Admiral Sochi said with a grin.

"That has to be the answer. But, still, why a provocation that far north? They have already destroyed the Chrysanthemum Project, there is nothing there for them to obtain."

"Did not the insurgents steal an atomic weapon from the Empire, admiral?" General Hammato asked.

Leave it to him to bring up problems we cannot solve.

"That is correct, general. However the weapon is still firmly in the hands of the resistance, who also seem to have a firm hold on Alaska Prefecture. How can one submarine triumph over those odds?"

"Perhaps they are scouting for a land invasion," Rear Admiral Konda suggested.

Admiral Hara nearly winced. "From a submarine, admiral? Wouldn't an aircraft be much more productive an alternative?"

Konda frowned and Hara knew he was thinking as hard as he could.

There are excellent reasons this man should never be in command of anything larger than a garbage scow, Hara thought, making sure his distaste didn't become evident to the others.

"They could be landing a small force of specialists to ferret out the location of the weapon," General Hammato said.

The room went quiet as the other three men pondered the idea.

"You may be correct, general." Hara scratched his head. "I wonder where they would be able to successfully and safely offload such a team close to a transportation system."

"If I were directing such a mission," Hammato said, "I would direct them to land in one of the smaller ports like Seward. The Alaska Railroad begins there and goes all the way to Fairbanks."

Hara revised his opinion of the general upward.

"The question that remains in my mind is why would they want the weapon?" Vice Admiral Sochi said. "One would think they have all they need from their own factories."

"The fissionable elements are more difficult to obtain in Europe than in North America," Hara said. "They may have depleted their stocks and are in desperate need in order to maintain their supposed military superiority."

"Should we field a team for the same reason, admiral?" General Hammato asked.

"This would not be an auspicious time to send highly trained people into Alaska Prefecture, general. Unless you have an excess and can afford to lose a few."

"If offered such a mission I have no doubt I would face an excess of volunteers," Hammato said crisply. "However, I have no intention of squandering *any* of my troops, no matter their level of training."

"My remark was entirely facetious, colonel, I did not mean to cast doubt about your attitude toward your troops."

"My sense of humor has always been lacking, admiral. I did not wish to create discord."

Hara waved a hand in dismissal. "Not to worry, general. The point is, we have suffered major setbacks in Alaska Prefecture and I have no wish to add to the magnitude."

"If we had not lost a generation in the Great Pacific War we would have a much larger military force," Hammato said bitterly. "At present we are hard put to maintain and man the equipment we possess."

"True," Hara said. "If the army would allow us to rebuild our depleted fleet as quickly as they rebuilt their equipment we would not have been so easily mauled in Alaska."

"The only gratifying aspect of the action in Alaska is it was the army who lost airfields and personnel to the insurgents," Hammato said with a ghastly grin.

"What do we need to do *now*?" Vice Admiral Sochi asked the room at large. "I am painfully aware we must act but have no idea how or where."

With no more suggestions forthcoming, Admiral Hara cleared his throat and his three subordinates all gave him their full attention.

"I suggest we withdraw all naval elements from Juneau in Alaska Prefecture and explore the possibility of an armistice with the Americans."

Rear Admiral Konda looked stricken.

Vice Admiral Sochi sucked in his breath in surprise. "Admiral Hara, with all due respect, that statement from a junior officer would mean his head. It reeks of–"

"Vision!" General Hammato snapped. "The Code of Bushido can be interpreted in more than one way. The interpretation Japan has followed all these years nearly lost us the Great Pacific War.

"Bushido taken in the right way may withstand a storm of this magnitude. We *have* to be flexible or we will lose everything we have gained since 1941. I rejoiced in our victory two decades ago when I was but a lieutenant hiding and starving on Tarawa and knew a miracle had taken place because we had been losing the war steadily since 1942.

"I agree with your suggestion, Admiral Hara. If this costs you your head I will be kneeling next to you to lose mine."

"That's high praise, general. Thank you."

Rear Admiral Konda appeared stunned. "I, I fail to see…"

"You are excused, Admiral Konda," Hara said and held his tongue until the door had shut behind the man.

"This concept is nothing short of revolutionary, admiral," Sochi said, obviously still mentally wrestling with the idea. "My only reluctance stems from the fact they have an atomic weapon in their hands. If we pull all forces out they will have the luxury of preparing it for delivery somewhere."

"Cogent thinking, admiral. Keep in mind they have no air force capable of delivering a weapon of that weight. They only have the sea and the trail they blazed through Canada. Both of those avenues can be closely watched and steps taken."

"We need to do this quietly," Admiral Hara said with finality. "Thank you, gentlemen, now I must convince the Imperial Army."

71

PT-245
Gulf of Alaska

Although the weather had cleared, the sea remained turbulent and the boat had to fight for every foot of headway in the massive troughs.

"How far are we from the Barren Islands?" Brian asked Lt Hart.

"Can't be more than thirty miles, skipper. I'm really worried about the fuel level."

"We can always hitchhike, John."

"Not a lot of friendly traffic out here, Brian."

"Somebody will come along, just watch."

"Skipper!" Chief Harris yelled, hanging out of the radio room. "I've got a message for you!"

"You have the helm, Lt Hart."

"Aye, sir, I have the helm."

Brian ducked into the radio room.

"Whattya got, chief?"

Chief Harris handed him the headset and he slipped it on.

"Commander, PT-245, this is *Bates*, do you read? Over."

"I hear you loud and clear, *Bates*, this is Captain Wallace, over."

"The Anchorage UL has attacked the Alaska Squadron. They have put one destroyer on the bottom so far. When the Japs come out of the inlet they're going to be moving fast. Over."

"Understood. Where do you want me?"

"We want you up north at Kennedy Entrance, the *Bonefish* and *Bates* will cover Stevenson Entrance."

"Roger that." Brian was hurriedly going over the chart Chief Harris held for him. "Are you at all worried they will exit through Shelikof Strait?"

"No. If they have trouble they will want to pull into Kodiak. They have a small naval repair facility there where our navy base used to be. I honestly think they will come through Stevenson Entrance. If they do we'll give you the tally ho and you come join us."

"What about aircraft, are they flying air patrols?"

"We have not seen any nor picked up any on our radar. We were worried about that, too."

"Let's hope they keep their birds at home. Please keep me informed. PT-245 out."

"Will do. *Bates* out."

"Skipper, it would mean us going into Cook Inlet, but we could always pull into Homer for a break. We could refuel, get dry land under our feet, eat some chow, and even go over to the Salty Dog for a beer."

"How far away from the Barren Islands is that?"

"Fifty miles, give or take. A couple hours travel time if we're in a hurry."

"If the Japs put up a combat air patrol they might see us."

"We'll pick them up on radar long before they could spot us. There are lots of little bays around here," he tapped the chart, "that we could duck into. Besides, they won't be looking for a PT Boat."

"Good point. I've never been there, have you?"

"Yeah," Chief Harris scratched his head and grinned. "Went there to see a woman a long time ago."

"She still there?"

"No idea, it wouldn't matter anyway. It's all in my wake now."

"You sure you want to go there?"

"You're the skipper, but I would love a shower."

Brian returned to the helm.

"You are relieved, I have the helm, Mr. Hart."

"I am relieved, captain. What's the chart for?"

He told his Exec about the conversation with the *Bates*. Then added, "Chief Harris said we could easily pull into Homer and take a break. Give the engines and crew all a rest, fuel up, maybe even grab a beer."

"How far does that put us from where the Japs would exit?"

"The chief says about fifty miles."

"But aren't the Japs sending ships up through Cook Inlet?"

"There will be Japs north and south of us, we can go either direction."

"So, that's doable, huh?"

"I think so, and I agree with him about getting a shower."

"Damn, that does sound good!"

Stoney Compton

72

Battle of Cook Inlet III

"Here comes that damned DE, everyone get ready for action!" Lt Mike Wingate said, watching the ship fire at the West foreland position. Leonard Hollar's piece had been taken out by the combined fire of the sunken DD, the DE now approaching, and one of the damned jets. He hoped his old friend made it out alive.

The DE had taken some hits from both sides of the inlet, but still seemed full of piss and vinegar.

Let's see if we can calm you down, asshole, Wingate thought.

"Tony, aim for the bridge!"

"Can do," Sgt Tony Mecklenburg said.

"Adamson, take out one of those fucking jets with one of our heat-seeking missiles."

"Oh, boy, I was hoping you'd say that!"

"You do realize there's more than one jet out there don't you, Mike, uh, lieutenant?" Tony asked.

"All I ask is that we put three rounds into the DE and scare off the jets with the missile. Then we all head for the shelter. Got it?"

Everyone in the emplacement answered in the affirmative.

"Carlo and Johns, make sure you load that 105 as fast as humanly possible."

"You got it, lieutenant. Ready when you are."

* * *

Lieutenant Yoshino, captain of the IJNS *Sakura*, could barely contain his terror. This little expedition into Cook Inlet was supposed to have been no more dangerous than visiting a shrine. The Americans had completely surprised them to the point of demoralization.

The thought had never occurred to them that the Americans would move their insurrection out of Anchorage. His charts were all nautical, he had no idea what was on the land or where. He dimly remembered seeing a map of the prefecture and noting how few roads it possessed. Now if he could just remember what he had seen!

Both insurgent positions had been neutralized. Yoshino knew there could be more and he was the biggest target out here.

"Captain, the *Hayashimo* just sank," the bridge watch said and continued sweeping the shore for signs of danger.

"Acknowledged," Yoshino said, knowing if he said more he would burst into tears. He had never seen combat until this day and he found himself wanting for courage. The only thing keeping him on the bridge was the fact he was the captain and the entire crew depended on him.

"The jets are returning, sir," the OOD, Ensign Tsuda said.

Thank the gods!

"All ahead full," he snapped. He wanted his ship out of this death filled inlet, the sooner the better.

The first shell hit them abaft the bridge and collapsed the radar and communications mast as well as destroying the radio room.

"Fire all batteries!" Yoshino screamed.

The second round hit the bridge and exploded.

Captain Yoshino found himself enveloped in pain, drenched with blood, and lying on the deck behind the number one gun mount. He realized he had been blown off the bridge. With great effort he twisted around and took in the shambles that had once been his domain.

A Fuji fighter shrilled overhead and he dimly heard more explosions. The ship lurched again as another artillery round found her port side. The deck listed immediately, slowly at first, and then it seemed to rush toward the sea.

His ship was dying and Captain Yoshino no longer felt fear in knowing he would die with it.

* * *

His world comprised entirely of blood and anguish, Lt Mike Wingate pushed himself upright and peered around with one eye. There seemed to be something terribly wrong with the other. His lovely 105mm howitzer, fondly named "Mike's Bitch", lay in large pieces across the emplacement.

He realized the bloody bundles of rags strewn about were his crew. Only one attempt to stand made him appreciate the solid earth beneath him. Warmth suffusing his hands brought his attention to his middle where intestines had sprung from his terribly wounded body.

Mike Wingate knew he was dying and wished he could spit on the enemy. But he lay down and relaxed instead. He had done all he could.

Stoney Compton

73

Juneau, Alaska Prefecture

Sitting in the observation post on Mt. Roberts, Sergeant Dina Spence tried to figure out what she was seeing through the binoculars. The SEAPA had established the post over ten years earlier as a way to watch the Japanese without being seen themselves. Abruptly she realized what they were doing.

"Patti, ring down and tell the operator that the Japs are withdrawing from Juneau!"

Patti Hult had been brewing tea on a small spirit stove. She looked up at Dina with a smile.

"What did you have for lunch?"

"I mean it! Here, look for yourself."

At that moment a massive Kawanishi sea plane flew in from the south and landed in the middle of Gastineau Channel. They watched it taxi up to the large military dock and men rushed out to tie it down. Two columns of Imperial Marines in full battle dress marched down the dock and waited for orders.

Dina bent down and spun the crank on the ancient telephone.

"Central." The disinterested tone of voice was standard procedure.

"This is Sergeant Dina Spence at the Mt. Roberts observation post. Pass the word that the Jap navy and army are evacuating Juneau."

"Did you hear that Mrs. Anderson died?"

Dina grinned, she helped create this piece of identification code.

"No she didn't, she's just out getting laid."

"All they have in port are patrol boats and the Kawanishi that just flew in."

"Central, I am watching though my binoculars. They are loading at least sixty Imperial Marines right now."

"Shit! Okay, Dina, I'll pass the word." The line went dead.

* * *

"So what does this mean?" Joe Coffey asked the room at large.

"Why are they giving up Juneau?" Betsy Phillips asked. "They don't even know they've lost the mine yet."

"According to the UL the Japs are losing their ass all up and down the coast. Their military is being attacked at every base they have and they're losing equipment they can't readily replace because of the loss of Tokyo and the bases around it," Addy Johnson said.

"They can no longer afford their empire," Dr. Anderson said. "They won't use non-Japanese in their military and they're low on manpower. If they pull troops out of their Asian holdings they face more rebellion."

"They believe non-Japanese are not worthy to serve the Emperor," Jerry Tanaka said. "That really works in our favor."

"Do you want me to ask Mr. Kimura to monitor their local traffic?" Andy King asked.

"What?" Joe said with a frown. "How could he monitor their traffic?"

Andy looked surprised and glanced at Betsy. "I, ah, I told—"

"He told me about Kimura and I haven't gotten around to vetting him yet," Betsy said.

"I've had him helping train the Chinese guys," James Flanagan said. "For some reason I thought we had already vetted him."

"Sorry, folks," Betsy said. "I dropped the ball on this one. I think the man could be an incredible asset but a lot has been happening and he slid down my list of things to do."

"How can he monitor their radio traffic?" Amelia Flanagan asked.

Andy explained about Kimura's past and his hobby of listening in to their official communications.

"Jesus wept, we need this man and his radio!" Joe said. "How did you get so addled you forgot this guy, Betsy?"

"I was worried about *your* dumb ass, okay?" Her voice ended with a catch.

Many exchanged glances, and raised eyebrows quickly lowered in understanding. More than one quick smile evaporated in an instant.

"So," Amelia cleared her throat, "how soon can we get Mr. Kimura's intelligence helping us?"

"Do you want me to get him right now?" Andy asked.

"I think we all would appreciate that," Dr. Anderson said.

"I vote we all meet again tomorrow. We're getting nowhere today and I've go things to do," Sue Ann Freeman said.

"Go ahead, Sue Ann," Betsy said. "We want to talk to Mr. Kimura today. But we will meet again tomorrow."

"Great, bye!" Sue Ann left the room.

She hurried to her little house on Starr Hill and immediately made the phone call she had promised herself for nearly a week.

"Dave? Sue Ann here. Are you busy? Can you come up to my place, I have something to share with you."

✳ ✳ ✳

"I'm so glad we finally did this," Sue Ann said in Dave Hammond's ear as she lay naked beside him.

"I have to agree," he said in a husky voice. "I had no idea this was in your mind when you invited me over."

"I thought you were always bedding women in your mind."

He laughed. "There's quite a gap between my imagination and reality, especially when it comes to women."

"I like how you fill needs, no matter if it's a SEAPA need, or mine." She kissed him and felt him respond.

Thank goodness, she thought rolling over onto him, *once is never enough.*

Some time later Dave asked in a drowsy voice, "How long have you been planning this?"

"Oh, probably a good month now."

He snorted in amusement. "I thought you just saw me as a tool."

"And you think that has changed?"
He laughed out loud.

74

Juneau, Alaska Prefecture

"Admiral Tanaka, Grand Admiral Hara is on the secure phone and wishes to speak with you."

"Put the call through immediately!"

"Yes, admiral." The signals yeoman quickly left the office.

The white telephone on his desk didn't finish the first ring before he had it to his ear.

"Grand Admiral Hara, how may I serve you?"

"First I want to wish you congratulations on your new command, enjoy it while you can."

"Thank you, admiral. I was very gratified to learn of your ascension to over all command in the Pacific States."

"We have much to cover, Jo, and I think you are the right man in the right place."

"I am ready to do as you direct, admiral."

"Is there anyone in Juneau who can speak for the insurgents?"

"In the past if we discovered they were an insurgent they lost their head, admiral. However, I believe there might be a person I can ask since I spared him from the Tokkeitai."

"How soon can you accomplish this?"

"The situation here is fluid. We are evacuating our people to Sitka per your instructions as we speak. I am sure the local populace have noticed the activity. Can you allow me twenty-four hours?"

"Yes. Contact me if you achieve results sooner than that, the situation is critical."

* * *

Joe Coffey and Betsy Phillips were lounging in his living room when someone knocked on the door.

"Are you expecting visitors?" Betsy asked.

"No. But with everything in flux…" he rose from where he sat next to her on the couch and went to the door. The Japanese admiral in his dress uniform and the two armed sailors with him gave Joe a start.

"Mr. Coffey, I am Admiral Jo Tanaka, I have a request for you."

"A request?" His mind immediately reeled and he wondered if everything the Japs had been doing was a ruse to eliminate SEAPA.

"May I come inside to talk to you? My men can wait out here."

He's the most polite Jap I've ever met, Joe thought.

"Of course, please come in."

When the two men entered the living room, Joe wondered if his eyes looked as astonished as Betsy's.

"Admiral Jo Tanaka, may I present my good friend–"

"Betsy Phillips, the librarian, if I am not mistaken," the admiral said.

"Joe," Betsy said, "what the hell–"

"You are safe, Miss Phillips. I am only here to make a request and then I will leave." The admiral glanced around.

"Please, sit down," Joe said pointing to the overstuffed chair next to the couch. "What is your request, sir?"

"My superior in San Francisco, Grand Admiral Hara, asked me to contact a spokesman for the insurgency."

"Contact, or *kill*?" Betsy said in a hard voice.

"Contact. He wishes to initiate an armistice in hostilities. When the Tokkeitai came to me with the list of Americans they had in custody and requested I sanction their summary execution, I refused. Not that I believed you and the others were innocent of everything the Tokkeitai accused you of, but because I knew we had to come to an understanding."

"What caused this incredible shift in attitude, admiral?" Betsy asked, her voice lighter but still brittle around the edges.

"It is very simple, and you both probably know more about it than I do. We are in a war with the Reich that both parties seem to have started at the same time. You both know about Tokyo and Berlin, yes?"

"Yes," Joe said quickly. He worried that Betsy would piss this guy off and he didn't want that, not yet anyway.

"Two days ago we lost a destroyer escort to submarine attack in the Gulf of Alaska. Why the Reich would go there to initiate hostilities is a hotly debated topic at the moment. The fact remains we cannot stave off a hostile Reich while battling insurgents inside the Pacific States and Alaska Prefecture."

"You want the insurgents to stand down so you can concentrate on the Nazis." Betsy's tone carried a hint of awe.

"Exactly. I came to you because the Tokkeitai had a great deal of evidence linking you to the insurgency, Mr. Coffey. I cannot ask for more than a mere agreement that you will put the concept of an armistice to the people engineering the current revolt against the Empire. I would like to add that we would be willing to seriously bargain about this. We are past the point of demanding anything from Americans."

"I can ask around," Joe said. "I can't promise more than that."

"Thank you. This is an auspicious beginning and I am grateful. Here is my card, just telephone that number and tell them who you are and they will put you through to me immediately."

The admiral stood and Joe and Betsy did likewise.

"Thank you for your hospitality, Mr. Coffey." The admiral gave them a brief bow and went out the door.

Betsy started to say something and Joe put a finger to her lips. He walked over and peered through a window.

"Wow, they really left."

"Holy fuck!" Betsy said with a smile. "They want to give up!"

"We can't speak for the whole damned Underground Liberation! All we can do is see if we can convince all the units in Southeast to agree to this. But the possibilities are incredible!"

"Don't telephone anyone," Betsy said. "We need to go around and contact people in person and have it passed on through word of mouth. This still could be a scheme to unearth the insurgency here."

"I know I haven't said this before, Betsy," Joe began.

"Said what?"

"I love you."

"You must think this armistice is going to work," she said with a smile.

75

Homer, Alaska Prefecture

"**O**ur picket boat says they're just steaming in circles down there!" Marion Matthews growled. "They sent their fucking jets over, but they hide, what chickenshits!"

Mike Armstrong laughed. "They know you're up here waiting to kick their asses, Marion. You've scared them."

Orin Beeder grinned. "Well, if that's the case they're smarter than I gave them credit for."

"The word from the north is that we lost four artillery pieces and a lot of good men. So why aren't they either going north or getting out of here?"

"Maybe they're looking for survivors, Marion," Mike said.

"In water *this* cold? Not even the Japs are that stupid!"

Mike decided he missed the old Marion, this new side of her abraded everything she touched, including him.

Mayor Orin Beeder sniffed loudly and winked at Mike. "What do you think we should do, Marion?"

"There's nothing we *can* do and you damn well know it, Orin. Don't start pulling my chain because the result won't be pretty."

"Marion, can I buy you a drink at the Salty Dog?" Orin asked.

"Yes," she said, visibly wilting. "I need a drink, this shit is boiling my brain."

Mike gave Orin a thumbs-up when Marion wasn't looking. Orin winked again.

They walked out of city hall into the dark evening.

Arnie theatrically expelled his breath. "Damn, she was getting dangerous."

Mike nodded. "You know, until this stuff happened I thought she was a very sedate woman. Goes to show what I know about women."

"You were smart enough to marry Jenny."

"That's true, I—"

Barney Benson slammed through the door. "You guys won't believe this!" he said, wheezing from exertion.

"Try us," Mike said.

"We just got word the Japs want to arrange an armistice."

"With whom?" Arnie asked.

"With *us*, the *insurgents* as they call us."

"Wait," Mike said. "Start at the beginning, where did you hear this?"

"On the *radio*, Mike. The SEAPA in Juneau just messaged all the units in Alaska and want us to vote, and fast, on whether or not to do it."

"Why do the Japs want an armistice?" Arnie asked.

"They are being overwhelmed by the UL units in all the Pacific States, and they think the Reich have started a shooting war with them."

"Really? Where?"

"They know a sub sank one of their ships, Arnie. Who else but the *Reich* would have a submarine?" Barney did a little dance. "I just love how unimaginative they are."

"Do we have the terms an armistice would cover?" Mike asked.

"I don't know anything about that. We need to elect a delegate for a meeting with the delegates from all the other outfits in Alaska."

"Barney, go get Orin and Marion at the Salty Dog. Find Big Bill—"

"He's on the radio," Barney said.

"Oh, good. I'll go round up Nels Pederson and Angus O'Neil. Everybody meet back here in one hour."

76

Tlingit Provisional Navy HQ
Angoon, Alaska Prefecture

"This seems to be a distinct possibility, gentlemen," Admiral Colby Williams said.

The men and women around the large table didn't respond as they waited to hear him out.

"Major Miamatsu, do you think this could be a trick?"

"No, admiral, I do not. They have effectively raised a white flag and asked for a parley. I know there were deceptive surrenders during the Great Pacific War with tragic results, but there would be no benefit for them to do that in this case. The request seems legitimate to me."

"It occurs to me this would be a very effective way for them to identify our spokespeople and capture them," Captain George said.

"I believe they are backed into a corner." Cdr Richards looked every person in the face before continuing. "They think the Reich sank their cruiser, that gives us a secret weapon in two forms. The underground in California and Washington have seriously crippled the Imperial Navy, and with the loss of their two huge bases in Tokyo they have no reinforcements to call on."

Major Ramona Didrickson raised her hand. "We also cannot afford to ignore the elephant in the room." They all looked at her blankly. "The Reich is a very real threat."

"But they're as tied down as the Japs are," Adm Williams said.

"Right now, yes. Keep in mind they have the luxury of fighting American insurgents with Waffen US troops. They have been indoctrinating American kids since 1946 and too many of the little bastards have been eating it up like gulls on rotten salmon." She favored everyone at the table with a scowl.

"No matter what happens between us and the Empire, we will end up fighting the Nazis in the near future. Creating a true alliance with the Empire would give us an edge on the Krauts. The thing we have to do right now is make sure we have autonomy and that we keep it after this war is over."

Major Miamatsu nodded to Ramona. "That is an excellent synopsis of our position, I agree with you."

"I have a question," Gabriel George said. "Who, *exactly*, is making this offer of an armistice? The military, the new Emperor, the navy, the army?"

They all went silent in thought.

"Damn good question, Gabe," Adm Williams said. "I would say that is the first question we get answered. Are we just talking about the Japanese here in North America or worldwide and for how long?"

"The SEAPA people in Juneau have the lead on this," Gabe said. "I suggest we send them a list of questions and wait for their answers."

Everyone agreed.

77

IJNS *Genda*
Cook Inlet

"Captain, this just came in from Admiral Tanaka in Juneau."
Captain Tatsuya Mihashi read the EXTREME SECRET message. Then he read it again. After some thought he reread the words a third time and smiled.

"Will there be a reply, captain?" the signals petty officer asked.

"No, Petty Officer Hirai, that will be all."

He sat in his cabin and considered the future of this conflict, the future of Japan, and the future of his career. The message gave him more hope than he had enjoyed in years. Elation coursed through him knowing there was another flag officer in the Imperial Navy who was of similar mind; who was not a follower of a strict interpretation of Bushido.

Hope flowered. He opened the door to his cabin and the marine on guard went rigid.

"Please ask the executive officer to join me, Corporal Yamashiro."

"Hai, captain! At once!" He saluted and sped away.

Two minutes later a knock sounded on his door.

"Enter."

Commander Kanegasaki entered. "You wished to see me, captain?"

"Yes, Kazuo, I have something I want you to read and then I want your *personal* opinion about the contents."

"As you wish, captain."

"Please sit, would you join me in a bottle of saki?"

"I would be honored, sir."

Mihashi gestured to a chair and the commander sat. He handed the officer the message and then busied himself with opening a fresh bottle of saki and selecting two glasses before returning to the small table between their chairs.

He poured the saki and eased back in his chair.

The commander wore a puzzled expression and seemed agitated.

"Before you say anything, be aware that I am in full concurrence with the message. I could have written it if events had transpired in that direction. Please, drink with me."

They held their small cups up to each other and threw back the contents. After a moment or two, Captain Mihashi nodded.

"Your opinion, commander?"

"We are to surrender?" he blurted.

"No. Not surrender. Call a truce, a much different thing."

"The Imperial Navy has never before done such a thing, captain."

"Does that mean it is impossible?"

"No, not impossible, merely improbable. I do not understand the reason for this action, sir. Have events unknown to me brought the Empire to these straits?"

"In essence, yes. Be aware that I do not know if the Emperor or Prime Minister feel the same way. However, my superior officer, Grand Admiral Hara, whom I know and highly respect, has sent this message to all units in North America."

"An *armistice*?"

"Put your personal feelings aside for the moment and look at the reality of our situation. In the past week here in Alaska Prefecture we have lost a heavy cruiser, two destroyers and a destroyer escort to enemy action. In the Pacific States we have lost an aircraft carrier, three cruisers and six destroyers, none of which left their moorings.

"The Imperial Army base in California has been all but destroyed as well as the Imperial Marine base in San Diego. We have lost over three thousand personnel in that disastrous week. Add to that the fact our cruiser up here was lost to a submarine.

"The only submarines other than ours belong to the Reich. We cannot enter open conflict with the Reich *and* fight the insurgents at the same time. We will lose!"

Commander Kanegasaki leaned forward and refilled his saki bowl, sat back and stared into an impossible distance, and threw back the drink.

"We would ask the Americans to join us in fighting the Reich?"

"That would be the most logical result, don't you think?"

"Would they be willing to do that after all this time under our subjugation?"

"That is an interesting question. I wish I knew the answer."

"Here is another interesting question; what would they receive in return after the culmination of a conflict between the Empire and the Reich? Full autonomy, Japanese citizenship, complete freedom?"

"If you had to answer your own question, commander, what would you say?"

"If we let them up now, there will be no turning back. We need to consider all the ramifications before we decide."

Stoney Compton

78

Imperial Headquarters
San Francisco, Pacific States

"Grand Admiral Hara, the Prime Minister is on the line for you."

Hara picked up his receiver and said, "Yes, Prime Minister?"

"What in the name of the Sun Goddess are you doing in North America?"

"I am saving the Japanese Empire much face and perhaps gaining an ally."

"They don't even have a country any more! How can they be an ally?"

"By ceasing what we have referred to as an insurrection, Prime Minister. They have depleted our fleet, our army, our marines, and we have no idea where to strike back other than through mass reprisals. They may not have a country but they sure as hell have an excellent organization."

"So, execute a mass reprisal!"

"Kill only Caucasian Americans or include Japanese Americans?"

"What are you talking about, admiral? Are you drunk?"

"I am sober as death, Prime Minister. What you don't seem to understand is that we are in a war with the Reich we would be hard put to win even if we didn't have a massive war at home to fight at the same time."

"We are fighting no war here in Japan. If you cannot contain your own populace then perhaps you need a different title."

"Before you extend your neck, please allow me to say three things."

"What are they?"

"You and the Emperor both left this continent with the sound of *enemy* artillery in your ears. We have Japanese-Americans who have lived here for a generation and do not see Japan as *home* any longer, but still revere the Emperor. And last, but definitely not least, I have secured the agreement to this plan from every military commander in North America, since they are in the trenches and on the sea, they know we must do this."

"So you are fomenting an insurrection to stop an insurrection?"

"That depends on you, Prime Minister. At the present time the Pacific States represent the bread basket of the Empire. If we declared independence the Empire would not be able to contest it militarily or economically."

"This is what we get for making a Christian the grand admiral," he said bitterly.

"All of the commanders in North America share the Shinto faith with you, sir. My religion does not enter the equation. Please, let us address the situation without fear. If we do not, I am sure Japan will lose this continent one way or another."

"I must speak to the Emperor about this."

"I am sure you already have, Prime Minister."

"You had better win, Admiral Hara," he said bitterly, "else your head will roll on the floor of your own office."

"I understand, Prime Minister. I thank you for agreeing with our plan."

The prime minister cut the connection.

Tameichi Hara replaced the receiver and leaned back in his chair. His face ran with sweat and he longed for a hot tub. For a brief moment he allowed himself to just breathe.

"Arimoto!" he yelled at his aide. "Get in here, we have much to do!"

79

Juneau, Alaska Prefecture

"Who's next?" Joe Coffey asked.

"The rep for the Denali Rangers and Central Alaska Coalition has been waiting for ten minutes," Betsy said.

"Christ, why did I agree to do this?"

"Because you can charm the pants off of a person." She winked at him.

Joe gave her a lewd grin and picked up the phone.

"Elstun? Joe here, how are you?"

"Doing great, Joe. Is this thing for real or are you smoking more than your share of marijuana?"

"Here's what happened..." Joe talked for twenty minutes and brought his old friend up to speed on the situation.

"What's the consensus from around the territory so far?"

"About half think we're setting ourselves up as ignorant tools who will end up losing our heads, and the other half thinks we would be stupid not to explore the idea and perhaps reclaim our country."

"That's pretty much what I'm finding up here, too. So many have hated for so long they can't change their way of thinking. I'm a bit dubious, but this is the first positive move by the Empire in my lifetime."

"I wonder what the folks in Osaka think about this," Joe said.

"Would the honchos in San Francisco do anything without an okay from Tok—, I mean, Osaka?"

"At this point, Elstun, I have no idea. The world has changed so damn much in the past three weeks I feel all bets are off."

269

"What if the home office in Japan says, 'no', what happens then?"

"My friend, we're all playing this one by ear, there isn't a scorecard to follow."

"Okay, here's the deal from the Interior. You set up a conference and I'll do my best to get there."

"Push comes to shove, if you need a way down we actually have an aircraft we could fetch you with."

"What kind of an aircraft?"

"Kawanishi flying boat. We stole it from the Japs."

Laughter poured from the receiver.

"I really want to hear that story over a beer!"

"I'd like that. I haven't seen you since what, '62, 63?"

"1962, when we had that training session out near Denali."

"That's right. When we killed the spy."

"Yeah. The fucker even had *me* convinced of his loyalty."

"Okay, my friend, I have more calls to make. I will keep you updated. Do we have a number where you can be reached?"

"Yes, but I'm not repeating it now."

"Understood. Be safe."

"You, too, Joe."

80

USS Bates
Gulf of Alaska

"I'm not sure I believe this, skipper," Lt Brad Phillips said. "Why would they capitulate after so few losses?"

"Probably because they haven't much left to lose," Lt Jeff Brown said. "From all I've heard, they didn't have a much of a navy to begin with, since the war, I mean."

"Jeff's right on this one," Captain Maher said. "At least that's the thinking up at TPN and Juneau."

"What about the Underground Liberation as a whole?" Lt Toomey asked. "Have they commented on this thing yet?"

"Good question, Jerry. I wish I had all the answers for you, gentlemen, but I don't. I'm not even sure the offer extends beyond Alaska."

"Aw, hell, skipper, it *has* to or it won't do them any good!" Lt Brown said. "What pisses me off is that here we are, ready to kick their asses and now this happens!"

"Jeff," Lt Phillips said gently, "there was never a guarantee we would pull this thing off."

"Twenty-two years we waited. Maintained, drilled, trained new people so we would be ready when the call came, and now they just *quit*! It isn't fair."

"Jeff, do you have any idea how honored I feel to be your captain?"

"You don't feel the same way as I do, skipper?"

"In part, yes. I have to say I was not looking forward to losing any of you in an engagement, even though I knew it was inevitable. You guys, and the gals back at Squid Cove, too, have become my family. I love all of you, and because of that I really hope this is a legitimate offer and ends our years of hiding."

"We are the nucleus of the new US Navy, right?" Chief Crockett asked.

"Is there still a United States?" Chief Payne asked. "I know there are the Pacific States, but anything east of the Neutral Zone is pretty much Nazified the way I hear it."

"Do we have enough people in Alaska Territory to declare a republic?" Lt Toomey asked.

"Think about it," Captain Maher said. "I doubt we can even get the people of Alaska Territory to agree on a government, how the hell would we pull the whole country together again? Losing the war changed everything for us, and it's not just waiting for us to pick it up and run with it. Everything has to be rebuilt."

The door opened and the OOD stepped into the wardroom.

"Captain, the bridge watch reports an aircraft carrier headed our way."

"Sound general quarters!" Maher snapped. "Gentlemen, let's go find out what the Japanese navy is up to now."

81

PT-245
Homer, Alaska

The PT Boat ran smoothly up the east side of Cook Inlet. All hands remained at battle stations and every man except Brian scanned their quadrants with binoculars. With the day edging into dusk the rocks lurked as an even bigger hazard than the Japanese Navy.

"Lights off the starboard bow!" Andy Didrickson shouted. "That's Homer!"

Brian popped the cap off the speaking tube to the radio room.

"Chief Harris, can you raise anyone on the radio?"

"Wait one, I'll check."

They continued onward into the darkening bay. Only three lights could be seen and one of them appeared to be a window in a structure. Suddenly a brighter light came on and in rapid flashes in Morse Code asked, *Who are you?*

"Dennis!" Brian shouted through the speaking tube. "We have a signal lamp on shore asking us who we are. Get up here and answer with the Aldis light!"

Chief Harris popped out of the door with a handheld signal lamp in his hands. He aimed it at the blinking light in the now dark town and flashed it four times.

"I sent them a 'V', skipper."

Lights flashed from the town.

Chief Harris answered, the Aldis lamp clacking in the night.

Another set of staccato flashes and the lamp went out.

"What did they say?"

"First round is on us."

Brian and Bosun's Mate Third Andy Didrickson stayed with the boat while it was fueled. Chief Walsh also stayed to go over the three Packard engines from top to bottom. They were his babies and he wasn't about to leave them uncared for.

The rest of the crew retired to the Salty Dog, an ancient bar that looked much like a lighthouse. Chief Foster said he would make sure everyone had no more than three beers, or the equivalent.

While Brian chatted with the fuel attendant, a man stepped up next to the hull.

"Request permission to come aboard."

"Permission granted," Brian said, walking over to the set of steps that served as a gangplank. "I'm Lieutenant Commander Brian Wallace, captain of the PT-245."

"Mike Armstrong, editor of the Homer News and member of the Homer Hellcats. I wanted to meet you and congratulate you on your action in Valdez."

They shook hands.

"How did you hear about that? It only happened a few days ago."

Mike grinned. "This magic thing they call radio…"

"What is the latest on the Japs? We don't get anything but short range messages."

Mike told him about the carnage north of them.

"All the Jap warships that went north didn't come back. I'm not at all surprised they want to call an armistice."

"They what?"

"You *have* been out of touch!" Mike quickly filled him in on the current situation.

"Why the hell didn't the *Bates* tell us about this?"

"Probably because you were out of range and you are all secret weapons at this point."

"My guys are going to be pissed, we busted our asses to get here and kill Japs, now we can't."

"Well, you can't *yet*. The jury is still out. Besides, you couldn't ask for a better place to tie up than Homer. You guys are all heroes as far as we're concerned."

Brian grinned. "I think I'll go have a beer, want to come along?"

Stoney Compton

82

USS Bonefish
Gulf of Alaska

"Take her down, chief!"

The dive klaxon blared through the submarine and the crew expertly went to their battle stations with the efficiency of a well trained team.

"Periscope depth, chief," Captain Edge ordered.

"Aye, aye, skipper. Periscope depth it is."

"I thought the Japs wanted to talk about an armistice," Lt Abel said. "Was that just a feint to allow them to attack—"

"Don," Edge said in a calm voice. "They don't know we're here yet. They haven't even put up a combat air patrol."

"So are we going to let them slip past? All they have to do is turn on their damned sonar and they'll find us, captain!"

"That's true. They also think the only possible sub out here has to be a Nazi, and they would do their best to sink us. Chief, set a course for Middleton Island. That's out of their way and we can still monitor the situation."

"Set course for Middleton Island, aye, sir."

"Captain," Lt Abel said, "Do you think the main reason the Japs are willing to make an armistice is because they think we are Krauts?"

"There is no doubt in my mind. If they discover us now it could upset the whole apple cart."

"So we go back to being a ghost."

"For awhile. I don't think we'll have to wait long to see how this plays out."

"You're the skipper. I also think TPN and the other outfits have this well in hand."

"I hope so, Don, I really hope so."

Chief Johnson came over and leaned on the chart table next to Edge.

"Skipper, we're running low on diesel. We have about five hundred miles worth left and not an inch more."

"Your recommendation, chief?"

"Find more diesel fuel, simple as that."

Captain Edge peered at the chart.

"Where is the closest place we could refuel without being seen by the Japanese?"

The chief studied the chart for a long moment.

"I wish I had a camel."

"What would you do with a *camel*, chief?"

"I'd smoke the son of a bitch, skipper."

Edge laughed and realized that the first time he done that in a very long time.

"So where do we go?"

"The closest place I can see would be Homer, second would be Yakutat but that would take us hundreds of miles away from potential action, and we can't have that."

"Homer, huh?"

"Yeah, I've met a couple of fishermen from there. They say it's a nice little drinking town with a fishing problem."

Edge laughed so hard he thought he hurt himself.

"We would have to go into Cook Inlet in the middle of the night or go in submerged until we arrived in Kachemak Bay."

"We have an aircraft carrier coming our way, remember?"

"How could I forget, skipper? We could get an island or seamount between it and us while it transited and then run like hell for Homer."

"If memory serves, it has a DD with it, so we have to watch out for that, too."

"Yeah, and they're going to be listening to the SONAR very closely. This is the area where they lost their cruiser."

"Once they are out of the way, I think Homer would be an excellent place to wait out this armistice decision."

"I concur, captain."

Stoney Compton

83

Sitka IJN HQ
Alaska Prefecture

Admiral Jo Tanaka walked down the dock with Colonel Hiraki after exiting the Kawanishi and received a full dress military welcome. Imperial Marines in their dress uniforms lined one side of the wharf, sailors in their perfectly aligned jumpers and shined shoes lined the other side, and all of the officers waited in two ranks at the end to greet him.

He felt like an imposter. He felt defeated. He felt like weeping.

Colonel Hiraki beamed at the spit and polish, he puffed his chest out farther.

Commander Issi, standing in front of the officer ranks, made a full half bow which Jo returned with a less stature bow.

"Welcome to the capital of Russian America, Admiral Tanaka."

"Thank you. I trust that Lord Baranof is not here?" He decided he liked the commander.

"Not for some time. Would you and the colonel like to inspect my officers and men?"

"We would be honored, commander." He reflected that this would be the first inspection he had ever performed as an admiral. Feeling it be a waste of time and energy, he had never held one in Juneau.

As he inspected the officers, he encountered two old shipmates who had been lieutenants last he saw them and now both wore the rank of lieutenant commander. The perfunctory inspection of officers finished, they moved down the enlisted ranks. He recognized a chief petty officer who had been a seaman on Tanaka's destroyer when the admiral was a junior lieutenant during the Great Pacific War.

"You have not yet retired, Chief Kanemoto?"

"No, Admiral Tanaka, I had yet to serve under your command. Perhaps after this enlistment ends I may go be a farmer."

The two old shipmates smiled at each other.

Commander Issi cleared his throat and Jo came back to the present.

"Excellent examples of the Emperor's navy, commander. Shall we retire and confer?"

"Hai, Admiral Tanaka, Colonel Hiraki. Follow me, please."

On their way back up the dock Jo noticed that all of the officers had disappeared. He stayed one step behind Commander Issi so he wouldn't have to mistake which way to turn and to give the man the prestige of being in charge for a little longer.

Admiral Tanaka turned to Colonel Hiraki, "Please oversee the unloading of the official files and records. Most are top secret."

The colonel straightened and smartly saluted.

"Hai, admiral. I will see to it immediately." The man departed at speed.

"This way, admiral." Issi led them into a three-story building on the waterfront. Once inside they climbed to the third floor and entered an office with a commanding view of Sitka Harbor. One more door and they stopped in Commander Issi's office.

"Please have a seat, admiral. Would you care for some saki?"

"That depends, commander," Jo said, dropping into a padded chair. He sighed deeply with the relief of being off his feet.

"Depends on what, admiral?" Issi said, sitting down behind his desk.

"Essentially, it depends on how you feel about what you've heard of recent developments."

"It is my understanding that your office was the source of a message promoting the concept of an armistice between the Empire and the insurgents. Is that true?"

"The original message came from Admiral Hara and General Kozuki in San Francisco. I was elated to receive the message with which I fully agree. I would appreciate your feelings on the subject.

"Please keep in mind that I understand your position in the military hierarchy is lower than mine by a few degrees, and therefore when dealing with this subject, I see us all as equals."

Issi stared at him for nearly a minute. Jo realized the man was looking through him rather than at him. He had a lot to sort out in a small amount of time.

"I admit that changes my official response, admiral."

"Another thing," Jo said with as sincere a smile as he could make, "...until we leave through that door I am Jo Tanaka, and you are Satō Issi. We are barring any consideration of Bushido for this discussion, and I want to hear what you *really* think. Please proceed."

Issi stood and unbuttoned his dress jacket, took it off, and hung it in a small closet.

Tanaka stood, copied the commander's movements, and handed the man his jacket.

Issi went back to his chair and sat, his face open and mind sussing.

"I say this in all sincerity, Jo. You are a lot more interesting than your predecessor."

"I was his chief of staff for three years. No one is more aware of the differences than I am. I loathed the man, he was a moral coward and a drain on the Empire."

"Is our situation bad enough to warrant an armistice? Really?"

"Yes," Jo said. He explained the events since the bombing of Tokyo and Berlin.

"I had no idea..." Satō said. "What is your decision on the saki?"

"I think it is called for at this moment in history."

Issi quickly cracked a new bottle and poured two generous cups. Handed one to Jo, and still standing, raised his cup. "To an auspicious future for our country."

Jo stood and raised his cup. "May it be ever honorable!"

They threw back the contents and both sat.

"We cannot win without the aid of the resistance?"

"It's not that simple, Satō. We have lived in their country for over two decades. They have watched us and learned our ways. They know how to hurt us, and they are."

Stoney Compton

"When the word went out that we hire Americans for low level positions, I worried that we might train them too well!" Satō said with great feeling. "It appears I was correct."

"In all honesty, do you blame them? They are a proud people, their nation is cut in half and they hate both the Empire and the Reich. If we can redirect that hate from us onto the Reich, we would be triumphant in the war we both know is imminent."

"But—"

"One more thing," Jo said. He could feel his pulse in his neck and he knew he was agitated and should be prudent with his words, but this was a unique situation. "The insurgents have managed to neutralize every military base of any importance we have. They have done this with minimal loss of life on their side and massive amounts on ours."

"So we have to make peace with them in order to win a war with the Germans," Satō said resignedly.

"Just consider it for a moment from a tactical perspective," Jo urged.

"Oh, it makes tactical sense. That it goes against every fiber of my being rather obscures everything else."

"More saki, please." Jo held out his cup and admired the commander's dexterity while under great mental pressure.

"Even though you said it was not to be part of this conversation, I need to know why you are turning your back on Bushido."

"I'm not. Along with the grand admiral and the general in San Francisco I am revisiting Bushido and examining what it says and not how the military has interpreted it for over fifty years."

"It is a warrior's code, Jo. We are warriors and Bushido is at the very foundation of our being."

"Foundations are built upon, they are basic and utilitarian, but they do not form the rest of the structure whether it be a temple or a geisha house. For two decades we have been ruling over the peoples of the Pacific and we have done a poor job of it. Warriors make poor governors because they understand war and distrust peace."

"Warriors maintain their abilities to insure peace."

"I agree. What the current view of Bushido does not take into account are the millions who are not warriors, the millions who are discounted or ignored at our very great peril. Satō, we must revisit compassion or we will all die by the sword."

Satō fell silent and regarded him with an expression Jo found unsettling.

"You do not agree, I take it?"

"Quite the contrary. You have brought up an issue I have struggled with for years. Unfortunately, the Prime Minister does not agree."

Jo carefully sat his bowl of saki on the desk.

"You know this from whom?"

"A former shipmate notified me Prime Minister Komura sent two teams to North America this morning. They are all Kempeitai assassins—"

"Assassins!"

"Yes, Jo. One team is to liquidate Grand Admiral Hara, and the other is to liquidate you."

"Are you a party to this, Satō?"

"No. Otherwise I would not have informed you. I had mixed feelings about all of this, but you have put the situation in perspective. I damn well don't want the Reich putting me in some labor camp I'll never leave."

"Are they already here?"

Satō glanced at the clock on his wall. "They arrived in San Francisco a half hour ago. The second team won't be here for another five hours."

"May I use your telephone?"

"Of course, admiral, you are my superior officer."

He grabbed the phone and snapped, "Operator, this is Admiral Tanaka, put me though immediately to Grand Admiral Hara in San Francisco. If you have to interrupt him in a call, do so. I accept all blame."

Buzzes and snaps echoed through the line. Jo wondered why the Empire had not perfected communications long ago. A loud hum came and went.

"This is Hara!" Jo recognized the voice.

"Admiral Hara, this is Admiral Tanaka in Sitka. I have just learned of forthcoming attempts on your life and mine."

"By whose orders?"

"Prime Minister Komura's. The team assigned to liquidate you arrived a little over a half hour ago in San Francisco."

"Thank you, admiral. I wish you luck on your end of this Kabuki farce." The line went dead.

Jo tapped the receiver cradle a few times. "Operator, put me through to my office in Juneau."

84

Juneau, Alaska Prefecture

Joe Coffey sat in the former office of the Japanese admiral who had moved to Sitka with his people. As a result Sitka was under heavy Japanese scrutiny and reports were few and far between. Now this office was used as an information hub where intelligence was received and passed on as needed.

SEAPA was waiting for the other Japanese shoe to drop. He had personally phoned the number Admiral Tanaka gave him and the person who answered wouldn't pass his call through.

"Pass on a message for me, sweet heart. Tell Admiral Tanaka that Joe called from his old office with very auspicious news, but you wouldn't let me talk to him. Got that buttercup?" and he had hung up.

A few hours ago the admiral had called Joe here in the admiral's old office. The admiral and Joe had a stimulating conversation and came to an understanding.

A large aircraft roared over Juneau. Joe flinched and peered out the window.

Are they going to bomb us? Old habits died hard.

A new Kawanishi bearing the rising sun insignia, with four reciprocating engines, plus a jet engine on each wing, flew down channel and then came back to land. It featured a dorsal turret with twin machine-guns and a tail gun, both manned. As it taxied toward the old military dock in the misting rain Joe was on the phone to the duty sergeant.

"This is what we talked about. Get the guys in Jap uniforms down there to tie that thing up. Make sure the armed people are out of sight."

"Okay, Joe, thanks for the advanced warning!" the line went dead.

Joe grabbed an old Browning .30 caliber machine gun and sat it on the cradle bolted to the floor. After slowly opening the double windows, he played with the sight as if it would actually be of benefit. Dave Hammond had outdone himself when he grabbed the Jap warehouses.

The Browning was one of forty they had. Cleaning them had been a treat for the vets they had called on to help put them back in service. *Those guys might have gray hair but they know what the fuck they're doing!* he thought with a fierce pride.

Three men wearing Japanese Navy foul weather gear ran down the dock and waited for the plane now closing on them. A hatch in the plane opened and a man shouted in Japanese at the line handling party. Joe felt his sphincter clench and wondered if he would be killing people in the next few minutes.

One of the men on the dock replied in Japanese and he knew it was Jerry Tanaka. All of Joe's senses focused on the man in the hatch. If the bastard showed a weapon he was dead.

Joe slowly inserted the belt of ammo and cocked the Browning.

Men threw lines from the plane and the men on the dock tied them fast. Two of the line handlers walked purposely back to the building. Jerry Tanaka stayed and talked to the men getting off the plane.

Joe watched Jerry to see which of the three pre-arranged signals he would make. So far he kept his hands down at his side. *Wait.*

Three men in civilian three-piece suits hurried off the plane and surrounded Jerry. The conversation looked animated and Jerry jabbed a thumb over his shoulder toward Joe.

Kill them.

Joe felt his eyes bug out. He knew there were people out of sight on the dock who just saw and understood Jerry's signal.

One of the suits yelled in Jerry's face. Jerry cocked his head toward the building from where Joe watched. While Jerry walked the other way, the three suits strode importantly toward the building.

Three quick bursts from Thompson submachine guns dropped them in bloody heaps on the wet dock. An Imperial Marine with a much newer machine gun jumped out of the plane and took aim at something out of Joe's sight. Jerry Tanaka dropped him with a pistol shot to the skull.

The turret gun swiveled but couldn't see Jerry on the dock. Joe covered the turret anyway, he was in the best position to eliminate it if needed. Jerry was shouting in Japanese at someone on the plane.

Suddenly Jerry stepped into view with the two pilots. He raised his right hand and shook it twice.

Everything is fine.

Jerry had them believing whatever he was saying and that was good enough for Joe. He shut the two windows and realized he was wet from the light rain and shivering from the cold wind smelling of winter. He covered the gun with a tarp and mopped up the water on the floor.

A few minutes later Jerry came through the door with the pilots.

"Joe, this is Lieutenant—" all Joe heard was pilot A and pilot B; he didn't plan to send them thank you notes and didn't need to remember their names. "This is Joe Coffey, the admiral's agent here in Juneau."

"When did this transfer take place?" Pilot A asked Jerry, completely ignoring Joe.

"Three days ago."

"By whose orders?"

"I have no idea, you would have to ask the admiral who has moved his flag to Sitka." Jerry was showing signs of agitation.

"This is most irregular, commander." Both pilots were eyeing Jerry with steely looks.

"The admiral received orders from San Francisco to evacuate Juneau and transfer to Sitka. That was three days ago," Joe said. "I have no idea what the rationale was, they didn't tell me."

"Why would *you* be the admiral's agent here, you're not even Japanese," Pilot A asked Joe.

"Because the admiral is exploring an armistice between the Empire and the insurgency. He asked me to help."

The two pilots spoke to each other in Japanese, alarm in their voices. One reached for his holstered pistol.

Jerry Tanaka snapped, "If you pull that weapon you are both dead men!"

"How is it that we are still alive if you are associated with the insurgents?"

"As long as the possibility of an armistice exists we will not harm the Empire or any of its personnel, *unless* they prove themselves dangerous or threatening."

"The three men we flew up here…"

"Were Kempeitai assassins sent to kill the admiral," Jerry said. "The admiral asked us to stop them. We did."

Surprise flashed over both men's faces.

"We did not know their mission."

"I believe you," Jerry said. "Now I must inform you that you, your crew, and aircraft are being interned until the situation is clear. You will be treated humanely as long as you both cooperate."

Bob Sylvester and Ken Burch stood in the door covering the pilots with machine guns.

"Do you agree to work with us?"

Neither man looked happy but both nodded affirmative.

Jerry spoke to Pilot A, "You and I will go back down to your aircraft and you will explain the situation to your crew. If they attempt to put up a fight they, and possibly you, will be killed. Do you understand, lieutenant?"

"I understand."

"Bob, you come down with us. Ken, please escort our other guest down to the holding cells. If he does anything he's not supposed to, kill him."

"With pleasure, Jerry!" Ken motioned to the man and both left the office.

Joe watched from the open windows with the Browning trained on the Kawanishi as the crew learned of the situation. Within minutes five other crewmen walked down the dock toward the building. Joe sighed with relief and closed the windows again.

He picked up the phone and called Admiral Tanaka.

85

IJNS *Genda*
Gulf of Alaska

Commander Kanegasaki stood next to the quartermaster, keeping one eye on the compass and staying aware of all functions for which the men on the bridge were responsible. One of their junior lieutenants was in sickbay recuperating from an appendectomy and the XO had readily agreed to stand a bridge watch every two days. Much to his relief, the weather had moderated, but the Gulf of Alaska was notorious for rough seas and that hadn't changed.

I wonder if I will ever have a command of my own. Everything is suddenly changing and there aren't many naval commands left.

The phone on the bulkhead rang and the duty bosun grabbed it.

"Commander, the captain would like to see you in his cabin."

"Thank you, bosun. Mr. Tagechi, you have the conn."

The ensign came to attention. "Hai, commander. I have the conn."

I hope he keeps us off the rocks, Kanegasaki thought with an inward smile. He knocked on the cabin door moments later.

"Enter!"

Captain Mihashi sat at his small desk that seemed overflowing with paper.

"Sit on the bunk, XO. This space isn't large enough for a visitor's chair."

"How may I serve you, captain?"

"You've had time to consider the possibility of an armistice, what conclusions have you reached?"

"I am torn, captain. Part of my being enjoys the position Japan holds in the Pacific and all the lands touching it. The other part of me knows that if the Reich hadn't dropped the bomb on the Americans we would have lost the Great Pacific War."

Captain Mihashi nodded. "And now the Reich wants to finish their war and turn the world into a labor camp for the benefit of the Aryan race. We are at a pivotal point in history and much of what happens now is up to us."

"We really have no choice, do we?"

"Not the way I see it. Unfortunately, Prime Minister Komura does not agree."

"What?"

"The prime minister dispatched two groups of assassins to kill Grand Admiral Hara and Admiral Tanaka. Both groups of three Kempeitai agents were killed before they got close to their targets."

"How?"

"It seems there is someone in the prime minister's office who didn't agree with him, this person alerted someone in Sitka."

"This means we are going against the wishes of the Emperor! How can we do that, captain?"

"We are going against the politics of Prime Minister Komura, *not* the Emperor."

"How can you be certain?"

"I have a relative who works in the prime minister's office. We exchange observations from time to time. It seems the Emperor is more interested in his forthcoming marriage than he is with his empire, and has given the prime minister *carte blanche* in the operation of everything outside the Home Islands."

Commander Kanegasaki stared at the deck for a full minute before he looked up into Captain Mihashi's face. "It seems we are facing a civil war, an insurrection, and an open war with the Reich all at the same time. How do you conceive of us persevering over all that?"

"There are but a handful of warships in the Home Islands and must remain there to protect home waters. The majority of our Navy is in the Pacific States and the fleet is under attack. If we conclude an armistice with the Underground Liberation we will gain an ally with military equipment and dedicated troops in the heart of the North American Reich, not to mention they will stop attacking us.

"The prime minister cannot fight a civil war without the knowledge of the Emperor, no matter how besotted his royal highness might be. This really *is* the only option we have, Kazuo."

"I concur, captain," Kanegasaki said with a sigh.

"Captain to the bridge! Captain to the bridge. Enemy warship in sight! General Quarters!" boomed over the speaker.

Stoney Compton

86

IJN HQ
San Francisco, Pacific States

"I summoned you here to explain what must be done else we lose the Empire, not just the Pacific States." Grand Admiral Hara ran his eyes over the hundred officers and senior enlisted men in the auditorium.

"Many of you in command positions have already agreed to our proposal. At my urging Admiral Tanaka in Alaska has opened talks with delegates from the insurgent factions. I wish to stress that: *factions*.

"It is not one unified organization, they are local and regional organizations but they talk to each other. I received a few suggestions that we take the delegates and execute them. Rather than do that we should all go ahead and commit seppuku to save time."

An Imperial Marine general stood, bowed, and in a loud voice asked, "What does the prime minister feel about this plan?" The general bowed again and took his seat.

"General Kobayashi, the prime minister does not fully agree with the plan, however he did not tell me to desist."

Murmurs swept the auditorium.

"But, he *did* try to have me assassinated." Hara grinned at them and a large portion of his audience openly laughed. "As you can see, I am still here, and I will do my utmost to see this plan through to fruition."

Everyone watched him with perfectly blank faces, not that he had expected else.

General Kobayashi stood again and bowed. "Admiral, what about the oath we all took to adhere to the Code of Bushido?" He bowed again and sat.

"The Code of Bushido, according to Nitobe Inazo, says, 'Courage is doing what is right', and, 'True patience means bearing the unbearable'. The *original* code spoke of benevolence, mercy, justice, character, self control, as well as loyalty and honor.

"Over fifty years ago the warlord faction cast the code into what we have been told is the way of the samurai, they changed it from bamboo to steel. They perverted a way of life. As the current leaders of the Pacific Ocean and all the lands touching it, we have a larger obligation to fulfill that is much more than mere domination.

"As a nation and a people we must move on or become superfluous to history as did the Romans. If we hold out our hand in brotherhood to the Americans we could garner an ally who to this day has not accepted defeat. The day is coming soon, far too soon I fear, when we will be in a shooting war with the Reich, and we cannot defeat them alone."

The general stood again, raised a pistol and fired at Hara. The alarmed man next to the general pushed him as he pulled the trigger and the bullet took off the admiral's left ear lobe. Three other officers piled on the general and two armed sentries hurried over and took the shouting man into custody.

A medic hurried over to Hara who had not moved or changed expression as blood ran from his damaged ear. He allowed the medic to apply first aid and bandage the ear without moving his gaze from the men in the room.

"That's twice in ten hours I have survived an attempt on my life. I am merely the messenger of a restored Bushido and one of the architects of a new Japan. General Kozuki and I worked together to insure the Empire would not die of hubris and we ask all of you to help us make a world free of the Reich a reality."

Suddenly the entire audience was on its feet, shouting "Banzai! Banzai! Banzai!"

Ten thousand years! Ten thousand years! Ten thousand years!

Grand Admiral Hara felt relief swirl thought him, followed by massive gratitude.

87

IJNS *Genda*
Gulf of Alaska

Captain Mihashi couldn't believe his eyes. The binoculars revealed a destroyer escort flying the old flag of the United States of America. The ship looked eminently sea worthy and her gun mounts tracked the *Genda*.

"Establish communications with that ship!" he ordered. "Make sure the radioman speaks English. Put the transmission on the speaker."

"IJNS *Genda* to unidentified American vessel, do you read me, over?"

"This is the USS *Bates*, I read you loud and clear, *Genda*, over."

"Our captain wishes to speak to your captain, over."

"Agreed, wait one. Over."

Captain Mihashi held the microphone and wondered at the feeling of surrealism washing though him.

"This is Captain Mihashi of the aircraft carrier *Genda*, who am I speaking to?"

"This is Captain Maher of the USS *Bates*, pleased to meet you, captain."

"Where did you come from, Captain Maher?"

"Out of the past, Captain Mihashi, and eager for the future."

"Have you heard about the potential armistice, sir?"

"Yes, we have. Is it true your Grand Admiral Hara suggested it?"

"That is what I have been informed. Are we two then at peace for the moment?"

"I sure as hell hope so, captain. I can see the fighters on your flight deck and have no wish to experience them any closer."

Mihashi laughed. "Not do we wish to see your torpedoes any closer than they currently are."

"I would say we understand the situation perfectly, captain. I see your remaining destroyer in your wake. Does her captain share our understanding?"

"Yes, he does. We are securing battle stations in the hope we are with an ally."

"I didn't think I would ever see this day," Maher said with feeling.

"Nor I," Mihashi answered.

88

USS *Bonesfish*
Gulf of Alaska

"Sure wish we could join the party!" Chief Johnson said in the quiet control room. They had all just listened to the transmission between the other two ships in their vicinity.

"We are a catalyst," Captain Edge said in a quiet voice. "If the Japanese find out we exist it could jeopardize the whole armistice negotiation. We have accomplished so much more by being quiet than we could have in any combat patrol no matter how lucky we were."

"So what do we do now, skipper?" Chief Johnson asked. "We need to reprovision in the next two weeks as well as refuel. We still gonna go to Homer?"

"Plot a course for Yakutat. I know they have fuel and a nice long dock and that puts us closer to the Gulf of Alaska as well as the Alexander Archipelago."

"Skipper, we can't submerge in there enough to be out of sight of a plane."

"I know that, chief. I don't think the Japs are going to be overflying Yakutat any time soon, they have bigger fish to fry."

"Here's the course, skipper," Chief Johnson said and pointed at the chart.

"Y'know, I think you should be an officer, chief."

"Dammit, no you don't, sir. I am a chief petty officer in the US Navy and that's all I want to be, sir."

"You get more pay." Edge grinned.

"The day any of us get our back pay will be one for the books, that's for damn sure."

"I'd buy a bar and take all the crew's money," Sparks Paskin said. "I'd never have to work another day in my whole life."

"I like a man who plans ahead," Lt Abel said. "Maybe I'll go in with you as a partner."

"Nothing personal, sir, but no way. This is *my* pipe dream."

"We'll be in Yakutat in four days, skipper," Chief Johnson said, "less if we surface and run for it."

"Get us a hundred miles or so away from the Jap navy, then we'll check out the surface."

"Aye, aye, captain."

89

Juneau, Alaska Prefecture

Rain fell in torrents from the leaden sky as the Kawanishi painted in USA colors landed on Gastineau Channel and taxied toward the military dock. Joe Coffey watched from the front of the Hara Building, their name for the old IJN headquarters. SEAPA decided it would be a good gesture toward the Japanese, and if it didn't work out they could always rename it.

The Kawanishi's landing ended a flight originating in Anchorage. Lt Ben Hooper had flown it from Yakutat to Anchorage, then to Homer, and finally Juneau. He had insisted on bad flying weather so he wouldn't have to worry about patrol planes, or fighters.

Ben's passenger list included the commander of the Denali Rangers and Central Alaska Coalition, a delegate from the Yukon River Militias by name of Doubtful Thomas, a gunnery sergeant representing the Anchorage Collective, and a Turk Babcock, the delegate from the Susitna Rangers. From Homer were Mike Armstrong and Orin Beeder. They stumbled off the plane stretching and rubbing their necks, backs, and butts.

When they got within shouting distance, Joe called, "Over here, folks, where it's dry!"

As one they ran for the protective overhang of the awning. Joe grabbed Elstun Lauesen's outstretched hand.

"Good to see you, my brother!" Elstun said with a grin.

"Welcome to our version of fall," Joe said.

He proceeded to shake hands and exchange names with each of the delegates. Turk Babcock made an issue of squeezing his hand as hard as possible, so Joe squeezed back. With twenty years of hard rock mining behind him, his grip could be close to crushing.

When Babcock finally winced Joe released him. "Welcome to Juneau."

Earlier in the day Captain Gabe George, Ramona Didrickson, and Katsu Miamatsu had arrived from Angoon, and Devon Bradley from the Queen Charlotte Group. All of the *insurgent* delegates had arrived. Once inside the conference room they all snacked on the smoked salmon and moose meat pies provided by the community.

Tables had been arranged in a large circle in order each person could clearly see the face of every other person. Each place at the table had a small card with a person's name.

"The Japanese are arriving!" someone yelled from the door.

They all went out and watched the Kawanishi H-19 glide down and touch the surface of Gastineau Channel before heading in to tie up at the dock. The rain abated for a moment and then returned in volume. In moments the plane was tethered to the dock and the delegates walked briskly toward the Hara Building.

Joe saw that more than one of the delegates glanced up at the three flag poles. The Japanese flag waved from the left pole, the American flag flapped on the right, and on the center pole, three times larger than the other two, was a white flag.

Jerry Tanaka ushered the Japanese into the building speaking English. The lead officer wore a bandage on his left ear and the rank of a grand admiral on his shoulder boards. As soon as everyone was inside and quietly staring at each other, Jerry said, "Please use the facilities, get something to eat and drink, and we'll get down to business."

Everyone found their names and sat in the chair indicated. The Japanese delegates were spaced between the American and Canadian delegates. After each delegate introduced themselves, Joe explained how the session would work.

"Since Grand Admiral Hara is our ranking guest, he will open with remarks on how we all came to be here today. After he has finished there will be a question and answer session. Each delegate will have the opportunity to ask one question and will yield the floor after it is answered. Everyone will have the opportunity to ask a question but cannot ask another until after every other delegate has had a chance to speak."

"What if we don't like your set-up?" Turk Babcock asked.

"Then you can leave. Or we will escort you out, your choice. This is our show and we're making the rules. Is everyone clear on this?"

Palpable distrust swirled through the room for the first two hours. Admiral Hara explained his position, the rationale for the position, and the fact that not every other Japanese agreed with him. He pointed to his bandaged ear.

"If the officer sitting next to the shooter hadn't pushed him, the bullet that took part of this ear would have hit me in the head. If we are not successful in this place the animosity on both sides will come back with a vengeance. I hope we are all finished with vengeance."

"If you do not speak for the Empire, what happens to any agreement we make here today if you lose your job?" Captain George asked.

"To a very large point, I do speak for the Empire, but only if we are successful here."

The session went on for four and a half hours.

When Admiral Hara said, "The tide of the war turned and were victorious—"

Babcock yelled, "We were kicking your asses and you know it!"

Joe stood and pointed at Babcock. "You just lost your next turn, sir. If you do that again you will be expelled."

Implacable hate suffused Babcock's face but he held his tongue.

Joe wondered why the man was here at all, he obviously didn't want to work with everyone else. When people spoke all of the other delegates made notes on the tablets provided. Joe wished could see all of the notes being made, that would tell him if this was going to work or not.

Elstun Lauesen stood to speak. "Admiral, what this all boils down to is to what extent will the Empire voluntarily back away from the American people and allow us to run our own lives? I would point out that if we are not granted full autonomy in our personal, local, and national affairs, this thing won't work." He sat down.

"Mr. Lauesen, I personally do not have an issue with any of those points. If they prove to be universal in negotiating with other factions of the *Underground Liberation*, then I am sure those points will be part of the agreement."

Elstun stood and raised his hand and looked at Joe, "Quick follow up, Joe?"

Joe nodded.

"Admiral Hara, you knew when you came here that we could only speak for Alaska and part of Canada," he nodded to Devon Bradley, the Queen Charlotte Group delegate. "Now it seems you need the entire, fragmented collective known as the Liberation Underground to all agree on what we say *here* and not speak for *themselves*? Before you answer, let me point out that you are pretty much on your own, too, if I read the situation correctly. Thanks, Joe, I'm done." He sat down.

The ghost of a smile crossed Hara's lips.

"I believe it would not be a good idea to play poker with you, sir. I take *all* your meanings and realize that I asked for too much. I apologize.

"All I can do is give you all you ask for, but only here in Alaska Prefecture and the Pacific States. This is where my authority lies and is accepted, *if* this works. It grieves me I must tell you this, my prime minister tried to assassinate my friend, Admiral Tanaka, *and* me." He gestured toward his left ear.

"There is more than enough distrust to infest all our houses, and therefore we need to establish geographic boundaries here in order to go further. Is that not logical?"

Joe stood. "We are concerned with Alaska Prefecture, Canada, and the Pacific States. As well as all of your gains in North America and Hawaii. If you want our help fighting the Reich we will accept nothing less."

Admiral Hara motioned to Admiral Tanaka and General Kozuki. They immediately went over to him and the three stepped away from the table and spoke in whispers.

Joe knew everyone in the room shared exactly what he felt; fear, hope and barely throttled elation. Something nagged at the back of his mind, distracting him from the culmination of years of bitterness and distrust. Then it hit him.

Babcock had disappeared. The only person in the room that Joe actively distrusted had slipped out. Joe couldn't leave.

He frantically glanced around. The back of the conference was thick with spectators, nobody wanted to miss this. He saw Dave Hammond and gestured to him.

Dave hurried over and knelt down next to Joe.

"You look agitated. What do you want me to do?"

"Delegate Babcock–"

"The asshole from Susitna? Why they sent him is beyond me, there are some good people up there."

"He's gone. I don't understand him or have any idea what his agenda is, but my gut is telling me to find out and fast."

"I have friends here, we've got this, don't worry." Dave vanished into the group of spectators.

Joe still felt apprehensive. Everyone in the room was unarmed, or supposed to be.

Stoney Compton

90

Juneau, Alaska Prefecture

Dave Hammond weaved though the crowd near the door and found two of his best fixers, Skip Gray and John Wilson. He explained the situation and told them what to do. They spread out and quietly went searching through the merciless rain.

Where would I go it I wasn't from here? Dave wondered and then grinned. *I'd go to a bar, but this isn't about having a good time.* Next to the Hara Building stood the two-story structure formerly housing the headquarters personnel of the IJN on the top floor. The bottom floor served as a supply depot. Dave hurried through the open front door and found the deepest shadows available.

Rain continued to pound the building. He waited, letting all of his senses open as fully as possible. Off to his left the floor creaked. He waited.

The floor creaked again, closer this time. He felt calm, holding a baton in his right hand and a Model 94 pistol in his left gave him all the assurance he needed. He also admitted to being ambidextrous.

Despite the front door standing open, the interior of the building lay bathed in unusual darkness for mid day.

Probably has something to do with the weather, Dave thought.

The floor creaked again and he wondered why the person didn't move onto another part of the floor. Something small moved in the shadow and Dave realized it was a pistol snaking around the corner.

The bastard knows I'm here!

With all of his strength he slammed the baton down on the wrist and the pistol spun into shadows across the wide passageway as a man screamed in agony.

"My arm, my arm! You broke my fucking arm!"

Dave stepped out and put his pistol to the head of the man slumped against the wall.

"What are you doing in here, sir? And why are you armed?"

"None of your fucking business! Who *are* you?"

"My name doesn't matter as I doubt we'd ever be friends."

Dave heard movement behind him and quickly turned.

"Just me, Dave," John Wilson said. "Is this the guy?"

"I'm a gawddamn delegate! You can't treat me like this."

"Too late, Mr. Babcock, we already have. Why did you leave the conference if you are a delegate?"

"I don't have to tell you a damn thing, fat man."

"You're just a petulant child, Mr. Babcock. Call people names and act like the deep-dyed asshole that you are. Let me guess, your daddy didn't think you measured up, did he?"

Dave laughed. "I think I agree with him."

"You won't be laughing when the bomb goes off, fat man!"

91

Juneau, Alaska Prefecture

#

D ave hurried into the conference room in time to hear Admiral Hara's statement.

"My colleagues and I have come to the only possible offer we can make under the circumstances. Our realm of responsibility only extends to the Pacific States and Alaska. Hawaii is not in our sphere and we cannot promise anything for or about the islands.

"It is our opinion that if your organization, here in the Pacific States and Alaska, assist us in repelling the imminent invasion by the Reich, the Empire would be grateful to the point you could achieve everything you ask for today. However, we cannot guarantee anything."

Dave blinked, *is that as good as I think it is?* He blinked again, he had to find Joe in the throng of people standing and applauding. He pushed his way through the crowd to where he last saw Joe.

Joe wasn't there.

Shit!!! What am I going to do?

He stood on a chair and scanned the room. Joe was on the far side of the room and everyone was talking, loud. Dave also possessed a loud, deep, commanding voice.

"Joe Coffey!"

Nearly everyone in the room went silent and stared at him. So did Joe.

"I need you to help me have everyone exit the building, there *might* be a bomb."

He had never before witnessed people panic while others did not. Standing on the chair gave him the perspective the situation called for.

"Please don't push!" he yelled. "There is a door there," he pointed, "there and there."

Joe rushed over and grabbed his leg.

"Are you *absolutely* sure?"

"Yeah. Babcock said there was a bomb. He hasn't revealed the location but it's being discussed as we speak."

"Why the hell would he want to blow this up? What could Susitna possibly gain with something as deadly and deliberate as this?"

"Joe, go over to the supply building *now*, that's where Skip and John have him squirming. Make him talk!"

Joe hurried out of the building. Dave glanced around to make sure nobody was still inside.

He couldn't have been gone more than ten minutes, where could he plant a bomb in that amount of time? He had to have brought it in his luggage, or it was his luggage!

Dave ran outside and shouted to the people searching around the building in the constant rain.

"Look for his suitcase, it has to be in there!"

He went looking for Lt Ben Hooper and found him wearing rain gear and admiring the new Japanese Kawanishi. He ran over to the pilot.

"They've made some nice modifications on this bird," Ben said and looked at Dave. "What's up? You look rattled."

"What did Babcock's suitcase look like?"

"Beat up, brown leather, has a black strap around it, it seemed heavy but he wouldn't let anyone help him with it. Why does it matter?"

"It's a bomb and he has planted it somewhere around the building, I think."

"It's a large suitcase," Ben demonstrated with his hands. "It should be easy to find."

"Help us look!"

92

Juneau, Alaska Prefecture

Grand Admiral Hara stood with his delegation inside a small office in the maintenance hangar. Admiral Tanaka remembered this had been the office of his lead maintenance petty officer, Chief Fukuda who always made sure the space was spotless. The remains of someone's lunch and two empty beer bottles in the corner attested to the lack of military correctness on the part of the Americans.

"Why would an American try to assassinate their own people?" Colonel Hiraki asked.

"Why, indeed," Admiral Hara said with a wry smile, touching his bandaged left ear. "Obviously they are all not in agreement on an armistice either."

"What bothers me," Commander Issi said, "Is how easy it would be for them to kill the five of us and eliminate most of the ranking Empire officers in North America."

"How would that help their cause in the long run?" General Kozuki asked. "Killing us would be very shortsighted and they have rather proven their mastery at the long game."

"All it takes is one madman, and they seem to have one here." Admiral Hara peered out into the downpour. "Although I believe they have apprehended him."

"If you don't mind, Admiral Hara," Colonel Hiraki said. "What is your opinion of the American delegates?"

Hara smiled. "They are a diverse lot. I cannot imagine any of them leading troops or planning campaigns, yet here they are. I admit to taking a liking to the delegate from Fairbanks, Dr. Pinky."

"Ah, Mr. Christenson," Commander Issi said. "Yes, he has a droll manner in phrasing questions and answers. More than once I wanted to laugh at his statements but worried that I would offend our hosts."

"I believe that is what he truly wishes; for people to laugh at his words." Hara said. "I would enjoy having him on my staff, but we are not allowed court jesters."

"The aborigine, Mr. Thomas," General Kozuki said, "is there some question as to his name?"

Hara laughed. "Yoshio, you are taking his name literally, it is 'Doubtful' and that is the case. His parents must have had a reason to burden him with such a name, but none of us had a say in what name with which we would face life."

"Doubtful Thomas." Admiral Tanaka shook his head. "What an intriguing person, he seems imbued with wisdom."

"I am impressed with the caliber of the American delegates," Hara said. "With the exception of the Babcock person, of course. His actions lack reason and responsibility. Why any—"

An explosion shook the building and screams and shouts filled the air outside their office.

93

Juneau, Alaska Prefecture

Joe Coffey stood with Elstun Lauesen and Mike Christenson as they stared at the shambles of the back portion of the Hara Building.

"Damn!" Elstun said. "Did we lose anyone?"

"They're trying to figure that out right now," Joe replied. "I hope not."

"If someone was killed," Mike Christenson said, "what will happen to Delegate Babcock?"

"We'll hang him," Joe said. "Simple as that. We have to show everyone that this is not a game to be leveraged through intimidation or bullying tactics."

"Do we need to give him a trial?" Elstun asked.

"I think a majority vote will suffice," Joe said. "Every person here was selected because they were smart, with the obvious exception of Babcock."

"Is there any way we can contact his people?" Mike asked.

"We have a phone number, if the line is working," Joe said.

"They need to know what happened here before we do anything final," Elstun said. "We at least have to make an effort to get them to commit to our actions."

Joe slapped Elstun on the back. "Now I remember why I liked you so much back in '62, you think things out."

Mike Armstrong slowly walked over to them, his face grim.

"Bad news, fellow delegates. Someone named Big Bill Thompson found the suitcase and must have opened it. There's not a lot of him left."

"He was a weapons expert,"Joe said numbly. "That sounds like something he would do."

Mike Armstrong looked at Joe. "Your guys got Babcock to confess he planted the bomb. What do you want to do with him?"

"I've given that a lot of thought in the past half hour," Joe said.

✳ ✳ ✳

"Ladies and gentlemen, I apologize for the disruption we have all endured." Joe quickly surveyed the faces of the delegates and found only solemn expressions. "I just spoke with the commanding officer of the Susitna Rangers and discovered that he had no knowledge of this conference, nor of Mr. Babcock's journey here.

"It seems that Mr. Babcock has his own agenda and does not care who suffers from its implementation. He is a 'loose cannon' and should be treated the same. Every person here on the American side was chosen by their peers. You are the jury.

"Does anyone here believe Mr. Babcock is innocent of planting a bomb and killing one of our people?"

Nobody moved.

"If you think Mr. Babcock guilty please raise your right hand."

All right hands went into the air.

During the proceeding Babcock sat in a chair with a smirk on his face and held his right hand carefully in his left.

"Mr. Babcock, do you have anything you would like to say? If you haven't figured it out already, you are on trial for your life." Joe stared down at the man.

"You idiots don't get it, do you?" Babcock said with a sneer. "Nobody in the Territory wants to give up any of their hard-earned rights for a central government to push them around!"

"The fact that we are all here rather says otherwise, Mr. Babcock," Joe said. "Even *you* can see that."

"All I see are dupes with an angle. Even you, Coffey."

"What would my angle be, if you don't mind sharing?"

"Power. You are all after power you don't deserve or know how to handle. You start with pissing on the Japs, then *maybe* pissing on the Germans, and if *that* works you start pissing on each other."

"Do you have anything further to say?" Joe asked.

"Yeah; *fuck you!*"

Joe looked at the other American delegates. "Do any of you wish to change your vote?"

"What vote?" Babcock said. "I wasn't asked to vote for anything."

"You voted first, with your bomb," Joe said. "And all the rest of us voted that you be executed for the murder of William Thompson, and the attempted murder of every other person in this room. Did you really think you could get away with this?"

"You can't execute me, you don't have the right."

"Guards, please escort the prisoner out," Joe said.

Eight beefy Chinese wearing old US Army fatigues marched into the room in two columns, picked up the chair holding Turk Babcock, and carried it back out the door and down to the dock. All of the delegates followed.

The Chinese sat him down and firmly tied him to the chair now weighted with sandbags and secured with a rope, regrouped, and marched back to the buildings.

Joe moved in front of Babcock.

"The only choice left to you in this life is how you wish to die, drowning, or a bullet?"

"Drowning, who knows, maybe I'll learn how to swim."

"Swim when you're tied to a chair?"

"You gotta let me have a chance!"

"You get the same chance as Big Bill. None."

"You do it, Coffey, or do you have the guts?"

"Do what, drown you?"

"Shoot me!"

"Happy to oblige." Joe lifted the pistol in his right hand and shot Babcock through the brain.

* * *

315

General Kozuki, watching the proceeding with his fellow officers, all of them at a distance from events, grunted.

"General?" Admiral Hara said. "Do you wish to share your thought?"

Kozuki made a wry smile and nodded.

"Yes, admiral, I will share. Those people will never be subjugated. We no longer have the troops to do the job. As they would phrase it, 'we are making a pact with the devil.' We will have to fight for our portion of hell."

"I concur, general," Admiral Hara said, "and it pains me to do so."

94

Yakutat, Alaska Prefecture

"Jimmy, this is Alex up at the lookout. There's a submarine coming toward the bay."

"What's on the conning tower?"

"The numbers 223, that's all."

"That's the *Bonefish*, she's one of ours."

"We have subs?"

"That's the only one I know of. Good work, Alex. I gotta go."

He rang up the duty radio operator.

"Thelma, use UHF and try to contact the *Bonefish*, it's on its way into the bay."

"Will do, Jimmy."

He hurried down to the radio room. "Put it on the speaker, Thelma!"

"...is *Bonefish*, do you copy Yakutat?"

"We copy you loud and clear, *Bonefish*, welcome to Yakutat. Do you require assistance in docking?"

"Just some people to catch mooring lines, Yakutat, other than that we can handle it, and we appreciate the offer."

Jimmy Walker tore down the stairs and into the common room. "We have a submarine coming in, help me greet it!" he yelled as he rushed through. Feet pounded in his wake.

Out in Monti Bay the *Bonefish* stopped and slowly turned in its own length. Once it faced Yakutat Bay it slowly moved backward to the dock. When it floated abreast of the dock, sailors threw lines to people waiting to moor it. The diesels on the sub rumbled down to a whisper and stopped.

Four people pushed a set of stairs down the dock and shoved it up against the hull. Two officers immediately descended and shook hands with everyone. Jimmy hurried over.

"I'm Commander Jimmy Walker, these are my people."

"Pleased to meet you, commander. I'm Lieutenant Commander Edge, captain of the USS *Bonefish*."

Jimmy shook the commander's hand. "The name's Jimmy. Great shooting up there in the gulf, sir!"

"Thanks. Allow me to introduce my crew..."

Men poured off the boat, grinning, glad-handing, slapping backs and laughing.

The dock quickly filled with locals and crew.

Commander Edge pulled Jimmy aside.

"Is there some place a bit quieter where we could talk?"

"Sure, follow me." Jimmy led Captain Edge into his office and shut the door. All of his people knew if the door wasn't open to try again later.

"Have a seat, captain. Would you care for a drink?" He held up a bottle of scotch whiskey.

"My word, yes! Thank you. What do you hear from Juneau?"

"Most of the information we get comes through Angoon, the TPN."

"Yes, me too. But I know they're having a conference with the Japanese in Juneau and I wondered if there was any news about it. We are still top secret as far as the Japanese are concerned, so I can't ask them myself."

"Yeah, them knowing about you and your boat could throw a monkey wrench into the whole thing down there. Unfortunately, I haven't heard squat from TPN or Juneau."

"How often does the Japanese carrier send scout planes over Yakutat?"

"They haven't done that since the Battle of Cook Inlet. I think after that they pretty much had their hands full. Are you worried about them spotting your boat?"

"Exactly." Edge sipped more of his scotch. "This is really fine booze, where did you get it?"

"It's out of Canada, we refuse to call it Nippon Columbia. Three brothers started a distillery over there and we are most happy to trade them fish for booze."

"Is there any place we could hide the *Bonefish* under cover?"

"Wow, that's a lot of boat to hide, captain."

"We pulled it off down in Klawak for over twenty years."

"How, can you draw me a picture?"

"Sure."

Jimmy provided some sheets of paper and a pencil.

Edge sketched with precise strokes, didn't erase a single line, and in a few minutes produced a cut-away diagram of their berth in Klawak.

"There you are. It took us a full two weeks, working as much as sixteen hours a day, to build it. We were lucky, the people of Klawak gave us all the help we could use and their cannery had a forklift that saved a lot of back-breaking work."

Jimmy studied the drawing.

"You're a pretty decent artist, captain. That is an impressive berth."

"Could that happen here?"

"Yeah, it could. It wouldn't be easy, but we could pull it off." He produced a chart of Yakutat Bay. "Right here, over on Khanfaak Island. There's Sea Otter Bay and it narrows down to nothing."

"It would mean a lot of work, Jimmy."

"Yeah, it would. But on the other hand, we would have a submarine base where nobody in their right mind would look for it. That really appeals to me."

Stoney Compton

95

Homer, Alaska Prefecture

"Brian, uh, captain, I just got word that the Jap carrier and destroyer have both exited Cook Inlet, they're in the Gulf of Alaska again."

"Thanks, Chief Harris. Any word on what they are doing?"

"Slowly headed south, skipper."

"Any word from Angoon or Juneau?"

"Not a peep. It's making me itchy."

"Ask the guys here in Homer to make a phone call. Mike's down there, isn't he?"

"He sure as hell is down there. Good idea. See you in a bit."

Chief Harris hurried off the PT-245 and made his way to the harbormaster's building. He went through the door and nodded to the young man sitting in the lobby reading a novel. Izzy Christenson nodded back. He had the sentry duty today.

If it had been someone Izzy didn't know he would have stopped them either with words or the Colt .45 automatic in his shoulder holster. His slight stature and angelic face belied his true abilities. Dennis made his way up to the radio room.

"Any word from the north?" he asked Inna Larsen.

"Not yet, Dennis."

"Brian wants to know if you can put a call into Juneau for Mike, ask for an update?"

"I can try." She worked at the switchboard for a moment. "Hello, Juneau? This is the Homer switchboard. Could I speak to Mike, please? Which one? Mike Armstrong, he's our delegate."

Inna looked up at Dennis, "He's checking to see if he's in the building."

"Hi, Mike, it's Inna. What's the situation down there?"

She held the phone to her ear, frowned, and began furiously taking notes.

"Why did he try to bomb it?"

More notes.

"What about the Japanese and the agreement?"

She abruptly stopped.

"Thanks for the news, Mike. I'll pass the word. Be careful, okay?"

She hung up the phone and looked at Dennis.

"We have an armistice! You guys can go home if you want."

96

Office of the Prime Minister
Osaka, Empire of Japan

"**P**rime Minister, we have a message from our man in Juneau." Akira Wada, the new head of the Intelligence Department bowed from the waist.

"Continue," Prime Minister Keizō Komura said, looking up from the paperwork on his desk.

"Grand Admiral Hara and *our* other delegates agreed to the basic conditions set by the Americans–"

"He surrendered our ascendancy in North America?"

"In essence, yes. However he did get them to agree to a timetable for removal of Imperial troops *after* the defeat of the Reich in North America."

"How long after?"

"Three years, prime minister."

"We can work with that. What else does he report?"

"There was an attempt to assassinate all delegates, but it was discovered early and only one American died in the bomb blast."

"I was led to believe that all our agents had been killed."

"They were, prime minister. The attempt was made by one of the American delegates."

Elation rushed through him; the Americans were not all behind this concept of armistice.

"What is his name? Can we use him in the future?"

"Not in this world, prime minister. The Americans executed him within an hour of the bombing. All of the American delegates voted on the matter and the death sentence was unanimous."

"So they *have* learned something from us."

"So it would seem."

"What are the other conditions the Americans secured from Admiral Hara?"

"The release of all political prisoners in North America with the exception of Reich agents and enablers. The release includes all conscripted workers from Asia and the Pacific Islands–"

"If we do that we are giving them a potential army!"

"They have already initiated military training of the former Chinese miners in Juneau, prime minister. They have yet to raise arms against the Empire, but they are said to be quite willing."

"You realize this isn't going to end in North America, don't you?"

"The potential of widening discord *had* crossed my mind, prime minister."

"We need to nip this in the bud. How many long range bombers are currently in our air fleet?"

"I believe the number to be between 230 and 260. The closest base is at Dutch Harbor. Where would we attack them without losing a staggering number of Japanese civilians?"

"Fortunes of war, wrong place at the wrong time. Besides, what did they do to thwart the insurgents other than hide their heads? We would hit them in Anchorage, Fairbanks, and Juneau."

"It is my understanding, prime minister, that the insurgents in the Fairbanks and Anchorage areas are scattered around the perimeter of the towns and even in Juneau there are not large numbers of insurgents in the commercial centers."

"We would deprive them of their infrastructure. Without food and fuel they cannot continue to defy the Empire."

"May I read the final proviso they made?"

Prime Minister Keizō Komura knew from the tone of Wada's voice that he wouldn't like what he was about to hear.

"Tell me."

"If the Empire of Japan reneges on this agreement, the Americans will join the Reich in the coming war and help defeat us."

"Those bastards thought of everything! Fortunately there aren't that many Americans in Alaska Prefecture."

"True, prime minister, but they have contacted the units in Nippon Columbia and the Pacific States about this conference, and all are avidly observing. The insurgents have already decimated our troop and fleet strength along the Pacific coast."

"I have studied the situation from every possible angle and have come to two conclusions."

"What are they, Minister Wada?"

"To effectively fight the insurgency in North America we would have to transfer the majority of our military from China, Australia, and the Pacific Islands. Even then our numbers would not be militarily overwhelming. In addition, it would take weeks to move the number of troops needed to any location in North America or even Hawai'i.

"Which could also mean potential rebellion in the countries we occupy and no way to put it down. I fear, sir, that we are going to have to live with Grand Admiral Hara's North American Treaty."

Prime Minister Keizō Komura thought his heart would explode.

"We have no choice, are you sure?"

"I welcome your thoughts on the matter, prime minister. If you can find a more auspicious solution I would be honored to hear it."

Stoney Compton

97

Juneau, Republic of Alaska

Bob Pavitt, Pat Henry, and Buddy Tabor harmonized on their guitars and everyone in the room started tapping their toes or moving their feet. The seaplane hanger bulged with people celebrating the end of a long nightmare. The presence of five senior Japanese officers attested to the dawning of a new age.

Joe Coffey, beer bottle firmly in hand, went from group to group chatting and laughing. He had never before felt so free and exhilarated. Betsy Phillips moved up next to him, she also carried a beer.

"How ya doing, sailor?"

"I feel overwhelmed, babe. I honestly never thought this day would come in my lifetime."

"You busted your ass to pull this off and everyone knows it. Have you thought about standing for office?"

"What office?"

Betsy laughed. "Christ, Joe, you can be so fucking thick sometimes. Political office. We need to put together a government and damn soon."

"You're jumping ahead a few moves, aren't you?"

"No more than two," she said, staring into his eyes.

"But we still have the Reich to fight, remember?"

"Yeah, but we're going to need generals and colonels and other straight thinkers to pull this off for the *free* Republic of Alaska."

"We have the TPN, and—"

"The Tlingit Provisional Navy is just that; *provisional*. We all have to get our acts together and form a permanent military council that answers to the will of the people. We need to do this *tomorrow*!"

"Damn, Betsy, you're right!" Joe glanced around the room with new eyes. "Excuse me, I need to go talk to someone."

"Damn right you do! I'll do the same."

He grabbed her and kissed her hard and long. When they pulled apart he looked into her eyes.

"Will you marry me before the shit hits the fan again?"

"I'll marry you no matter what hits the fan, and damn soon, buster."

Grinning, he walked over to where Admiral Colby Williams and Captain Brian Wallace were laughing at each other's jokes.

"Gentlemen, I salute you. You both did fantastic jobs in making all this happen."

"It's not every day that the chessmen are congratulated by the master," Colby said with a wide grin. "We couldn't have done anything as monumental as this without you and the Juneau folks pulling strings and working miracles."

"We all did this together, *Admiral* Williams. Brian here literally put his ass on the line and made our adversaries realize they really had a war on their hands."

Brian shook his head. "It was my *crew* that—"

"Yeah, I heard that already, Brian. But you led them. Now I want to change the subject."

Both men laughed.

"What now?" Joe said, looking from one to the other. "We need to put together a functioning government, and we need to do it fast. As of today we are the Republic of Alaska, and we need to keep it that way. Got any ideas?"

* * *

Sue Ann Freeman leaned against Dave Hammond's side. "You ever thought about a partnership, Dave?"

"Not really, I decide everything and tell other people what to do to make it happen. Why would I want a partnership, other than a lot of investment money up front, of course. Why do you ask?"

"I didn't mean that kind of partnership."

"Oh…!"

* * *

Grand Admiral Hara frowned at the American delegate in front of him.

"*What* is it you wish to know, Mr. Armstrong?"

"I want to know what you, and the Empire, would have done if this conference didn't work?"

"Why do you ask such a thing?" Admiral Tanaka blurted, much to Hara's relief.

"Because I know that, as military men, you had a back up plan, what to do if this didn't work, and I would like to know particulars of that plan."

"Mr. Armstrong, what is it you do for a living?" Hara asked.

"I am a newspaper editor and I write novels, admiral. Why do you ask?"

"I wished to know your frame of reference. We would have lost North America if this conference did not end auspiciously. It is my fervent hope that your nation and mine will become friends and allies to face the future together."

Armstrong frowned and gave him an odd look.

"Where the fuck were you twenty years ago?"

"Honestly? Celebrating victory. My crew and I knew we would die in the final invasion of Japan."

"I was just a kid," Armstrong said. "It's just that so much anguish and misery would have been forestalled if wiser heads in Japan had prevailed."

"Keep in mind that they also thought they would die, and very soon. Our forces had been beaten back for two years and seppuku was on everyone's mind. It took us a bit of time to get over that universal feeling and I regret your countrymen absorbed much of the transitory abuse."

"Interesting way to put it," Mike mused. "So what now? How do you make a military alliance with a nation you previously conquered but now need to save your Empire?"

"You are very astute, Mr. Armstrong. Suffice it to say that we will be waiting to hear from the representatives of the Republic of Alaska."

"Damn," Mike said with a wide smile, "that *does* have a ring to it!"

* * *

Addie Johnson ran into the hangar, her eyes moving over the throng frantically.

"Betsy!" she shrieked, cutting through the chatter and ambiance, "where the *fuck* are you?"

Betsy materialized next to her, grabbed her arm, and whispered in her ear, "I'm right here, Addie. What's wrong?"

"I just heard from the Underground Liberation in the Queen Charlottes, the Nazis are pouring through the Neutral Zone and attacking the Pacific States right now!"

59499015R00185

Made in the USA
Columbia, SC
06 June 2019